HOW TO WORK FOR AN IDIOT

SURVIVE & THRIVE...
WITHOUT KILLING YOUR BOSS

By

John Hoover

CAREER
PRESS

Franklin Lakes, NJ

HOW TO WORK FOR AN IDIOT

EDITED AND TYPESET BY NICOLE DEFELICE

Cover design by Lu Rossman/Digi Dog Design

Printed in the U.S.A. by Book-mart Press

To order this title, please call toll-free 1-800-CAREER-1 (NJ and Canada: 201-848-0310) to order using VISA or MasterCard, or for further information on books from Career Press.

The Career Press, Inc., 3 Tice Road, PO Box 687,
Franklin Lakes, NJ 07417

CAREER
PRESS

www.careerpress.com

Library of Congress Cataloging-in-Publication Data

Hoover, John, 1952-

How to work for an idiot : survive & thrive— without killing your boss / by

John Hoover.

p. cm.

Includes bibliographical references and index.

ISBN 1-56414-704-5 (pbk.)

1. Managing your boss. 2. Executives—Psychology. 3. Office politics. 4. Interpersonal relations. 5. Psychology, Industrial. I. Title.

HF5548.83.H66 2004

650.1'3—dc21   2003054652

How to Work for an Idiot

Survive & Thrive... *Without* Killing Your Boss

Dedication

To my father, Robert J. Hoover (1925–2001), who showed me how we can change the ways we think and act.

Acknowledgments

I want to thank Career Press publisher, Ron Fry, for having the courage to publish the confessions of a recovering Idiot Boss and examine the sometimes unsightly underworld of employee/employer relationships; Career Press editorial director, Stacey Farkas and editor, Nicole DeFelice, who transformed a raging torrent of ideas and personal illustrations into a readable document that actually makes sense; my mother, Ruth Schultz Hoover, a gifted writer herself, who examined early drafts and said, "Listen to your editors"; Sandy Wilson, a gifted training and development professional, who read an early draft and confirmed that the issue of Idiot Bosses needed to be brought out of the closet and into the daylight where we could all have a good laugh. Thanks also to author and leadership expert, Danny Cox, for being an inspiration to me and to so many. And special thanks to Pamala Davenport for her encouragement to see this through to the end.

Contents

Introduction

After studying Idiot Bosses for nearly two decades, I finally understand why females in certain species eat their young. The experience of working for an Idiot Boss is so universal and the feelings of frustration so widespread that the mere mention of this book title resonates throughout the human race. It does not resonate, however, with Idiot Bosses (code name: "I-Bosses"), not because they take exception to the name-calling and innuendo, but because I-Bosses just don't get it—any of it.

I once failed miserably trying to market a seminar titled, "How to Manage People who are Smarter, More Talented, and Productive than You Are." My mistake was advertising to Idiot Bosses who needed the seminar. If I had advertised to people who could anonymously enroll and send their Idiot Bosses, I'd be a multimillionaire. *How to Work for an Idiot* might not be a seminar to which bosses will eagerly send their employees, but as a book, the potential audience of highly motivated revenge seekers is huge and as ubiquitous as oxygen.

Speaking of omnipresence, on the seventh day, God relaxed and thought back over the productive week He had just completed. Suddenly remembering that He forgot to fix the Idiot Boss malfunction, God winced and said, "oops." Not feeling the problem was annoying enough to create an eight-day week, God let the idiot thing slide, and the rest is history. Then again, God doesn't have to work for an idiot.

Idiot Bosses are the mutant hiccups of organizational evolution with cockroach-like immunity to calamities that wipe out truly talented and creative people. Although idiots are barnacles on the ship of executive survival, they can nonetheless serve valuable functions— as long as they're not in charge. The bad news is they usually *are* in charge. The good news is, talented and dedicated people can rise above the situation and thrive in spite of their I-Bosses. If *How to Work for an Idiot* doesn't provide you with the knowledge and awareness to deal with this vertical mobility challenge, it might at least keep you from going postal.

Nearly everyone now works or has worked for an I-Boss. Despite the liberties this book takes with archetypal Idiot Bosses in the tradition of Dagwood's Mr. Dithers or Dilbert's despicable department head, it also suggests some methods and techniques to help you deal with fools in positions of power more easily. You'll encounter pearls of wisdom in the pages ahead. But, at times, you'll need to follow a herd of swine to find them.

Isn't that how real life works? I'll lead you through many of my own experiences so the truths will be revealed in the appropriate context. You'll learn to reflect on your own life experiences and, in doing so, potentially make your relationship with idiots tolerable and even productive. You'll begin by activating and enlarging your empathic capacity, thus rendering Idiot Bosses powerless to increase hostility, blood pressure, or the likelihood of homicide. I-Bosses only have as much power over your mood as you allow.

For most, the terms *empathy* and *idiot* don't often appear in the same thought. But what has resentment done for you lately? Resentment causes your heart to shrivel and your veins, arteries, and capillaries to harden. While all that's happening to you, your I-Boss's heart is merrily pumping away, forcing oxygenated blood though veins, arteries, and capillaries as wide open and free-flowing as a Los Angeles freeway at 3 o'clock on a Sunday morning.

By sharing some of my good and not-so-good life experiences, and inviting you to reflect on your own memorable and forgettable experiences, you'll begin to see how your I-Boss came to aggravate you so much. How aggravated we allow ourselves to become is more about our own attitudes than the external persons or circumstances committing the alleged aggravating. The key to surviving and thriving without killing your boss (as the subtitle suggests) is to take control over the only thing you have control over: your emotional response to the things other people say and do as well as things that go bump in the universe.

How to Work for an Idiot is as irreverent as it is therapeutic, as satirical as it is sensible, as lighthearted as it is heartfelt, and treats the classic hierarchical management model with all of the dignity and respect it deserves in a progressive private sector—none. Chapters such as "Idiotspeak" and "Idiot-eat" are replete with tales of bungling and stumbling attempts at leadership; mostly my bungling and stumbling attempts at leadership.

If I can help you become more comfortable with your frail and imperfect humanity, I've helped launch you on a path toward a serene and comfortable coexistence with the idiots in your personal and professional lives. With empathy comes increased tolerance, patience, and a sense of peace. Facing truths about our own flirtations with stupidity can sometimes be difficult. That's why I've chosen to lace this book with wall-to-wall humor. If a spoonful of sugar helps the medicine go down, a barrel of laughs can wash down the big pills you might need to swallow. I've had a bitter pill of self-aggrandizement lodged in my throat for years. I gag on it to this day if I eat too fast.

There is no guarantee my anecdotal approach to surviving and thriving despite your Idiot Boss will make you taller, better looking, increase your intelligence, or lose weight. I do guarantee that I write from a position of authority on the subject. If you read my biographical sketch on the back cover, you know that I hold a Ph.D. I also have two Master's degrees and years of experience as a worker bee, middle manager, executive, entrepreneur, consultant, and mental health clinical intern. More important than any of that is the fact that I'm an idiot. More accurately, a recovering idiot. The operative word (in case you didn't notice) is recovering. Once an idiot, always an idiot.

There is an enormous difference between an active idiot and a recovering idiot. An active idiot isn't aware of his condition and the effect he has on others. In that state of ignorance, active idiots aren't doing anything intentional to change. Recovering idiots are actively engaged in improving their awareness of what makes them tick and how their thoughts, words, and actions affect others.

Active idiots carry their dysfunction into positions of leadership and remain oblivious to the havoc they wreak. Recovering idiots carry hope and ever-expanding awareness wherever they go, including positions of leadership. Recovering idiots are not perfect. We never will be. But we're working on it. Wouldn't you like to hear your I-Boss say that?

The chapters ahead contain a rare glimpse at the inner workings of the idiot mind and reveal why the term "inner workings" is truly an oxymoron. For more than a decade, I've written books on leadership, creativity, and organizational performance. I've traveled far and wide extolling the virtues of flattened organizations, collaborative leadership, and shared responsibility in the workplace. My clients welcomed me and nodded approvingly as I taught the principles of empowerment, teamwork, and open communication. They politely waited until I finished and left the building before ignoring my advice.

How to Work for an Idiot was supposed to be my revenge. However, accepting my personal powerlessness over stupidity and that my life had become unmanageable, I found in my 12-step program for recovering idiots a roadmap leading from the brink of suicide to idiot-free serenity. I invite you to join me as I journal my recovery. But first, a Legal Disclaimer:

Reading this book in a meeting when you are supposed to be paying attention is not recommended, as laughing out loud can be grounds for termination. (You might be laughing at yourself, but your I-Boss won't know the difference.) Reading this book during church sermons, funerals, or commencement speeches is not recommended if you ever want your spouse or children to speak to you again.

Do not leave *How to Work for an Idiot* lying around the office unless it's on your worst enemy's desk. If you ever thought the only way to survive an Idiot Boss was to medicate yourself, quit your job, or grind up your medication and lace your I-Boss's coffee, *How to Work for an Idiot* offers hope for your spirit, strategy for your mind, and a money-back guarantee when and if Bill Gates ever files for personal bankruptcy.

You are welcome to contact me through *idiotworld.org* and vent your spleen about your Idiot Boss, nominate an Idiot of the Month, or vent about this book. If you're going to complain, however, I doubt you'll be telling me anything I haven't already heard. Writing this book isn't the first mistake I've ever made.

Read slowly, chew thoroughly, and swallow carefully.

—Dr. John Hoover

1

Confessions of a Recovering Idiot

Author John Irving advises aspiring writers to write about what they know. I published five business books before I realized I had yet to write from my personal ground zero. Now, standing in a pile of shards where a glass house once stood, I can't remember who threw the first stone. Maybe it was me. Maybe not. It doesn't matter. The stone-throwing got so intense that I forgot why they were being thrown to begin with.

Oh, yeah. I remember. I was pointing my finger at others and accusing them of things for which I was equally, if not more, guilty. For every stone I threw, a bigger one came back at me. I felt justified in my accusations and victimized by the criticism of others. Dishing it out came naturally and felt righteous. Taking it seemed unnatural and felt unfair. Just because I lived in a glass house didn't mean I wanted others to see through me. Or did I?

Mi Casa Es Su Casa

Are you living in a glass house? Are you accusing your I-Boss of things that you can just as easily be convicted of? These are not easy questions. Nor are they questions we routinely ask ourselves. That's why I'm asking you now. Things that annoy us about others are often characteristics we possess. Our own flaws are especially irritating when they show up in someone else's words and actions. Our own flaws are almost indescribably irritating when they show up in the words and actions of someone with power and authority over us.

Now that my glass house has been shattered, I'm able to write about false confidence, false security, and false pride. I know them all. Somewhere in the beginning, my wires were crossed. If not at birth, soon thereafter. Was it nature or nurture? Genetics or environment? It doesn't matter. Now I pray daily for the serenity to accept the nature and the courage to change the nurture. Like the prayer says, wisdom is the ability to distinguish between the two. All self-actualization aside, I can't help but be a little disturbed and perturbed that nobody explained these distinctions to me until I had already messed up a major portion of my life. But, that is blaming. I might as well bend over and pick up another rock.

Recovery is a Test in Itself

Who or what pulls your trigger or tends to set you off? If you pause and think about your pet peeves or things that cause you discomfort, you are compiling a laundry list of personal issues that need addressing. This is especially true in your professional affairs. Your chances of stopping people in positions of power and authority from pulling your triggers are next to nil.

You have a far greater chance of removing or disarming your internal triggers, thereby diminishing the likelihood that your I-Boss or coworkers will upset you. Consciously disarming your triggers is the best way to build immunity to aggravation. What do you care how much power an idiot has as long as he doesn't use it to annoy you? Reducing your I-Boss's ability to annoy you, whether he does it intentionally or unintentionally, is a tremendous form of self-empowerment. And no one can take it away from you.

Dealing with a trigger puller

"My name is John and I'm an idiot," I tell the group in the big tile-floored room in the church basement.

"Hi, John," the chorus responds between swigs of coffee. Some say it clearly, as if to welcome me. Others mumble, as if speaking unintelligibly will mask the fact that they're present.

"I used to think that my glass house was the perfect place to live," I continue.

"Speak up," one of the mumblers spouts, suddenly very articulate. "We can't hear you."

Annoyed by the interruption, my instincts tell me to attack him with a toxic mixture of sarcasm and innuendo, impugning his intelligence and, should I be sufficiently irritated, his ancestry. That's what we do, those of us who consider ourselves super smart, orbiting high above the stupidity. We impugn other people's intelligence—especially after we've been caught doing something stupid. But that would be my disease talking. That's why it's called recovery. At least now I can catch myself before I throw the stone. Most of the time anyway.

I still instinctively bend over to pick up stones and formulate poison blow dart questions such as, "Did someone forget his medication this morning?" But now I can regain control before opening my mouth and letting it fly. In that moment, when the stone would have been en route to its target, the truth floods over me like acid rain, eating away my pretenses. I was mumbling. Guilty as charged. If I'm at a meeting of recovering idiots, trying to get beyond the thoughts and behaviors that have imprisoned my personal and professional potential all of these years, why am I mumbling?

The acid burns away another layer and I decide to share my stream of consciousness with the group. "I learned that living in a glass house is not a good idea if you're going to throw stones."

"How original," Mr. Mumbles blurts.

I quickly pick up another stone and suck in some additional oxygen, not to calm myself, but to have enough breath support to achieve maximum volume. That's when I notice the others are glaring at him. "Don't interrupt," a woman scolds. "You know the rules."

"Yeah," I think to myself. "What she said." I feel relieved, comforted, and protected. Somebody stood up for me. Somebody cared. Instantly, the anger begins to drain from my body and I feel a tinge of compassion for Mr. Mumbles. He slumps back in his metal folding chair and picks at the edge of his Styrofoam coffee cup. When I feel like someone is on my side and cares about my right to occupy space in the universe, toxic thoughts dissipate, and in their place are curiosities about how others came to be the way they are. I even begin to wonder how I came to be the way I am.

Your Idiot Boss needs to feel that someone is on his side, in his corner, and has his back. Never forget that you and your Idiot Boss are both human beings. He will have the same basic responses to feelings and situations you do. This is important because, when you feel unsupported or even undermined, you tend to grasp tighter, fight more intensely, become more suspicious. Your Idiot Boss does the same.

Find ways to support your Idiot Boss, especially in his times of uncertainty and doubt. When you do, he will feel as I did when the woman spoke up against my detractor at the recovery meeting. I had a new best friend. Recall how you felt when someone spoke up or took up for you. You can engender the same feeling within your boss towards you. Try it and feel the tension evaporate. Send an encouraging e-mail, mention in the hallway how well you thought he handled a situation. Keep it all in the context of the department's goals and objectives so as not to seem syrupy.

Watch for Signs Your I-Boss is on the Mend

If you consider your boss an idiot, yet you notice him exercising restraint, you might consider changing your diagnosis. An out-of-control idiot will never consider the big picture of how his management pronouncements and edicts will affect the lives of others. If your boss appears to be giving any conscious thought to the consequences of his actions or how he managed to get into his current condition, listen, pay attention, and try to notice clues that he is undergoing some type of self-improvement initiative. If he is, encourage him. He needs all the support he can get.

I went on to share with the group how I learned to receive in kind what I am willing to give—good or bad. Getting back some measure of the good I give is an "iffy" proposition. Sometimes it happens. Sometimes it doesn't. Regardless, I've learned it's best to do good anyway. Having been raised a German Lutheran in the doctrine of the worm I feel guilty if good things happen to me for no reason. If I send out goodness, I feel more comfortable with the good that comes back to me.

Nevertheless, I still resent it when nothing good comes my way. Lurking beneath my recovery are the remnants of my selfish inner worm. Everything, all the time, just because I'm here. That's what I want. And so does your boss.

Would it hurt to pretend a little? I'm not suggesting you kiss up or go along just to get along. I'm more mercenary than that. I suggest going along to get whatever you can. In the murky world of office politics, resisting what your I-Boss wants might give you a moment's satisfaction as you thwart his will and expectations. But it doesn't buy you anything on your long-term wish list, assuming your wish list includes more respect and acknowledgement around the workplace, a raise, or a promotion.

That's a Mirror, Not a Window

Before I stepped across that line between active idiocy and recovery, I didn't understand that seeing other people as nincompoops was actually a self-indictment. I didn't necessarily want my boss to stop being an idiot. I wanted to be the Alpha Idiot. I didn't really want to stop him from antagonizing me with impunity. I wanted the power to antagonize others with impunity. I wasn't on a mission to create a kinder, gentler workplace. I coveted the power to make lives miserable.

When I first realized that other people could see me for the idiot I am, I felt naked. Worse, I felt as if I had been living a naked dream for most of my life without knowing it. It is embarrassing to reflect upon, but what can I do about it now? Get comfortable with my nakedness, I guess. That or stitch together some fig leaves. Building another glass house with thicker walls won't help. There will always be big enough rocks to shatter them.

I can write about being an idiot from a position of knowledge because I fell into the trap. More accurately, I skipped down the road to hell following the siren's song of success. Back then, success meant having the freedom to do whatever I wanted to do, whenever I wanted to do it, and having unlimited resources. I also wanted complete anonymity on demand, no accountability for anything I might choose to do, and I wanted all of the above without lifting a finger to make it all possible. I wanted to be a hybrid of William Randolph Hearst, Jr., Howard Hughes, Donald Trump, and Ted Kennedy. I wanted the proverbial silver spoon.

Just because I'm in recovery doesn't mean I don't still secretly want all of those things. What has changed is my attitude toward them. I can now accept that I will never live like any of the aforementioned silver spooners. Better yet, I can be grateful for the things I have. If I ever achieve anything remotely close to the financial status those guys enjoy(ed), it will result from my efforts and the grace of my Higher Power. I could always win the lottery. But that's my disease butting in again. As a recovering idiot, I live a happier, more peaceful, and satisfied life. Despite how messed up I allowed my past to be, I still have time to live a large and enlightened future.

Idiots, Idiots Everywhere and Not a Thought Worth Keeping

Part of a large and enlightened life is accepting there will always be idiots among us, recovering idiots like me, and those who don't know they're idiots. Idiocy is sometimes defined as a permanent state of stupidity. I disagree. As a recovering idiot, I know I'll always be vulnerable to stupid thoughts, stupid words, and stupid deeds. But I can reduce my dependence on them. That might sound stupid, but I've lived in spite of my stupidity my whole life. I can exercise some control, minimize the debilitating effects of stupidity, and be less annoying to others.

In an ideal world, we would have idiot colonies and only allow idiots off the island after they receive a one-year sobriety pin. Recovery would be hard, especially in an idiot-rich environment. Without intervention, the idiots would wander around looking at one another and wonder why they're there. Active idiots do not engage in denial; they're just plain clueless.

In most cases, practicing idiots don't make life miserable for the rest of us on purpose. They're not likely to feel as if they're on the island as a form of punishment. They'll probably think they're there for a Tom Peters seminar, which, in a way, is not a bad idea. If Tom yells long and loud enough, some of them might start seeing their fellow detainees as idiots, which is the first step to recognizing the idiot within.

"Wait a minute," they might think to themselves. "If they're all idiots, what am I doing here?" It's a long shot, but it might work.

Imagine for a moment what your organization would look like if the Idiot Police showed up one day and hauled off all the idiots. Which offices would be vacant? What things wouldn't be done? Would any positive activities cease? Would any negative activities cease? If you found out where your I-Boss was being held, would you send him a postcard? Would you even...

...notice he is gone?

...care that he is gone?

...miss him?

...feel sorry for him?

...wonder what became of him?

Back in the real world, there are no Idiot Police. We're on our own to deal with the idiots among us. At least those of us who are recovering idiots know what we're dealing with. Active idiots will remain oblivious to the damage they cause, and non-idiots will just keep tearing their hair out. That's why this book is so critical to your survival. Keep reading. There is hope.

Idiots: Stranger than Fiction

We can watch Jim Carey depicting an idiot in a film like *Dumb and Dumber* and laugh. But when dumb and dumber are running organizations, corporations, and government agencies, it's not funny anymore. The ugly truth is that active idiots are lurking all around us. The tentacles of their stupidity reach deep into the lives of millions. Their power is indescribable. Fortunately, idiots are largely unaware of how much power they wield. If I-Bosses knew how many bullets they have in the chamber, things could really get scary.

All idiots might be created equal, but there is a wide disparity in how they are endowed by their Creator. Through some mysterious quirk of nature, cosmic hiccup, or an evolutionary belch in the universe, some idiots are granted the freedom to do whatever they want to do, whenever they want to do it, and have unlimited resources to do so. They will also receive complete anonymity on demand, no accountability for anything they might choose to do, and not lift a finger to make it all possible.

Why is there such power in stupidity? The answer will roll out in front of you like a red carpet as you read on. It's too much to capture in a single sentence or clever phrase. Contexts must be built. Paradigms must be shifted. Thoughts must exit the box.

Cosmic Questions

We all need to form a pact. I have a list of questions for God that will never be answered unless I meet Him face to face. I suggest you do the same. At least one person reading this book is likely to get through the Pearly Gates if I don't. Whomever among us manages to interview God first can send the information back to Earth. Here are some sample questions:

- Why did You create idiots in the first place?
- Why must intelligent people suffer from worry, fear, and anxiety while idiots sleep well at night?
- What purpose is served by keeping idiots oblivious to the carnage they create?
- What is the purpose of idiots, anyway?
- How do idiots fit into the big picture?

The question on the mind of every working person the world over is, "Why does God allow idiots to become bosses?" In a world where basketball players are paid more than scientists working to cure cancer and people actually care what Hollywood actors and multi-millionaire musicians think about global politics, the fact that idiots become bosses seems like the cruelest trick of all.

Testing the Theory

You can clearly see why such profound questions must be addressed incrementally. Shamu couldn't swallow such a big pill in a single gulp. An important initial question to ask, albeit one you might not want to ask, is, "Am I an idiot?" The following quiz can help determine whether or not you fall into that category. If it makes you too nervous to consider yourself as a potential boob, go ahead and use the quiz to assess your boss. Answer the questions honestly. You'll decide whether the test is accurate after you determine if the results jive with your preconceived notions.

1. When something goes wrong at the office I...
   a. Automatically blame it on someone else.
   b. Drop important work and focus on damage control.
   c. Send out for pizza.
   d. All of the above.

2. When I receive orders to cut my staff I...
   a. Check the batting averages of everyone on the department softball team.
   b. Cut the people who challenge me the most to think and innovate.

c. Send out for pizza.

d. All of the above.

3. When I receive orders to increase production I...

   a. Threaten to fire the people who challenge me to think and innovate.

   b. Start a list of employees to blame for low production.

   c. Send out for pizza.

   d. All of the above.

4. When I receive orders to cut costs I...

   a. Cancel the departmental holiday party.

   b. Force employees to provide their own office supplies.

   c. Force employees to pitch in for the pizza.

   d. All of the above.

5. When I'm told to reward employees for good performance I...

   a. Check the batting averages of everyone on the department softball team.

   b. Allow employees to order extra office supplies.

   c. Order extra pizza.

   d. All of the above.

We really don't need to go any further. If you tried taking the quiz for yourself and you threw your pencil across the room before you finished, there is hope. If you took the quiz with your boss in mind, here's how the scoring goes:

Each (a) answer is worth one point; each (b) answer is worth two points; each (c) answer is worth three points; and each (d) answer is worth four points. Four points: Just Plain Stupid; five to 12 points: A Real Idiot; 13 to 19 points: A Complete Idiot; 20 points: A Colossal Idiot. How did your boss do?

Self-Employment: Will the Cure be Worse than the Disease?

Abraham Lincoln pointed out that representing oneself in a court of law guarantees a less-than-gifted lawyer with a less-than-intelligent client, or words to that effect. To quit a job that pays regularly and provides benefits for you and your family in order to work for yourself and set the world on fire is roughly the same thing. I never realized what it was really like to work for an idiot until I started working for myself. Thank goodness I went into recovery. It was the best thing that ever happened to my employee.

People often turn to self-employment as a way to liberate themselves from their I-Bosses. But they often find out too late that their new boss is a bigger idiot than the one they just insulted on the way out the door. Consider some potential pitfalls before you tell your boss to take this job and shove it:

- Once you walk out that door, is there any chance of coming back?
- If you can come back, will they start you in the mailroom?
- Can you pay yourself salary and benefits equal to those you're leaving?
- Can you pay yourself without using up your savings and college fund for the kids?
- Do you understand what deficit spending is?
- Are you ready to spend more hours working than ever before?
- Does your spouse want you around the house all day?
- Will your spouse allow you to turn the spare bedroom into an office?
- Are you certain that you have the organization skills and self-discipline to be productive?
- Will you be as brutal on yourself as you were on your I-Boss when things screw up?

If you answered no to any of these questions, you might want to think twice about quitting a sure thing only to discover you've shot yourself in the foot.

The Birth of an Idiot Boss

The vast majority of us never receive any formal education or training in the art of leadership. As we claw or stumble our way into positions of authority, we use what we know, which is essentially nothing.

So we do what any inexperienced person does and imitate the authority figures we have encountered and observed. But even our observations are not exactly "educated."

I worked my way through college as a musician. In one of my first enterprising moves, I started a trio to play at the Top of the Tower restaurant and lounge at the downtown Des Moines Holiday Inn (circa 1972). About that same time I went to see a new movie called *The Godfather*. Most people would have identified with the characters portrayed by Marlon Brando or Al Pacino. Not me. I identified with Moe Green, the evil egomaniac that ran the hotel/casino in Vegas and got whacked with a bullet through his right eye in the final reel.

There was a prima donna piano player at the Top of the Tower who I needed to deal with. He showed up late for rehearsals and was otherwise irresponsible. I came down on him one night before the show. He complained later about being publicly humiliated in front of the singing waiters and waitresses. "Chester," I said, lighting a cigarette and exhaling a long stream of smoke for effect (back then it was cool to smoke). "I'm running a business here, and sometimes I have to kick a little ass to make it run right."

Chester laughed in my face and went on acting irresponsibly. I was mystified. The line was straight out of the film and nobody laughed when Moe Green said it. Chester did change one thing. Instead of disliking me intensely, he hated me from that point on. In my first true professional leadership challenge, I became an instant I-Boss. I was a monkey who watched Moe Green look and sound tough when he got in Pacino's face on the movie screen. Monkey saw, monkey imitated—poorly.

The imitation myth

Most bosses are promoted without the benefit of leadership training or formalized personal development. It's common for Idiot Bosses to merely imitate the leadership styles and practices of their predecessors. That's how we learn to be parents, isn't it? We either do what our folks did or do the opposite, neither one of which is likely to be the best choice.

Although they seem oblivious to nearly everything, I-Bosses can be insecure. If an employee does something wonderful, an I-Boss might feel a twinge of humiliation, rooted in his inability to match competencies. He might not be able to put a finger on the feeling or its origins, but he can take steps to make the employee feel what he's feeling. That's why no good deed goes unpunished and team members who do good things are routinely embarrassed or humiliated by their I-Bosses.

If an I-Boss isn't sure whether something a team member does is good or bad, he is likely to err on the side of bad and seize control of the situation, just to be safe. I'm embarrassed to admit I've done it. I've joined in conversations on subjects I knew nothing about just to appear informed. I picked up terms and phrases foreign to me and dropped them into conversations. If no one reacted, I knew I got away with it. If everybody stopped and looked at me, I'd act as if there was something caught in my throat. Trust me, there are better ways to win the confidence and respect of your team members than to wear your ignorance on your sleeve.

The student becomes the teacher

Because virtually no I-Boss is prepared, trained, or otherwise acclimated to the best practices of effective leadership, it's up to you to train them. You can't let your I-Boss know you're training him. That's your little secret. Just prepare your lesson plan and be consistent.

A psychology professor was teaching the concepts of classical conditioning to his class when they turned the tables on him. An insidious conspiracy formed and the students agreed to sit forward in their seats and pay rapt attention when the professor was on the right side of the room. When he wandered to the left side of the room they leaned back, slumped in their chairs, and acted disinterested. Without realizing why, he was soon delivering his entire lecture from the right corner of the classroom. I know because I started the conspiracy.

You can do the same with your I-Boss. Be perky, attentive, appreciative, or whatever else will please him when he does what you want him to do. Ignore him, work slowly, or act generally rebellious when he is behaving in ways that displease you. If you've paid attention to what makes him happy and unhappy as far as your behavior is concerned, it won't take long to start influencing what he says and does.

Become an amateur anthropologist. Pretend you're a CSI detective. Observe what pictures he hangs on his office walls, and what artifacts he proudly displays on his credenza. What animals are pictured on his wall calendar? Listen to the words and phrases he uses. Is he literate? Can he operate a computer? Can he build a computer? Can he write software? Can he spell "software"? Is the child in the picture on his desk indescribably ugly? Can you bring yourself to compliment him on all of the things he so obviously holds dear, including the {gag} cute child?

Be patient. It doesn't happen overnight. If nothing else, it will give you something to look forward to at work. You can also feel smug satisfaction that you are improving the working environment for all of your peers. Don't feel dirty or guilty for kissing up. It's survival. Think of yourself as a missionary to the clueless.

You're Not Invisible

Remember: You're being watched all the time. If you feel invisible or ignored, it's likely what you're doing isn't sufficiently impressive or important to those around or above you. But they're just pretending you don't exist. Put your detective skills to work again and note what types of behavior they approve of and start behaving accordingly. Even if you don't plan to alter your personal style and work habits over the long term, the experiment will prove what you do and say are noticed more than you thought.

Please people and you'll get recognition. As in the behavior modification episode with the psychology professor, you need to distinguish between what your I-Boss perceives as positive and negative behavior. In sufficient quantity, both positive and negative behaviors will make those who feel invisible visible. If you don't elicit much attention from your I-Boss, you know whatever it is you're doing falls into his dead zone.

Idiots lack imagination. That deficiency, coupled with the tunnel vision Idiot Bosses are famous for, means the ship will be submerged before they realize it hit an iceberg. If you want attention, you not only need to say or do things that warrant attention in the idiot's eyes, you need to exaggerate them so much he can't possibly fail to notice. If you're trying to impress your I-Boss by watering the plants around the office, drag in the fire hose from next to the elevator. If you want him to notice you're vacuuming the carpet, remove the muffler from the vacuum cleaner so the noise will deafen people two floors away, and then run a couple of circles around his desk.

Become an Influencer

A former president of the Maytag Company told me he couldn't drink coffee at work in the early years when his office was down the hall from Fred Maytag, Jr. To reach the restroom, he had to pass Fred's office, and he didn't want the grandson of the founder to see him making multiple trips to the john. So, he literally gave up drinking coffee in the morning. How far are you willing to go to improve your situation? The ex-coffee drinker was trying to avoid making a negative impression. I'm suggesting you develop and employ some tactics of your own to intentionally and systematically engineer the impression you want:

- If you're willing to help look after the office plant life, do it when and where the boss will see you.

- If you see trash on the floor, pick it up. You never know who's looking. If you have a chance to police the area when your boss is present, make a reasonable and believable demonstration.

- If an opportunity arises to lend the boss a hand with something, from carrying a large box to helping reboot the computer, graciously offer to help.

- Bring the donuts once in a while. When you do, don't just drop them in the coffee area. Walk past the boss's office, display the box, and say, "You can have first choice before I put these out for the masses."

- If your boss articulates frustration with a situation to which you can bring a reasonable solution, offer to help. Don't get pushy and aggravate his insecurities; make suggestions in the form of questions. "Would it help if..?" "What if we tried..?"

- In all things and at all times, be positive. Not, over-the-top giddy, making everyone sick—just positive. This means finding ways to get along with difficult people, greeting your boss's directives with a "can do" attitude, and making sure the boss knows you're a team player.

- Come in early and go home late. If you don't want your family life to suffer, drop into conversations that you polished up that proposal last night at home or got up early to work on it before coming to the office.

Throughout the humorous anecdotes and advice I've put together in this and future chapters, you'll find a constant theme: Your success when working with difficult peers and difficult people in positions of power all comes down to attitude—yours. "But, John," you complain, "I have serious problems and I need serious solutions." I agree. I've been there, done that. No matter how miserable your situation, your solution starts in your head and works its way out through your hands. Deliberately scheme how you can be a positive influence in your working environment.

If you think it sounds cheesy to tidy up the coffee area within your boss's view or to offer first dibs at the donuts, you don't understand how a boss's brain functions. Henry Ford said he was willing to pay more for a person's ability to get along with others than any other quality. If you think shedding resentment and hostility, and replacing them with a positive and helpful demeanor are for Boy Scouts and Girl Scouts, you're not seriously interested in improving your working atmosphere. There is no more powerful way to impress a boss than to be a supporter. There is nothing more miserable to a boss than a detractor.

Think this through to its logical conclusion. That's your office you're tidying up. You enjoy those plants along with everyone else. A happy boss, idiot or no idiot, is key to a pleasant working environment. Be honest and real about it. You are doing these things, as silly as some of them sound, and purposefully altering your attitude to improve your professional living conditions. Aren't you worth it?

Hard Work Makes Friends and Enemies

If idiots in positions of authority annoy you, it could be your I-Boss is holding you back from hard work. To my credit, I have always been a dedicated, hard worker. Ever since my first job as the pro shop boy at the Newton, Iowa Country Club (I've been paying income taxes every year since the age of 11), I've felt, if I must work, I should get into it so intensely that when I come up for air, it will be quitting time. It's hard for me to take a breather and then dive back into something with the same intensity I had before I took the break. Like a helpful and positive attitude, I've found that working hard benefits me as well as my employees.

I moved to California in 1977 and went to work as a union audio and lighting technician at Disneyland. It wasn't long before my work habits attracted some attention. One day I was on a crew of three or four, unloading sound equipment from a truck. Big Mike, the union boss, joked with several of the other fellows I was working like a human forklift. He suggested a couple of times that I should slow down before I blew a gasket. I chuckled with them and worked on until I felt a sharp tug on my arm. I had a microphone stand in each hand. "Put those down," Big Mike grumbled. I could see by the veins bulging from his neck that he wasn't joking anymore. I must have looked at him funny because he said it again, louder.

I set the microphone stands down and reached for some more gear on the truck. He grabbed my arm harder and swung me around. I was about to apologize for not working hard enough when he said, "Stand over there against the wall." I began to suspect my befuddled expression didn't please him as he shoved me against the wall. "You watch from right there," he growled. "Don't let me see you touch another thing."

It was one of the most excruciating experiences I've ever endured. Every synapse in my nervous system was firing, trying to get back into the unloading process. But I stayed put. The other stagehands kept doing their thing and I watched them helplessly as Big Mike watched me. When the truck was finally unloaded, he gave me permission to move. "Next time I tell you to slow down," he snarled menacingly, "slow down."

With that, he stomped off toward the commissary. The other guys turned and walked away, too. I remembered Big Mike hinting I should slow down a couple of times before, but I thought he was making a joke. After all, there was no reason for him to be concerned about my health. In the locker room later that day, one of the other guys expressed his displeasure that I had made them look bad by working so fast and left them unloading the truck shorthanded while Big Mike had me pinned to the wall. I was nicknamed the human forklift, which was not a term of endearment at the union hall.

Not long thereafter, Bob, the management guy came backstage between shows and took me by the arm. "Come with me, John," he said. "I want to talk to you." I was sure he going to fire me for slowing down on the job, even though I only did it when Big Mike was around. "I've been watching you and asking around," he went on.

"Here it comes," I thought to myself.

"We want you to head up a new department that will bring the union technicians under the jurisdiction of the Entertainment Division."

"What the...?" I thought. The International Alliance of Theatrical Stage Employees personnel had been part of the Maintenance Division since Walt opened Disneyland in 1955. Here it was 1978 and they wanted me to team up with another person and effect one of the biggest organizational changes in the park's history. I was to be in charge of audio, and an engineer from WED (the Disney design firm in Glendale named after Walter Elias Disney), was to be in charge of theatrical lighting. I thought this was all good and couldn't understand why the union guys weren't happy. After all, I couldn't pick up equipment anymore.

Idiot Oblivion

I share my professional experiences with you so you'll know you're not alone. How much of your professional good fortune resulted from your best-laid plans? How much of your bad fortune resulted from your best-laid plans? I'm guessing that you, like most people, enjoy successes and disappointments that occur more often in the randomness of the universe than as intentional outcomes of a well-thought-out strategies. Understanding and accepting how much our fortunes resemble corks floating in the ocean doesn't mean we should stop trying to position ourselves by doing the right things at every opportunity.

Without my knowledge, the same work ethic that upset the union boss at Disneyland had impressed management. And I hadn't set out to make an impression on either one of them. I was just trying to stay busy until quitting time. Disney management thought I was something on a stick and my 85 or so union employees thought I was an idiot. Being a true idiot, I didn't realize how much I was despised. Even after a couple of big guys from the union office came by and demanded my union card (my membership had been involuntarily terminated), I still didn't get it.

I managed to stay oblivious to the sneers and verbal jabs taken at my expense as I set out to move the technicians from the Maintenance Division to the Entertainment Division. Once again, my nose was close to the grindstone and I didn't intend to come up for air until

quitting time. I didn't realize there is no quitting time for management. Sometimes I worked into the wee hours and slept on the floor
of my office with the Anaheim Yellow Pages for a pillow.

Your I-Boss Might Care More Than You Know

Fatigue might have helped bring about my epiphany. The jeers and
jabs slowed down somewhat due to the relaxed working schedules and
other work environment improvements we were able to enact on behalf
of our technicians. As time passed, the audio, video, and lighting technicians liked being part of the Entertainment Division and felt more at
home. It was a major change, and we made it work because we were
working for the team, not the other way around. We hacked our way
through the bureaucratic underbrush to make working conditions better for them, and they responded. Attitudes improved, even though I'm
sure they still considered me an idiot. At least I was their idiot.

Your I-Boss might have a greater emotional investment in getting
things done right than he is willing or able to admit. An I-Boss's failure to communicate effectively can result from cluelessness about
important matters or simply from an inability to express himself.
People who are not formally prepared for positions of leadership are
not taught effective communications skills. Stay alert.

One of our Disneyland stage technicians was chronically late. She
was one of our brightest people, but she also had an attitude with a
capital A. After three or four late appearances in a row, I asked her to
come see me in my office, well away from the stages where her peers
were working. She came in, slumped down in a chair, and dropped her
tool belt loudly on the floor. I immediately recognized Chester the
piano player's loathsome attitude. But whatever part of me that once
admired Moe Green was gone. Instead, I started to cry. Not a big
boo-hoo, but I teared up and a minute passed before I could speak.
Maybe it was Moe's "bullet in the eye" thing.

My unusual demeanor surprised us both and got her attention.
Though she tried not to let her tough countenance down, I could see
she was curious. To my amazement, I really didn't care. What was on
my mind sort of materialized on my tongue as I spoke. I honestly
didn't fully realize what was on my mind until the words came out. I
know I had a picture in my mind of all the other technicians working
away down on the Space Mountain stage. "Personally," I said in a

calm, assured voice, "I don't care if you come in early, late, or not at all." I listened to myself closely because none of this was premeditated or rehearsed and I might need to remember what I said later.

"All I care about is the rest of the techs down there setting up for tonight's show. Those are your friends, the people you go out and drink with after work, and some of the people who took you under their wings to teach you the ropes when you started here. They won't say anything to you, so I'll say it for them. They get here on time and cover for you when you're late. From now on, if you decide to come in, I hope you'll be on time. Not for me or the company—I hope you'll be on time for them."

She was never late again. And her attitude changed to a lower-case "a." She seemed happier and more enthusiastic, which pleased her teammates. I stood at a distance and watched them work together many times. I'm not exactly sure what got through to her, but it resonated enough to make a change in her attitude and behavior; even if it did come from an idiot. Even a broken clock is right twice a day.

That was a turning point for me. As clumsy and unanticipated as it was, my epiphany gave me enough of a peek at the Promised Land to never return to complete idiocy. Your I-Boss is no exception. Even idiots tend to retain bits and pieces of knowledge. If your I-Boss stumbles into a good move, something that is truly helpful to you or those around you, reinforce it the way we reinforced our psychology professor's behavior. Rewarded behavior is repeated behavior—even if it's accidental.

The Stupid Gene

Be cautious with your idiot diagnosis. Sometimes what appears to be an idiot is just a regular person with idiosyncrasies. We all have them. Idiosyncrasies become exaggerated with exhaustion and dehydration. If a person arrives at the office wearing a different color sock on each foot, he might be a genius, a fashion setter, or color blind. Most likely though, he's an idiot.

Stupidity is different than alcoholism, drug addiction, or smoking. Well, maybe not entirely. But that's a different discussion. The analogy I'm about to make borrows liberally from 12-step recovery programs. I'm not disparaging 12-step programs, mind you. The point is that stupidity is a wide-spread disease. We have no control over stupidity in others. We didn't cause it, we can't cure it, and we can't control it. The only stupidity we can deal with is our own.

Steps to Stop Stupidity

Once you've become a transcendent idiot—one who can reflect upon his personal condition and circumstances—you can no longer wander back into the idiot population and disappear. Your intelligence, such as it is, will torment you night and day. You'll suffer from sleep deprivation (which will exaggerate your idiosyncrasies), begin experiencing psychotic episodes, be involuntarily institutionalized, sprung by an A.C.L.U. lawyer without your knowledge, put back on the street, and worry your family to death until your dog finds you sleeping in your garage.

The only reasonable alternative you have left is to accept the inevitability of stupidity in the form of idiots. Welcome to the real world. You can sooner change the weather than have any effect whatsoever on the number and distribution of idiots on this planet. Sometimes it seems as if idiots in human bodies have invaded Earth. Maybe it's a cosmic conspiracy to keep us from extended space exploration beyond our own neighborhood, which occupants of neighboring galaxies have written off long ago as depressed real estate.

You're here. I'm here. Wherever they came from, idiots are here. They're the only ones who don't know it. Can't we all just get along? I say yes...sort of. Our focus must be on our personal journeys toward recovery, enlightenment, and enrichment. Genuine idiots won't be reading this book, so it's kind of like a private conversation. The good news is that we can live fulfilling lives and have rewarding careers in spite of the idiots we work for.

The bad news is we must do all of the work. Don't get mad at me. The idiots don't even know what's going on. How can they help? But isn't a fulfilling life and a rewarding career worth the effort? I say yes...absolutely. With that, I take you to step one of our journey to idiot-proof (so to speak) nirvana.

The First Step:
"I admit that I am powerless over the stupidity of others and my life has become too stupid to manage."

Don't let this first step depress you too much. Stupidity might not exactly be a disease, but it should at least be classified as a syndrome. We can't begin our journey of recovery until we first confess how much trouble we're in. Feeling, much less admitting, powerless is intolerable to some people. It implies a loss of control (which they never had anyway) and they just won't go there. Meet the living dead. These zombies walk around thinking that they can change the idiots in their lives. I say we need to succeed in spite of the idiots in our lives.

Life is unmanageable if you try to control stupidity other than your own. Do I need to say it again? It's too big. Let it go. God can handle it. You and I need to invest our resources in managing our own stupidity. Now we're talking manageable. Maybe. If we keep the whole universal idiot thing in perspective and context, there is hope. Trying to manage our own stupidity issues without deference to the stupidity around us is like driving the wrong way down the freeway. You're asking for trouble. Driving in the right direction, minding your own business, even driving defensively doesn't guarantee that some idiot won't run into you. Each one of us is a single car in heavy traffic. Keep one eye on your rearview mirror.

Confession is good for the soul. Even if the confession is somewhat of a stretch, go with the flow. It's easier to push off toward the surface from the bottom of the pool. Admitting powerlessness is the first step to recovery. Subsequent steps will reveal who has the power and how you can tap into it to achieve your own serenity.

Think about what I've said in the context of managing yourself. You are ultimately your own boss, even if you report to someone else. Are you your own I-Boss, as I am? How effectively you interact with your boss is your choice. Will you be a monkey see, monkey do kind of person? Or will monkey see, monkey think better of it? Will you be able to give yourself an emotional break, even if others won't?

In the chapters ahead, we'll get down to brass tacks and examine the whole idiot issue and the roles we play in it. It makes dealing with your I-Boss at the office much easier if you can see the parallels to your own experience. I don't suggest the type of reflection that leads to regrets. But changing your thinking and behavior doesn't happen naturally or effortlessly. Contemplating your past will serve only to predict your future unless you consciously decide to follow another road.

2

Will the Real Idiot Please Stand Up?

Not every boss is an idiot and not every idiot is a boss. Idiot Bosses are not all bad. Most every one of them is good at something. They're just no good at being bosses. Even though not all bosses are idiots, once you learn more about some of the other boss types, you might be grateful to have an Idiot Boss.

It's a mistake to assume your boss is an idiot if she is not. Using idiot modification techniques on a non-idiot will prove about as effective as snorting Vick's Nasal Spray to pass a kidney stone. Depending on the type of boss you work for, using the wrong approach might leave you wishing you were passing a kidney stone just to brighten your day.

I have organized the world of bosses into eight sub-categories:

- Good Bosses.
- God Bosses.
- Machiavellian Bosses.
- Masochistic Bosses.
- Sadistic Bosses.
- Paranoid Bosses.
- Buddy Bosses.
- Idiot Bosses.

As we examine each boss type, arrange all of the bosses you have ever worked for in their appropriate category, including your current boss. You might find out that your boss history reveals a disturbing

37

pattern. Having been both an Idiot Boss and an Idiot Employee, I have found if there are prominent boss patterns in your professional life, it could mean:

A.   You are attracted to a certain type of boss to fulfill a subliminal desire for self-punishment.

B.   There is a dominant type of boss in your industry.

C.   You are chronically unlucky.

D.   You are the idiot.

E.   All of the above.

Good Bosses

As hard as it is for some to believe, there are Good Bosses out there. If you see a coworker leaning back in her cubicle with her eyes closed and a silly grin on her face, chances are she is taking a vacation of the imagination in which her thoughts have drifted back to a happier place and time when she worked for a Good Boss. Those who have worked for Good Bosses often wax nostalgic. Those who have never had that pleasure of working for a Good Boss can only imagine.

It's surprisingly simple to be a Good Boss, which makes me wonder why more bosses don't get it. I'll wager you know at least one I-Boss who hasn't done anything right since the Carter administration. Then again, it took me a long time to get it. The ways in which we humans think and act are like the tires on your car. You never give them any thought until one goes flat. For Idiot Bosses to change, and they can, some incident or series of incidents of sufficient magnitude need to occur before they will know there is a problem. Once they are aware a problem exists—and they are it—they can begin making the transformation from Idiot Boss to Good Boss by adopting the surprisingly simple yet profound golden rule of leadership:

Lead the way you like to be led.

Simply put, that's what Good Bosses do. In most human interactions, the simpler something is, the more effective it is. We all want simple answers, the easy road, and the easy money. If we are convicted, we want to do easy time. Have you ever heard an ad on the radio that said, "…in just three hard payments?"

Good Bosses have the self-awareness to understand how they like to be treated and the common sense to figure out that other people probably like to be treated the same way. How we communicate with one another is a good place to start. Good Bosses provide a constant flow of clear and concise information and encourage you and the rest of your team to do the same. Good Bosses don't like to play 20 questions in order to discern what you're talking about; they don't want to read your mind in order to learn what you're withholding; and they don't expect you to read their minds as to what they expect.

If you make your boss play a round of Jeopardy in order to learn what you're doing, you have a problem with that person and vice versa. Making someone guess at what you want or to gain important information you have in your little clutches is passive-aggressive behavior. It's resentment playing itself out. We tend to be passive-aggressive with people we want to punish. When was the last time you gave the silent treatment to someone you were happy with? The concept is easy to test. Just reverse the situation and consider how you feel when your boss withholds information from you.

Your imagination starts running wild. Doesn't she trust me? Does she think I'm too stupid to let me in on the big secret? Is she afraid that I might do something I will get praised for? All kinds of thoughts might run through your mind—none of which produce warm and fuzzy thoughts about your boss. If your boss is likewise filled with doubt, how warm and fuzzy can you expect her to feel about you?

Uncertainty always leads to uneasiness. How often do people go to lunch together and speculate about what's going on around the office? How often do you hear whispered conversations with hands cupped over the telephone mouthpiece? Have you ever found yourself sitting in a bathroom stall when your boss came in with another of her management level? You kept very still, hoping you might overhear some tidbit of information that would affect your job, didn't you? Are you aware of how often you strain to overhear what is being said in a conversation in the next cubicle or around the corner?

Adjoining bullpens

My first office at Disneyland was not a conventional cubicle. It had tall walls, but no ceiling. I could easily hear one end of telephone conversations in adjoining offices, as well as full conversations. I didn't give it much thought at the time, but looking back, there were certain people who spoke up robustly as if they didn't care who overheard them. These were the open personalities who didn't make it a point or policy to be secretive. I always felt relaxed around those people. They spoke positively about others, which gave me the feeling they probably spoke positively about me in my absence.

The same principle holds when reversed. Disney was the first big corporate atmosphere I ever worked in. The human dynamics of the workplace were a fascinating and frightening thing to behold for a single young person with delusions of grandeur and no polished skills to achieve it. Through experience, I learned that people who habitually speak positively of others tend to do so in all circumstances. Those who criticize others in your presence and recruit you to agree with their cutting remarks will probably criticize you when you're out of the room.

There were those who always had muffled and subdued conversations in their ceilingless offices. Someone would come into the office, the door would be closed (which was a cue that some secret information was about to be exchanged), and the whispering began. I don't remember ever being able to decipher what was being said, and I didn't want to be caught standing with my ear pressed to the wall or tippytoed on top of my credenza, straining to hear what was coming over the wall. Those conversations will forever remain private. But they piqued my paranoia and sure sounded important at the time.

The whisperers might have been trying to cloak their conversation from any number of people in the surrounding, ceilingless offices. Perhaps they were aware that the apparent secrecy of their conversation made the information, whatever it was, incredibly enticing. Maybe they knew the effect of whispered conversations and didn't actually say anything—just whispered to bust the neighbors' chops.

None of this is a problem if people are open and honest. There was a secretary for one of the other Disney executives who took secretiveness to an extreme. Whenever anyone, not just me, walked near her workspace, whether to talk to her or just pass by, she dove on top of the papers on her desk to hide them. I had to pass her desk on my way to the restroom. The next nearest restroom required walking downstairs, out the door, and into another building.

Whenever I walked past her desk, I repeated to myself, *Say nothing. Don't slow down. Don't look in her direction.* It didn't matter. The moment I rounded the corner, I heard the papers rustle and a dull thud as she landed on the desktop. She lay there, sprawled out, glaring at me, until I was out of sight.

I always wondered what was so important about her boss's work to warrant such secrecy. He was a good person, a mid-food-chain manager, like me. He seemed to be an open communicator. The effect of her sprawling performance was curious, though. It created the illusion that whatever was contained on those papers was top secret, which it probably wasn't, and that she considered me a threat if I found out what was there.

Maybe I should have been flattered that she thought I had so much power. I felt like she had some reason to be suspicious of me, even though I knew she didn't. Obviously, she felt she had reason to be suspicious of me. Other people had similar experiences with her and she spent a lot of time on top of her desk (especially an hour or so after the first pot of coffee disappeared). Yet, I only worried about what I might have done to warrant such treatment.

Good Bosses are aware that sharing information in a thorough, timely manner makes people feel included, respected, and acknowledged for their ability to contribute. They make open communication a priority. They keep everybody informed all the time. And they are receptive to feedback. Not just between 3 and 4 p.m. every third Tuesday, but all of the time. It's so remarkably easy that bosses who don't do it should undergo psychiatric examination and electroshock therapy if necessary.

The equitable treatment of all team members is nearly as important in the workplace as communication. I say nearly as important because, if people are going to be treated inequitably, it's better to be told up front about it than to pretend it's not happening. The real sting from preferential treatment of some at the expense of others comes from the charade that everyone is being treated equally. People don't mind being Cinderella before her run of luck as much as they hate being promised the whole prince and pumpkin thing with no follow-through.

Good Bosses are fair

Fairness in the office simply means applying the rules fairly, equally, and without regard for workplace political alliances. Even if the rules are stuffy and cumbersome, applying them fairly across the board builds good relationships. Holding some people's feet to the fire while giving others a pass produces hostility, resentment, and payback if it goes far enough.

Communicating openly and honestly with people and treating them fairly is no more than treating them the way you like to be treated. It sounds overly simple, but it works. It's not hard and it doesn't cost anything. It also works on everybody, regardless of where you are on the food chain. Good Bosses treat those with more power the same way they treat those with less power. People are people. Yet, how often do you encounter a double standard? Worse, how often do you practice a double standard?

Good employees tend to make Good Bosses and Good Bosses make good employees to those above them because the same factors apply to both. Positive behaviors that produce good relationships work in all directions. Self-indulgent employees usually make self-indulgent bosses. People who screw the little person are just as likely to screw the big person, given the opportunity. If you're not a fair person or you don't communicate openly, you're not going to be the person the cubicle daydreamer with the silly grin on her face is dreaming about.

Managing in all directions is an important concept to comprehend because the implications are so far reaching. If you have a Good Boss, chances are she is also a good employee. The values she demonstrates in your presence are likely to be the same values she demonstrates when you're not around.

Being a Good Boss is so easy, it makes you wonder why anyone would invest the extra effort and energy required to be a bad one. I guess it all could come down to not knowing any better, monkey see/monkey do, or choosing the wrong role model out of the available options. As much as go-along-to-get-along social butterflies around the office want to believe that animals and small children, left to their own devices, never hurt each other, there is always the ever-present hidden agenda or the ever-popular ulterior motive. When you have a bad boss, chances are that somebody is up to no good.

Thicker Than Blood

When the owner's kid is working for the company, you'd be a dim bulb indeed to not figure out she is special-rules material. I knew a guy once who drove a limo in New York City for a wealthy business family. Specifically, he worked for a father and his two sons. He was sure his employers liked him so much they were going to cut him in on the family business one day.

That day never came. I tried to warn him it would never happen. Just because somebody likes you, with or without good reason, doesn't mean they're going to adopt you. You don't have to study much history to learn, blood is thicker than water and family money is thicker than blood. I've seen heads of families bypass talented, capable, loyal, dedicated, lifelong employees to hand their businesses over to a son or a daughter whose mental faculties have been significantly reduced by generations of inbreeding.

The diminished capacity often contributes to the demise of the enterprise. Typically, the first generation establishes the business, the second generation grows it, the third generation barely sustains it, and the fourth generation destroys what's left. Not just mom-and-pop shops, but big firms, with hundreds of millions in revenues. Go figure.

There are exceptions. I know of several fourth generation owners who are still growing their family businesses. Like so many things I once rebelled against, nepotism is now on my 'Get Over It and Get On with Your Life' list. Even when nepotism is the order of the day, open and honest communication, along with fairness in everything else, takes away much of the sting. Working for a family-owned business can be a rewarding experience.

God Bosses

There are people who think they're God. No one is sure how or why some people come upon self-deification. It could be an extreme case of choosing a role model. There is nothing wrong with emulating God-like qualities, but to imagine you're the big guy Himself—to think you are the voice from the burning bush—now you're scaring me.

A God Boss is not an Idiot Boss in the classical sense. Somehow, thinking you're God transcends cluelessness. It's like believing you're Napoleon Bonaparte and then some. For their own safety and the safety of the population at large, God Bosses should be locked up, with the key dropped in the deepest river.

Fortunately, God Bosses appear most often in church settings or in missionary organizations where the real God is considered boss to begin with, so the whole thing winds up as a power struggle with you-know-who coming up short. The misguided mortal in such cases merely tries to usurp the authority. God probably doesn't consider God Bosses a threat as much as an annoyance. You should take a deep breath and do the same, unless you work for one.

If you have a God Boss, I hope and pray that he is a loving and gracious lord. Fire and brimstone in the wrong hands can ruin your day. Hopefully, the lunatic doesn't expect you to put on sackcloth and sandals. Then again, the more powerful the God Boss, the more important it is to find a way to coexist.

If you find it is expedient to appease a God Boss, pray for pardon from your real Higher Authority and then play church. Upon seeing your God Boss for the first time each morning, bow slightly. When he acts down or depressed, take up a collection around the office and deliver tithes and offerings unto him. If your God Boss indicates you have disappointed him, don't argue. Beg forgiveness. Use the Old Testament as a guidebook to making him happy. Old Testament antics are as a rule more over the top than New Testament behavior.

When your God Boss is angry, find something or someone to sacrifice on his desk. Johnson, the internal auditor from Accounting, will make a decent burnt offering. Just be careful not to grind ashes into your boss's carpet.

Use your imagination. One of the many reasons God Bosses annoy you might be that you can't believe the real God would create such a megalomaniac. Believe it. Leave room for the possibility he is playing God to compensate for a tremendous lack of confidence. In either case, it pays to consider what will please him and deliver. Trying to subvert or compete with a God Boss will invariably leave you the loser.

- Make sure you address your God Boss as he wants to be addressed. If he wants to be called Mr. Smith instead of Joe, do it. Resistance will only cost you peace of mind and whatever influence over your working conditions you hope to achieve.
- Follow his rules. Even if his rules conflict with company policies, find the middle ground and present him with

the illusion that you are doing things his way—from formatting e-mail to the types of pictures you hang in your cubicle.

- Lose the battles and win the war. God bosses are about power, usually because power hides incompetence. Your goal is to create a pleasant and rewarding working environment to the best of your ability. Battling a more powerful foe over the little stuff will leave you unhappy and resentful.

- Offer him sacrifices. Seriously. It might cost you less than you think. If he likes donuts, as I mentioned in Chapter 1, show up at his door and offer the whole box. If he likes granola, bring him granola (and eat it yourself around him). These are silly little things, but God Bosses firmly believe that, if you're not for them, you're against them.

- Ask forward forgiveness. It's not that hard. By saying things like, "If it's okay with you…" or "Would you mind if...?" What your God Boss will hear is, "You have the power to grant…" and "It's your will that matters most around here."

- Acknowledge his presence. God Bosses don't think of themselves as invisible. Don't make the mistake of ignoring him. When he comes into a meeting or the cafeteria, welcome him verbally. If you don't have the floor at the moment, make eye contact and nod your head to let him know you noticed his arrival.

Your comfort in professional situations begins with your boss's comfort. Your attitude, if it is sufficiently positive, will put him at ease. His ease is your ease. If your attitude is resentful, he will bring thunder and lightning on your head and the heads of your coworkers. I won't go so far as to advise fearing your God Boss. He doesn't wield that much real power. But it's worth your while to respect the power he does have. Not to do so is to bring a plague of locusts on yourself.

Machiavellian Bosses

Machiavellian Bosses don't think they're God. They are extremely intelligent and know better. But they will end you for soiling the carpet in their offices. Machiavellian Bosses are ticked off they can't bump God out of His job and don't mind taking out their frustration on the rest of us.

Machiavellian Bosses view the universe as an enormous pyramid. There is one spot at the top and it belongs to them, by divine right. Machiavellian Bosses have committed every ounce of their being to achieving the top spot. They don't care what or whom they must climb over to get there. They simply won't be denied.

If you are run over, run through, or otherwise become a casualty of the Machiavellian's race to the top, don't take it personally. It's not about you. It was never about you. And it will never be about you, except for the moment you are actually in her way. That moment is yours and will live over and over again in your nightmares.

The only time Machiavellian Bosses will ever be content or benevolent is when they are in the top spot. Even then, it's a coin toss. They might have read somewhere that there is a higher spot to acquire. As long as there is more power to be had, Machiavellian Bosses will not rest. Moreover, they will leave no maneuver or weapon of mass destruction unused in their quest for the top.

Machiavellian Bosses are too intelligent and shrewd to be considered Idiot Bosses. They are not clueless, except for things that don't matter to them—like the health and well-being of other people or the goals and objectives of the organization. They are highly focused, highly driven, and highly efficient. Translated, that means lean, mean, killing machines. They remove obstacles from their path by whatever means are necessary and readily available. Don't cross the street in front of a speeding Machiavellian, even if you have the light.

If you find yourself working for a Machiavellian, there are several ways to protect yourself. You can say things like, "You know, boss, the carpet in the CEO's office matches your eyes." If the CEO of your company drives a Lexus 430 LS you can say, "You seem like a Lexus 430 LS kinda person to me, boss." You can skip the symbolism and appeal to his insatiable appetite for power with, "This organization would run like clockwork if you were in charge." Telling God and Machiavellian Bosses what they want to hear is always your best bet.

Realizing the Machiavellians perceive the universe as a pyramid, you must take care in all you do to avoid competition. More than avoiding competition, which she will assume, you need to frame your language and behavior in ways that indicate you understand and accept her right to the top spot. Like the God Boss, the Machiavellian is dead serious about her self-perception and has little or no genuine regard for you. On the up side, presenting the proper attitude and actions to your Machiavellian Boss will make your working environment as pleasant as possible and, on a more positive side, possibly keep you from getting run over.

- Use the words "for you" often. To merely say, "I'll take care of it," can actually be interpreted by a Machiavellian as a threat to go over her head. You might have no such intention. But if a Machiavellian Boss suspects that you're going over her head, she'll have yours served up on a platter. To a Machiavellian, saying, "I'll take care of it for you," sounds far less threatening, almost as if you're doing it in her name.

- Use "for you" in the past tense. In describing anything you did, include the words, "for you." This makes the Machiavellian think that you are acting on her behalf, even when you're out of her sight, and her comfort level around you will improve.

- Alert her to intelligence. When you find something out, tell her. Send an e-mail or mention it in passing. Being in constant competition with everyone, Machiavellians appreciate information that might be useful to them. The information might not mean much to you, but you're not engaged in her struggle for supremacy.

- Copy her first. Make sure your Machiavellian Boss is in the loop on everything. Even if it seems like a trivial piece of information to you, let the Machiavellian tell you if she doesn't want to hear it. If she senses that you are withholding information, she'll conclude you are competing with her and things will get unpleasant. This is about detoxing your environment, remember?

- Accept her invitations. It might disrupt your schedule, but turning down a Machiavellian's invitation to lunch or an event can be interpreted as resistance or a possible power move on your part. Be reasonable in the context of your own life, but understand that disinterest on your part can be a threat to a Machiavellian.

- Frame your contributions in terms of whom she can impress. "That oughta make Mr. Big a happy camper," is much better than saying, "I hope Mr. Big likes what I did." When complimenting a Machiavellian, be aware of the people higher on her food chain and construct your comments in terms of how they will be impressed and appreciative of what she did, even if you did it.

As with all of these tactics, you must use your best judgment and balance your needs with the sacrifice you're willing to make. Just be aware of how your attitudes and behaviors appear through your boss's eyes. Although you and your boss might march to different drummers, the boss sets the rhythm around the office. Learning a new cadence will serve you better than forming your own drum line. You'll probably just frustrate yourself and your boss, who in turn will drum you out.

Masochistic Bosses

Saying what a Masochistic Boss wants to hear,—"You're a piece of slime..."—is not exactly appropriate and could come back to haunt you if overheard. Unfortunately, complimenting masochists only annoys them, and they usually respond by doing something particularly despicable to set the record straight.

As the name implies, masochists have developed a belief that they should be punished...must be punished. Who knows why? The important thing is that they will suck everyone within their sphere of influence into their sick behavior. Their need to be punished is so intense that they will punish themselves if nobody else will. In extreme cases, nobody else can do it well enough to be trusted.

Masochistic Bosses attract codependents like flies to a Sunday picnic. The codependents try like crazy to fill up the black hole in the masochist's soul, which is impossible. Yet, the Herculean effort continues day-in and day-out. The codependents shovel affirmations down the masochist's throat for all they're worth and the masochist vomits them all back up. Masochistic Bosses are not idiots in the classical sense. But they're about as uplifting as a boat anchor.

Departments run by Masochistic Bosses are easy to spot. For starters, nothing ever gets done except for the occasional 911 call. Getting something accomplished might mean a reduction in pain and misery, so that's out. Masochistic Bosses make sure their departments fail so upper management will deal out punishment.

The best way to deal with a Masochistic Boss is to get out. There is no way these people will ever feel good about themselves. Neither will they ever allow you to accomplish anything that might make them look or feel good. When you accomplish something that makes you look or feel good, your Masochistic Boss is likely to say, "Oh, swell. Good for yo-o-o-ou. I suppose you're going to get promoted now and knock me off the management ladder. Well, go ahead. Do what makes you happy." It makes you want to take your accomplishment, wad it up, and throw it in the trash. Except that your Masochistic Boss will probably have already put the trashcan over his head and will be beating it against a wall.

Once again, the secret to surviving and thriving in a Masochistic Boss's department begins with attitude, followed by language and behavior. You must learn to be positive without smiling. In fact, being positive in a masochist's world means getting the focus off his pain as often as possible.

- Frame your comments in the context of avoiding problems. If you have a proposal you want to advance, say, "This will assure we're in compliance with the organization's parameters without drawing any undue attention our way." Your Masochistic Boss will hear in your comment an absence of reward and appreciation, which to him is the next best thing to actual punishment.

- Point out possible down-side outcomes. Saying, "This could result in some negative consequences that we'll have to deal with," can be a perfectly honest and truthful statement. Your Masochistic Boss will hear the possible negatives, while your fellow team members will simply take it as a heads up.

- Don't engage your Masochistic Boss's negative conversation. Listen respectfully, but don't pick up the negativity. You don't want any more negative energy around you than necessary. He wants to wallow in it. You can strike a compromise of sorts by being attentive when it's appropriate and steering clear whenever you can.

- Acknowledge what can happen. Your Masochistic Boss will tell you repeatedly what bad things are likely to happen in any given scenario or initiative. Note for future reference what he is most afraid of, to hear him tell it, and point out up front the possibility that his specific fears could be realized. Then offer that it might turn out another way by the luck of the draw.

- Include but don't invite. Copy your Masochistic Boss on all e-mails and announcements of activities that you cook up with your coworkers, but don't specifically invite him. Issue a blanket invitation. The last thing you want to do is act as if you're cheering him up. Don't specifically exclude him either.

- Give him a virtual hug. Physical contact is rarely appropriate in office settings, but a well-timed nod of the head, sigh, or shrug of the shoulders can have a similar effect. A virtual hug for your Masochistic Boss is a nonverbal way to say, "I know you're under an immense amount of pressure that you don't deserve and I'm powerless to help you."

I rarely advise quitting, but, as W.C. Fields said, "If at first you don't succeed, try again. Then give up. There's no use being a damn fool about it." Or words to that effect. The best way to deal with a Masochistic Boss is to get out. There is no way these people will ever feel good about themselves. Neither will they ever allow you to accomplish anything that might make them look or feel good. My advice: Get out before you injure yourself on a booby trap he has set around the office for himself. Get out that is, unless you're a sadist. Then you can play with the masochist the way a cat plays with a defenseless mouse.

Sadistic Bosses

Hello, Cruella. Telling Sadistic Bosses what they want to hear, like "...ouch," will only get them charged up to lay on more punishment—sometimes overt and sometimes subtle. Take for example the practical joker Sadistic Bosses that put up signs reading, "When I want your opinion, I'll give it to you." Ha-ha. What these morons apparently don't realize is people see through the pseudo-humor for what it is—a reminder of who has the power.

If it's so funny, why isn't anyone laughing except the boss? There's always the suggestion box with no bottom placed strategically over a wastebasket. Do you hear anyone laughing? I'll never understand why people think making light of power disparity in the workplace is supposed to make it okay.

Like the mouse that has been caught, but not killed, the Sadistic Boss won't let you get away. She will keep you alive to torture you. If you try to transfer out of her department, she will show up at your door holding your transfer request with R-E-J-E-C-T-E-D written across it in big red letters. You'll pinch yourself to wake from the nightmare only to find that you're just pinching yourself and she is still standing there—with an evil smile. If you try to go around her or above her head, she will go to the Pope if necessary to get your transfer request rejected.

Working for a Sadistic Boss is the closest thing to hell I can think of. Forget about working your way out of the problem. The harder you work, the more she'll pile on you. Forget about insubordinating your way out of the problem. The more you goof off, the more justification you give her to beat you. Forget about bleeding your way out of the problem. Injuring yourself is a waste of time, not to mention painful. Pain is like catnip for a sadist.

Working yourself to near death, goofing off, or self-inflicting wounds only play into the Sadistic Boss's game. But it's not hopeless. Try pretending you're a masochist. If your performance is convincing and the sadist thinks you're enjoying the pain, you'll be out in a flash. Only the pain and suffering of others will charge a sadist's batteries. Take a cue from Brer Rabbit. He put the fox in a paradoxical bind when he pleaded for the solution he wanted as if it were punishment by saying, "Please don't throw me in the brier patch." Of course, the brier patch is where Brer wanted to be. In laymen's terms, a paradoxical bind simply means damned if you do and damned if you don't. It worked for Brer Rabbit and you just might be hippity hopping to freedom before you know it.

There are ways to deal with Sadistic Bosses to improve your working environment. As always, knowing what you're up against helps.

The maxim, "Keep your friends close and your enemies closer," doesn't apply here. You need to keep as much distance as possible without provoking the sadist to jerk your choke collar.

- Develop ways to assure your Sadistic Boss that her workload is indeed oppressive, even if it's not. In real terms, if she thinks you're skating through anything, she'll associate that with failure to sufficiently burden you. It sounds silly, but there are many bosses who truly believe any happiness or frivolity around the office can only mean one thing: jailbreak. Jail keepers deal with jailbreaks in one way: lockdown.

- When a Sadistic Boss calls, come. Disobeying a Sadistic Boss, or even delaying your responses, gives her an excuse to lash out. She has enough motivation to cause pain without you adding more. Understand that, to a sadist, pain is power. Your pain—her power. Fighting her power plays into her game. Always be ready to respond quickly, although not merrily, to a Sadistic Boss. You will get through the day more painlessly.

- Assure her that pain is a good motivator. Many employees think it's a mission from God to convince the Sadistic Boss that her methods are unsound. Not only will you lose that argument every time, you have just given her a reason to prove all over again how powerful she is. Smart workers will hand in their work with an acknowledgement that the pressure she exerted accelerated the process. Refer in your e-mails and other correspondences to the fact that workloads are weighty, but you're continuing your struggle.

- Don't organize activities in a Sadistic Boss's department. Keep them underground and ad hoc. Organizing a sports activity or a party is like serving her a punishment opportunity on a silver platter. This means, don't dress up in your softball uniform before leaving the office. If your Sadistic Boss sees you're on your way out to have fun, you'll wind up working late and missing the game.

- Act busy. Idleness invites punishment in the form of exaggerated workloads. I'm not saying fake working. To create a better working environment for yourself, you want to work on important and personally rewarding activities. In a sadistic environment, just make your work appear excessively burdensome. If you've ever tried to kick back and lighten things up around a Sadistic Boss, I don't need to remind you what happens.

- Watch her eyes. Pain begets pain. The Sadistic Boss is probably the victim of pain imposed by another sadist, either in her family or elsewhere. This is not a happy person thumping on you for no reason. Whatever pain she dishes out, she has felt it before from someone more powerful. For whatever reason, pain has become a way of life. Sometimes, making eye contact will open an unspoken corridor between you and she'll back off a little. If making eye contact only makes her rage out at you, disengage.

You are best served in a Sadistic Boss's department to appear busy and focused without good cheer, not that a serious attitude will be hard to come by. This doesn't mean you can't be upbeat and positive when you're outside of the sadist's orbit. Being positive and upbeat will enhance the possibility that someone might recruit you away from your Sadistic Boss.

The fact that your boss is a sadist is probably not news to anyone, inside or outside of your department. People up the food chain know more than you might think, despite the fact they don't acknowledge it when you're around. If you are sour and dour everywhere with everyone, they won't know if the problem is you or your boss.

Never talk your Sadistic Boss down in front of her superiors. If others see you being positive when away from your boss, they'll feel sorry for your situation and might even admire your tenacity for keeping a stiff upper lip in the face of such negativity. With a Sadistic Boss, play it smart, but play it nonetheless.

Paranoid Bosses

A Paranoid Boss is a piece of work. To Paranoid Bosses, everything and everybody is out to get them, including you. Working for a Paranoid Boss can be a real treat. Anything you do, for whatever reason, is an attempt to subvert your boss, or so he thinks. What can you do?

Very little. Paranoia is a sticky wicket. It exists largely in the paranoid's imagination, which is not a sector accessible to you or anybody else.

Paranoia can feed on itself and become a self-fulfilling prophecy. The Paranoid Boss spends his energy searching out and exposing the conspiracy against him. Sometimes he actually finds one. But most of the time, he has to invent one. Either way, the focus and leadership that should have been committed to departmental objectives is wasted and the whole operation goes in the tank—thus confirming the paranoid boss's contention that someone conspired to sabotage his operation. He doesn't need to have any evidence, only a failed operation. That's enough to feed the paranoia until next time.

Escaping the Paranoid Boss is not hard. If you can make him believe you're part of the conspiracy, he will do everything he can to have you punished, which in most organizations will result in your transfer because termination is such a litigious exposure these days and everybody knows he's paranoid anyway.

Although it's ethically suspect, you might want to try coughing at meetings. Your Paranoid Boss will immediately stop whatever he's doing and say, "What? What's going on?" Look around the room and say, "Nothing." Approximately 90 seconds later, signal one of your coconspirators to cough. Tap out Morse Code on the top of the conference table and have one of your coconspirators tap back. When your Paranoid Boss turns and asks, "What? What's going on?" shrug your shoulders. The more you deny his accusations the more he will suspect you and work to have you removed from his department.

Times and circumstances change. For most professionals, the employment landscape is nearly unrecognizable from what it was a few years ago. Industry-wide fiscal setbacks, corporate cutbacks, and downsizing often limit the options you once had to move easily and freely around the organization. If escaping your paranoid boss is not as easy as you had hoped, you can employ tactics to make the relationship tolerable.

- Keep your activities in plain sight. It might not occur to you that a Paranoid Boss can see an innocent conversation by the coffee machine as a threat. Once again, use your imagination. These people don't think like you. Stay one step ahead of your Paranoid Boss by intentionally avoiding the appearance of secret activity.

- Like the Machiavellian Boss, copy your Paranoid Boss on everything. Let him tell you when to stop. A constant flow of information serves two purposes. First, he will think, by its sheer volume, information is being disclosed more than withheld. Second, he will be sufficiently occupied with reading the information that he'll have less time to ruminate about conspiracies.

- Spend more time with him. It's hard for a Paranoid Boss to imagine you conspiring if you're in his face. Imagination is a key term because that's where the conspiracies exist—in his imagination. If creating a more copasetic work environment is your main objective, invite your Paranoid Boss to spend time with you and your coworkers.

- Share the knowledge. Use terms and phrases indicating that you not only share information freely with your Paranoid Boss, but also with the rest of the organization. Indicate in your correspondences how widely you distribute information. Come right out and say, "As I shared with [so-and-so]..." This will decrease his anxiety level, knowing that information shared over a larger population reduces the probability of a mass conspiracy.

- Share secrets. Disclose to your Paranoid Boss some of your inner thoughts, within reason. Demonstrating your trust for him will invite his trust in return. It's hard to distrust someone who demonstrates trust in you. Paranoids are not completely hopeless. Sharing will also demonstrate a new way of being for a person who might adopt a new attitude around you, given enough encouragement. Be a genuine listener if he decides to share with you.

- Put on the uniform. Rather than herd out of the office for the company softball game, which your Paranoid Boss will interpret as a sure sign you're all on your way to an underground meeting, put on your softball uniforms first. Not that you can't conspire against your Paranoid Boss while dressed in softball uniforms, but it at least appears that you're doing something legitimate. And of course invite him to come to the game. If he doesn't, bring pictures and a post game report to the office the following morning.

Like any other personality disorder, you have no real control over a Paranoid Boss. But you can do a great deal to influence the environment in a positive way. That much power you do have. Deciding not to intentionally do things to shape your environment the way you prefer it to be will help bring about the environment you don't want. Inaction around the office is not innocuous.

Buddy Bosses

I don't need any more friends, do you? Buddy Bosses are so determined to occupy the same space in the universe with you that you'll welcome any excuse to elude them. This includes working. "Sorry boss," you rehearse saying in the mirror, putting on the most pitiful face you can conjure. "The CEO just gave me a deadline directly." Logic like this places a Buddy Boss in the same type of paradoxical bind Brer Rabbit laid on the fox. If you are fired, she loses a buddy and has to break in someone new to replace you. So distressed is she that you're not available, she doesn't even question why the CEO might be giving you orders directly.

Your Buddy Boss wants to hang with you, but she doesn't want you to get in trouble and not like her. If she has the power to relax a deadline or get you out of a tough assignment altogether, it might be worth kicking around with her a bit. With most Buddy Bosses, however, people prefer to double their workload rather than becoming joined at the head.

Buddy Bosses can be aggravating and annoying, but they are also some of the most malleable bosses around. You can exert positive influences on them more effectively than with almost any other type of boss. If you are equally as emotionally needy as your Buddy Boss, it could be a marriage made in heaven, although I would rather go to another heaven.

- Invite your Buddy Boss to everything. She is going to come anyway. Trying to sneak events around a Buddy Boss can be disastrous. She'll be hurt if she finds out you didn't include her and you'll be saddled with a sulking boss, which would only appeal to a sadist.
- Share information openly with her. This will make her feel included. Sharing information openly is a sound organizational practice. Remain mindful, though, that these

various boss personalities—with the exception of the Good Boss—are not concerned first and foremost with best practices. In a practical sense, you can bind up a Buddy Boss to a degree by flooding her with information, which in turn keeps her out of your way temporarily while you try to work.

- Request meetings. A Buddy Boss might enthusiastically gather her chicks around her, but if it's always at her suggestion, she might eventually become annoyed and even saddened. If you request a staff meeting at least once per week, the time can be put to productive organizational use and your Buddy Boss will be pleased that you took the initiative. To her, it means you care. She'll gladly let you plan and conduct the meeting, which puts the ball in your court to shape the environment.

- Post pictures with her in them. Visual demonstrations and reminders of her inclusion in all things will assure her emotionally. Buddy Bosses are generally lonely people and a little attention can go a long way. A departmental bulletin board featuring photographs of her with various groups of team members can fill the empty spaces diminishing her need to bug you constantly.

- Target e-mails and other correspondence to remind her that she's not alone. It doesn't take very many words to say, "Hi." The "How are you doing?" is implied. Sending pictures and funny stories to her e-mail address also promotes her sense of inclusion. If you know her home e-mail address, include that on the cc line and make sure the net of friendliness captures her wherever she is.

- Beware the confessional. Your Buddy Boss will devote endless hours to hearing your confessions and making hers to you. This is a potential disconnect from getting any appreciable work done. When a confession begins, ask politely if you can hear it later because there are too many pressing issues at that moment to give her your complete and undivided attention. This is a true statement and allows you more control over when you can be distracted. She will be pleased with the anticipation of your conversation.

- Set time limits. When your Buddy Boss asks, "Do you have a minute?" Tell her you have three. This behavior modification technique is generally effective if applied consistently. If every time she asks for your time, and you set a limit, she will tend not to ask when her intention is to engage you in an open-ended conversation.

Your Buddy Boss, if you can stand being around her, is not the most intolerable department head or supervisor you can work for. Getting along with her simply requires ignoring everything you're being paid to do and hanging out. Dedicated workers get hit the hardest by Buddy Bosses because they must work nights and weekends to do the things they would have done if they weren't discussing news, weather, and sports with their Buddy Bosses. You will probably just need to suck it up and work around your Buddy Boss' situation. With luck, you might get transferred to an Idiot Boss.

Idiot Bosses

Thank the Lord for small blessings. Unlike the God, Machiavellian, Masochistic, Sadistic, Paranoid, and Buddy Bosses, the I-Boss is simply a chronically clueless mutant from the evolutionary journey of the species. The wagon of human development hit a bump somewhere and the I-Boss was left sitting in the middle of the road, in a cloud of dust, rubbing the bump on his head. From there, he wandered into a nearby office and before long was running it. Welcome to Idiot World.

Although there will be some occasional references to the various boss types, the rest of this book is mostly a guide to understanding I-Bosses, for there are so many. The good news is your I-Boss probably won't think he's God, be shrewd enough to surgically slice her way to the top, mutilate himself and bleed all over your desk, cause lacerations leaving you bleeding all over your desk, see blood droplets on the carpet and think they mark the way for Ninjas to sneak in and attack when he is not looking, or plug her umbilical cord into your fuel cell and start living off your energy.

The Second Step:
"I realized that the challenge of an Idiot Boss was too big for me to handle by myself and I needed a power bigger than all Idiot Bosses combined to keep me from going crazy."

I believe that God loves I-Bosses just the same as the rest of us. If not, why make so many of them? They are here to test our faith, secure our sanity, and teach survival skills. You see, all things work together for good. We might start thinking we really can control the world around us were it not for idiots. Our sanity depends on how sincerely and completely we turn our I-Bosses over to the omniscient, omnipresent, and omnipotent care of God, as we understand Her.

Idiot Bosses keep us honest. If we don't have them around, how can they enrich our lives? Like the country song says, "I can't tell you how much I miss you if you won't go away." Be thankful for your I-Boss. He might be the easiest to work with and the least threatening to your health of all the other boss types. A reminder: Make sure your boss is an I-Boss before you start applying I-Boss intervention methods and techniques.

Attempting to use I-Boss solutions on other boss types is like running a cross-platform application with incompatible software. At best, you will crash the system. At worst you might set off an intermolecular reaction causing the planet to implode, creating a black hole sucking all known matter in our galaxy into nonexistence, leaving only Idiot Bosses in charge after the next Big Bang.

Not every boss is an idiot and not every idiot is a boss. The best you can do is be prepared to deal with whatever comes your way. Let go and let God. But remember you are His arms and legs. When He asks to borrow them, let Him.

3

The Making of an I-Boss

The perennial argument rages: Are idiots the product of nature or nurture? Are Idiot Bosses a fly in the ointment of evolution or God's sense of humor? God has a sense of humor. Have you ever seen a duck run? I'm personally leaning toward the 'big bang' theory in the evolution vs. creation argument. However, the Big Bang theory still doesn't explain whether or not God was playing with firecrackers one day and boom—we had birth, death, and taxes.

If life on this planet was set into motion by one enormous explosion, then it would make sense that Idiot Bosses were the leftover shrapnel. I was taught in Sunday school that God created everyone and everything with a purpose, and a purpose for everything and everyone. Apparently, the first I-Boss was in the john when God was handing out assignments. What purpose can there be in stupidity?

The Third Step:
"We decided to turn over our lives to our Higher Power—as we understand Him."

Understanding how your background has set you on a course of tolerance or intolerance for stupidity is essential if you are to become more adept at dealing with your Idiot Boss. Without self-reflection, framed in the context of your Higher Power, how will you ever know if the discomfort and frustration you attribute to your I-Boss is real or a product of your imagination?

Most likely, it is a combination of both. A refreshing swim in the Pacific Ocean is a welcome thing if you're vacationing in a Maui beach condominium. What if your sailboat capsizes five miles off shore? Same water, same temperature, different psychological response. How well you will be able to thrive in spite of your Idiot Boss depends on how aware you are of your own temperament and the chemical reaction when you and your I-Boss are in the same room.

Your Higher Power is important to your understanding because He created you and your I-Boss. You're both swimming in the same water, so to speak. You are different creatures within the same system. But how different are you? You might fit together in some cosmic way you just haven't figured out yet. As you follow my journey to enlightenment, consider your own. Don't be surprised if you start feeling more peaceful and sleep better at night, which means you're getting it.

Choosing Cool Role Models

My horizons were internal for the most part. I was a nerdy Iowa kid, imagining great wonders for the future, all through the lens of Hollywood. I could have emulated Charlton Heston in *The Ten Commandments*, but I didn't. He wasn't cool enough for me. Without some moral absolute about who this Higher Power should be and what He should look like, it's possible to travel well down the wrong road before figuring out that anything is askew.

Cool is a natural condition, not a conditioned nature. Cool just is. God decides who gets to be cool and who doesn't, which has been a thorn in my theological side for some time now. All of my righteous indignation on the subject aside, as a rule, I-Bosses are not cool. Their uncoolness is a natural omission, just as other people's coolness is a natural gift. To what degree is coolness an inside-out issue vs. an outside-in issue? Does coolness emanate from within certain individuals or does it exist only in the way others see them? Maybe it's both intrinsic and extrinsic. My list of questions for God is getting longer.

Think of your I-Boss. Who did he select as a role model? Is the role model cool or uncool? Can you guess from his personality and behavior? Can you believe that thousands of managers bought the book *Leadership Secrets of Attila the Hun*, dreaming of someday having a reputation on the street like Attila? I don't have the exact numbers, but I doubt that *Jesus as CEO* sold as many copies as *Leadership Secrets of Attila the Hun* or the sequel, *Victory Secrets of Attila the Hun* because hardcore business types didn't think the Savior had his profit motive in the right place.

Origins of Idiot Power

With a little power, I-Bosses can drive you crazy. With a lot of power, they can terrorize the planet. Not because they are evil, but because they just get certain bizarre thoughts in their heads. And that's dangerous in a head not designed for thinking. Where does idiot power come from to begin with? Is there a mother of all idiots? Is there a higher power reserved exclusively for the feeble minded? Is there an idol from ancient mythology all idiots worship? Do Idiot Bosses have little statues of their idiot gods hidden in little shrines in their closets? Do they have pictures of their idiot gods hidden in their underwear drawers? Are there secret, underground meetings of I-Boss societies, with lots of chanting, incense burning, and draft beer?

There must be some common, cosmic thread running through all workplace idiocy. Idiots at work all tend to think alike. Idiots at work all tend to walk alike. Idiots at work all talk alike. Most people can spot an I-Boss from 100 yards with their eyes closed. They all appear to be cut from the same cloth, if you can call Velcro cloth. When I was at the zenith of my career as an Idiot Boss, I always had something stuck to my shoe or the back of my pants.

Nature or nurture?

The belief that I-Bosses occur naturally in the random selection of nature raises some interesting questions. If becoming an I-Boss is a natural progression then the disorder must have its origins in the prenatal equation. For those who skipped their psych classes in college to catch up on sleep, the prenatal equation means in the womb.

Was it a chemical imbalance or oxygen deprivation? The former is a pervasive, ongoing condition that can possibly be treated with medication. Neurological damage is harder, if not impossible, to overcome. In either case, it's people working for I-Bosses who need medicating. Sometimes Mother Nature deals some nasty cards. However, with early detection and extensive therapy, I-Bosses like me can turn it around and transform our oversupply of lemons into lemonade. Some I-Bosses can eventually conduct meetings and stay tuned into what's being said throughout, whether or not they understand or comprehend.

If I-Bosses are caused by nurture instead of nature, the questions change. (That's environment vs. genetics for those that slept through Psych 101.) What did the child see when he first opened his eyes? Was there a "Wash your hands after using the restroom" notice on the wall of the delivery room? Did the kid look directly into the bright light? Something started the snowball down the hill. What if babies are switched in the nursery? What if the cool one goes home with the nerdy parents or vice versa?

What effect does breast-feeding have on coolness vs. ultimate stupidity? There are babies who can't figure out how to suck on a breast when it is presented. Perhaps that's an early sign of management aptitude. If so, we're right back in the nature camp. To the advocates of the nurture argument, the influence must come incrementally, beginning in early childhood.

When the post-World War II parents let their children watch Rowan and Martin's *Laugh In*, the fate of the next generation in the workplace was sealed. Iowa Basic Skills Tests, *Petticoat Junction*, Lucille Ball's seventh sitcom series, sock hops, sleepovers, hippies, dippies, yippies—somewhere in the middle of it all, the I-Bosses took control while the rest of the workforce was distracted. Once control of the workplace was lost, it became nearly impossible to get it back.

How the cards are dealt

Beyond the nature vs. nurture argument about how an idiot came to be an idiot, the larger question is, What can be done about it now? An idiot didn't become an idiot on the job. He arrived in that condition. Our characters are forged and galvanized long before we punch our first clocks. The characteristics of a good boss are rooted in some mysterious combination of biological and social influences. Despite the research and inquiry we can conduct in the fields of psychology and neurological science, God still holds the human development equivalent to the Coca-Cola formula and He's not sharing it with us.

Even the God Boss type has its origins in early childhood. If you really want to spend your time researching the God Boss syndrome, their moms might be a good place to start. If the God Boss ever hopes to enter recovery, he must accept and acknowledge there has been a slight case of mistaken identity. To expect a God Boss to ever acknowledge and accept such a thing is a tall order. After all, if you really believe you're God and then discover you're not, the only direction to go is down.

The Machiavellian Boss was Machiavellian in kindergarten. Whatever made her aspire to the top spot started early and was well established before she stuffed the ballot box and was elected class president for the first time. Whatever made the Machiavellian think there is only room for one at the top of the pyramid came early on. Having been a substitute teacher in kindergarten classrooms enough to develop a nervous twitch in my left eye, I've observed young children don't naturally take to sharing. Kindergarten is a German word that means 'this is why you drink.'

Not only do 5-year-olds not share, they have no innate respect for the property of others. Two statements I heard a lot in kindergarten classrooms were, "Dr. John, (So-and-so) hit me," and "Dr. John, he took my (fill in the blank)." The most common statement out of a kindergartner's mouth is, "Dr. John, I have to go to the bathroom." This paragraph conjures images of offices I've managed.

It might be all children are born with the Machiavellian gene and lay claim to the mountaintop. Then they start getting knocked off one by one. If an older sibling doesn't do it first, their kindergarten classmates will. Some give up right away and occupy themselves with isolated activities on the periphery of life. Some try to climb back up the mountain only to be knocked off repeatedly.

Gradually, over the years, each child abdicates his claim to the top spot, leaving only the most passionately driven Machiavellian to acquire and hold on to it. It's not a matter of brute force. Machiavellian children learn quickly that physical strength is not the key to success. Cunning is a much more valuable skill.

If you notice a child in a kindergarten classroom sharing candy with another student, don't be seduced into the liberal mindset that there is inherent generativity (niceness) in everyone and it will blossom if only given the chance. The "benevolent" child is more than likely a Machiavellian Boss in training, and she is practicing the fine art of manipulation. I promise, if you teach a kindergarten class for one day, you will see more unholy alliances formed and betrayed than 50 years at the United Nations. Yet, if a Machiavellian ever hopes to enter recovery, she must acknowledge and accept that there are other ways to view success. Maybe there is room for a group shot on the mountaintop.

More Than One Way to Create a Personality Disorder

After the Machiavellian and God Bosses are separated from the flock, everyone else is a candidate for Idiot Boss. Or are they? Where do Masochistic Bosses acquire their little idiosyncrasies? Again, in early childhood. Somehow, the child gets fixated on punishment. If you have experience with young children, ages 6 through 12, you've seen for yourself that the self-punishers are already at it. We all capture fragments of our parents' personalities and etch them into our own. Why we chose certain ones and not others is another question for God.

Thankfully, most children don't become masochists. Unfortunately, those that do carry masochism into the workplace. Some become bosses, but most just stay slaves because slavery is consistent with their self-image. If Masochistic Bosses ever hope to enter recovery, they must acknowledge and accept there are other ways to deal with self-indictment. And leave the rest of us out of it, please.

If you're keeping count, the portion of the population left available for just plain stupidity is shrunk even more by the emergence of sadistic personalities in childhood. If you've ever worked for a Sadistic Boss, you know it doesn't take much of a stretch to imagine her torturing small animals as a child. When little Sammy brings his fuzzy bunny to class for Show and Tell, look around the room for the pupil with the narrowing pupils. See Sally over there, leaning forward in her seat, focused like a laser on the furry creature nonchalantly munching on lettuce? Don't leave Sally alone with Mister Big Ears.

In extreme cases, Sadistic Bosses have been known to bring small animals into the office for entertainment. Sadistic Bosses sometimes have elaborate aquariums filled with pet piranhas. Sometimes they keep snakes in a terrarium just to enjoy watching them kill and eat furry creatures. Sadistic Bosses are not recommended as managers at zoos or animal shelters.

In the absence of innocent animals to torment, innocent human beings will do. If you have a Sadistic Boss, look at the bright side. You can consider yourself a living sacrifice or human shield, making it possible for another innocent creature to enjoy one more day.

Like the other boss types, sadists don't pick up this behavior in the workplace. They arrive with it. But torture can come from any boss, depending on the circumstances. If you hear blood-curdling screams from down the hall, it's just as likely that an Idiot Boss has asked someone to put aside productive work and rewrite the medium-range plan, again. Certain tasks cause immense pain, whether a Sadistic Boss or an Idiot Boss instigates them. The main difference is that the sadist enjoys the suffering of others. The idiot is oblivious to it.

Both idiots and sadists are likely to form teams upon which to inflict excruciating pain. The I-Boss does it because he has heard and read the word "team" so many times he thinks it's a cool thing to do—putting people on teams. And that anything an individual can do is more fun for everybody if they get to do it as a team. The Sadistic Boss relishes the opportunity to stand back and watch a group of people writhe in agony. To her, any pain an individual can suffer is more fun to watch as a group activity if everyone on the team suffers.

If Sadistic Bosses ever hope to enter recovery, they must acknowledge and accept that other people have a right to live in comfort and peace. But don't hold your breath. Many factors conspire to keep Sadistic Bosses in power. For one, the rush they get from watching others suffer is so intense that to buy enough narcotics to deliver a comparable rush would cost millions. The habit is simply too much to give up and too expensive to replace.

Another reason Sadistic Bosses are here to stay is that corporate environments, especially those with hierarchical organization charts, are well suited for sadists. Sadists need a disparity of power to operate. The Napoleonic, militaristic, mechanistic, bureaucratic, hierarchical structure in most companies and government agencies guarantees sadism just as surely as leaving your teenager alone at home while you and your spouse vacation out of the country guarantees a party.

Paranoid Bosses thin out the field for potential Idiot Bosses. Like everyone else, the peculiar thinking and behavior of Paranoid Bosses can be traced to early childhood. It's not common, but it shows up in the kindergarten classroom. There have been occasions when I've heard, "(So-and-so) hit me," only to find out that so-and-so is not in school that day.

Paranoia, like any other undesirable characteristic, starts early. Paranoid Bosses are tough to work for because they suspect everything you do is part of an insidious conspiracy against them. They think everything you don't do, but imagined you should have done, is part of an insidious conspiracy against them.

By contrast, Idiot Bosses don't suspect anything. An I-Boss can encounter someone coming out of his office, greet the person warmly, go inside to discover someone has hacked into payroll records, and left the payroll screen on the computer. "Hm-m-m-m," the Idiot thinks. "I was playing solitaire when I went to the john. Oh, well."

If Paranoid Bosses ever hope to enter recovery, they must acknowledge and accept that other people aren't always conspiring against them. Unfortunately, there are enough situations when people are conspiring against them to justify a Paranoid Boss's paranoia. More than any other leadership flaw, paranoia is a self-fulfilling prophecy. The more paranoid you act, the more justified you will be. Like the sadist, paranoia didn't start in the workplace, but the workplace is a fertile environment for it to flourish.

Buddy Bosses and I-Bosses are often indistinguishable. However, to the trained eye, Buddy Bosses are probably aware they don't have any naturally occurring friendships, which is why they so desperately pursue you. Idiots think everybody is their friend. The Buddy Boss's phobia about being friendless is also rooted in early childhood. There's an old joke that says his mother had to tie a bone around his neck to get the dog to play with him. I know that's a tired joke, but it illustrates the plight of a friendless child.

Animals are not judgmental and it doesn't matter what you look like. With the possible exception of great white sharks and other insatiable predators, if you're kind to animals, they'll be kind to you— except for cats. Cats live on a one-way street. They might curl up on your lap. But only a King or Queen of Denial can pretend the cat's behavior has anything to do with making you feel good. Dogs, on the other hand, are great for loving lonely children. The sight of a child with an overzealous puppy is a joyous scene to behold.

For the most part, dogs are idiots, which should help dog lovers understand how innocent and innocuous I-Bosses can be. Dogs think that anything they're doing is the most important thing on Earth at that moment. Unless some illness, degenerative breeding, or perceived threat has altered their dispositions, dogs are perpetually in an insufferably good mood. They love to eat and will eat nearly anything with no regard for expiration date, table manners, or social etiquette. Most I-Bosses stop short of sniffing their dinner companions, but they will repeat mindlessly unimportant activities over and over. Worse, yet, they expect you to join in their never-ending shenanigans and will hound you (no pun intended) unmercifully if you refuse.

If you know how to be kind and encouraging to a dumb animal, you possess the majority of skills required to handle an Idiot Boss. If you have a Buddy Boss, be her buddy and get over it. Have a heart. There are probably some dead animals in her past following her encounters with sadists. An I-Boss won't characteristically carry such emotional baggage. There is an opportunity for joy, even serenity, in cluelessness. I yearn for the days of innocence when I was an aggravation only to others and not to myself. Don't let anyone tell you that recovery is an easy road.

What happened to us during the handoff from childhood to adulthood? When we were kids, we didn't accept Idiot Bosses unless they were thrust upon us. We never lined up behind those who appeared to be stupid. If for some miraculous reason I had been made captain of a team, perhaps through a generous bribe of some sort, I would have picked the biggest, strongest, and coolest kids to be on my squad, while my fellow nerds stood in line and watched. Only the cool ruled. Why in adult life do cool people wind up so often working for the uncool? Another question for God.

Idiots vs. Intelligents

Why do the super-intelligent wind up reporting to idiots? I-Bosses are often overwhelmed at the extent and complexity of the information being discussed by their team members at meetings. In these situations, it's common to see the I-Boss's eyes glaze over. He might be starring straight ahead with his focus fixed somewhere between 12 feet and 20 miles beyond the opposite wall for a few seconds to 30 minutes before anyone notices. When this happens, the team members usually signal each other with subtle sign language and file quietly out of the room confident that, if the I-Boss doesn't regain consciousness before everyone else goes home, the custodial crew will clean around him.

Sometimes I-Bosses become so overwhelmed by the complexity of what's being discussed around them that they require hospitalization. This is becoming an increasingly significant economic issue for companies with spiraling major medical premiums. Progressive organizations are training their security personnel and HR staff in recessitation techniques to avoid costly institutionalization.

Too bad the Accounting Department hasn't yet found a way to quantify the cost savings incurred when an I-Boss is incapacitated. It might be that a hospitalized I-Boss's department becomes remarkably efficient in his absence and the medical costs are a wash. How can the organization save the most money? Revive I-Bosses on the spot or leave them in a catatonic state? Further research is called for.

Hopefully, you're beginning to appreciate the complex challenge your Idiot Boss presents to organizational designers. Idiot Bosses can be real whack jobs. Even if that deer-in-the-headlights glaze over their eyes at meetings was caused by early childhood trauma, shame, or guilt, they're still idiots. And you must learn to deal with them. The road to idiot recovery is worth paying attention to, especially if you're not the idiot. Accepting things that can't be changed is a big part of it.

Embarrassment: A ray of hope for idiots

While I was still at Disneyland, I lobbied hard to replace my WED associate, who had resigned in protest over a Machiavellian's power grab, with a person I felt had been underappreciated for years. Big Steve was a lighting technician and easily could have become a union thug. He had the size for it. As it was, he was smarter than that. Even so, you didn't give any lip to Big Steve.

I lobbied everybody I encountered around the office about how great it would be to move Big Steve into management. Perhaps I secretly wanted a personal bodyguard. The truth is, I really liked the guy. I even mentioned what a great asset he would be to the secretary sprawled out on the top of her desk on my way to the restroom one day.

My new Machiavellian Boss was dead set against it. "Over my dead body," was a typical comment. Then one day, he suddenly reversed himself and Big Steve was in. To this day, I don't know what brought about his change of heart. One of the stage managers and I took Big Steve out to celebrate. Doug and Steve towered over me as we hit bar after bar in the swaggering city of Anaheim.

We started about 6 o'clock with a few tagalongs and our little group got smaller and smaller with each bar until it was just the three of us. The last bar was a bustle of activity as they prepared for their featured 9 p.m. entertainment: Female mud wrestling. All three of us were about paid out, even with something as enticing as mud wrestling only moments away. We hit the john in preparation to leave just as the contestants were being introduced.

I came out of the restroom ahead of the other two and nearly ran into a big woman in a bikini who was collecting dollar bills in various parts of her costume. Doug and Steve emerged a moment later and we fought through the crowd and left. I'm no snob, mind you. Female mud wrestling is near the top of my all-time favorite spectator sports. We just had enough noise, smoke, and beer for one night. And Big Steve had to be at work the next day wearing a clean shirt and his first necktie.

About a week later, I noticed people pausing at the doorway of the office Big Steve and I shared. They paused, snickered, and moved on. Soon thereafter, they escorted someone back with them and they'd both snicker. When I finally walked out from behind my desk and approached the door they scattered like cockroaches when you turn on a light. I stepped into the hall and there hung a huge picture of me with the bikini-clad woman starring down at me in the nightclub.

Timing is everything. A reporter from a local paper had been there that night doing a story on female mud wrestling in local bars. If the reporter had snapped his picture five seconds before that fateful moment, now forever suspended in time, or five seconds after, nobody would have been snickering in my office doorway. As it was, the photo made it look like I was part of the show. One of our technicians had clipped the photo from the paper, mounted it impressively on poster board, and hung it on the wall.

"I'd take that down if I was you," a Crystal Cathedral parishioner advised as she walked past. Taking it down was my first instinct. But I decided to act as though it didn't embarrass me and left it up. After all, it wasn't like I was out trying to hook up with female mud wrestlers. I was celebrating Big Steve's promotion with Doug. As I turned to walk back into my office, Big Steve and Big Doug appeared out of the woodwork with several others, all of them laughing and taunting me.

"What are you guys laughing at?" I insisted belligerently. "You were there, too."

"Yeah, right, John," they roared. "Keep dreaming." I turned and took a closer look at the photograph, which must have been 10 inches high and four columns wide. The photographer's timing had been impeccable. Steve and Doug hadn't come out of the bathroom yet when the picture was snapped. I was standing alone with my face about level with her bikini top. I knew my battleship had been sunk. I had nowhere to run and nowhere to hide.

I went down to the Main Street Emporium, bought a pair of Groucho glasses with the fake nose and mustache, and wore them for the next two years. Yes indeed, only suckers get sucker punched. But sometimes suckers are just in the wrong place at the wrong time. It was the kind of incident that scars people for life.

The lesson in this vis-à-vis your Idiot Boss is embarrassing things happen to everybody. Bad things happen to everybody, some more than others, but to everybody nonetheless. As I've matured, I've learned it's okay. All things can work together for good.

I took the poster down the following morning. Perhaps the school-teacher part of me thought, the technician did such a nice job of cutting it out and mounting it, I really should let everyone see what he's done. Of course, I didn't think that. For whatever reason, a wee small voice popped into my head and reminded me whatever doesn't kill me can make me stronger. I'm not exactly sure where the voice came from quietly advising me to leave the photograph mounted on the wall outside my office for 24 hours. But I'm glad I listened.

An Opportunity to Build a Bridge

The recollection of embarrassing moments in your life can be an emphatic bridge between you and your I-Boss. He no doubt does a lot of embarrassing things. To be more accurate, things that would embarrass a normal person. He probably has no clue that anything he does warrants embarrassment. He might, however, wonder why people are laughing at him. In my experience, it is far better to be conscious of the fact I've embarrassed myself than to not know why people are laughing at me.

In those desperate moments when everyone else is laughing at your I-Boss, you can rest your hand on his shoulder and say, "Don't worry about it, boss. I've done a lot of really stupid things in my life, too." There is a possibility he'll take offense to your transparently double-edged comment. On the other hand, the fact that you are the only person in the room not laughing at him is bound to increase your equity to some degree.

Dealing with embarrassment has become part of my recovery from idiocy. I eventually came to accept that I was never going to completely stop bad or potentially embarrassing things from happening. How they affected my life was up to me. I realized I only had control over things I chose to do and how I chose to feel about them. And I wasn't about to give up female mud wrestling just because of a little ridicule.

Privately, Doug and Steve apologized. Well, sort of apologized, as men do. They took me out for a pizza after work one night and rehashed how the whole incident had been such a God-given setup and they had to play it out at my expense. It's a male thing.

An Opportunity to Grow

The ancient Eastern philosophy teaches us, "When the student is ready, something will happen to embarrass him," or words to that effect. If we are never challenged in our lives, we won't grow very much. Maybe that's not important to you, but you might never have been an idiot. It's the seminal lesson. Making peace with your inner idiot is the first step on a long road to recovery, bringing you personal peace and a peaceful coexistence with other idiots.

Look at your Idiot Boss through new eyes. He wants to be important. In many respects, he's already more important than you want him to be. Work smart. Don't wait for your I-Boss to conjure up some ridiculous scheme to keep him, and you, busy. Examine your departmental and organizational objectives and suggest plans that will make them so. When your I-Boss takes credit, let it go. Plan your work and work your plan. Be ready for opportunities when they come.

I'm not suggesting that you sit and ponder the origins of your I-Boss's thinking and behavior. Accept he has a history just like you and is a product of some combination of nature and nurture, just like you. Working for this person might be an opportunity for you to grow and develop into a Good Boss when your turn comes.

If you are the boss, remember that business is about people. People make the stuff other people buy and use. People provide services other people need and pay for. Good Bosses never forget that. Nobody starts life more important than anyone else. I believe that no soul is more precious to the One who created it than any other at any time. Everybody has a situation suitable to their unique talents and abilities. Find yours. Find the optimal opportunity for your team members to be actualized. There is no more effective way to pump up the bottom line.

4

Idiot Procreation

The term *idiot procreation* doesn't mean male and female I-Bosses get together at trade shows and mate. Idiot procreation refers to the strange yet universal phenomenon that occurs as naturally and frequently in organizations as cancelled bonuses. A glimpse into the I-Boss's day will help you understand how their population grows.

As I travel around the country attempting to save organizations from themselves, I sometimes arrive too late. Between the time I receive the panicked telephone call, book my flight, and pull my rental car in the parking garage, the entire organizational population is likely to have crossed over into the I-zone—a state caused by the fusion of neurological synapses, usually following an attempt to apply logic and reason to an Idiot Boss's thinking and behavior.

Those who are suddenly and unexpectedly adrift in the I-zone have not become idiots. Their mental faculties have merely been disconnected from their power sources. The experience is similar to typing away at your computer late at night when the power goes out. Everything is instantly dark and silent. In the I-zone, your brain goes dark and silent along with everything else. You become one with the power failure.

It's an internal virus from which few recover. Imagine being in good health and of sound mind and body as you arrive for work. You present your I-Boss with the brilliant mid-range plan you stayed up for three days and nights rewriting. He looks at it with a blank expression and asks, "What's this?"

A voice inside your head screams, *It's the mid-range report you asked me to do over again for the third time, you idiot!*

"Why are you wasting time on this instead of doing important work?" your I-Boss continues, oblivious to the voice inside your head. Your inner voice tries to scream again, but nothing comes out this time, even inside your head. A pop-up window on your mental desktop reads: This program has committed an illegal operation and will be shut down. It's too late to do anything but watch your sanity disappear. Everything goes quiet and your internal monitor screen winks out.

I often find people in the I-zone: Weary workers, shoulders slumped, bags under hollow eyes that have peered once too often into the corporate abyss. Standing among these zombies as they wander aimlessly through sterile corridors, I wonder how much sooner I would have needed to arrive in order to prevent the wholesale destruction of gray matter, broken souls, and irreversible nerve damage. There is no sound to accompany the macabre scene except a low moaning that doesn't seem to come from anyone in particular. It's like the poorly looped soundtrack from a "B" movie.

As I stand in the hallowed halls of American enterprise, a mob of moaning, walking corpses parts around me like the Red Sea. I can't imagine how they manage to avoid running into me as I stand there. They must have Flipper's sonar, I think to myself as I slowly shake my head and wonder what might have been. The lifeless expressions worn by the zombies is the opposite of the perpetual smile so many I-Boss's wear. I've never been able to figure out how perpetual smilers manage to bite and chew their food, much less talk, without moving their jaws.

Just then, I feel a slight tug on my sleeve. I turn and there is a ghostly looking young woman, once vibrant, now gaunt and sallow. "Why do they make idiots into bosses?" she asks, staring off into space. Her voice is monotone and scratchy, as if someone pulled the ring attached to the string in her back a hundred times too many. Her cavernous eyes search the angles where the walls meet the ceiling as if the answer to her question might be written near that junction of horizontal and vertical surfaces.

I've been here and done this too many times to hazard a quick response. I just wait. As I suspected, she doesn't wait for an answer to her first question before asking a second. "Why do Idiot Bosses multiply like rabbits?" Her voice is still raspy. This time she looks at me, but I realize she is sensing my presence more than actually seeing me. I step slightly to the side. Her eyes don't follow.

Suddenly, the door swings open to the men's room. Her Idiot Boss strolls out in a limber, almost cavalier manner contradicting the moaning masses around him. "Hey, Dr. John," he calls out to me, zipping his pants at the same time. The ghost person releases my sleeve and wanders back into the river of walking dead.

How can he be so glib? I think to myself. *He must see these people. Why doesn't he acknowledge them?* By then, he's on me, extending his hand for me to shake. Yech.

"We haven't seen you in a long time," says he, referring to a brief appearance I made five years earlier to help develop a corporate communications strategy. Before the strategy could be implemented, the company's earnings hit a bump in the road, top management panicked, and all extravagances were cancelled, especially those they needed most.

"Too long," I say flatly, scanning the morbid scene around me.

"What do you mean?" he asks innocently.

Instead of amusing me, his sheer stupidity invokes an angry response. I feel as if he is taunting me, trying to bust my chops intentionally. *Nobody can be that stupid*, my inner voice snarls. "Didn't you call?" I ask aloud, trying to sound genuinely curious. I am curious. If you're going to receive payment for your consulting, it helps to know who hired you.

"Oh, yeah," he recalls. "I did call you. People were really starting to go bonkers around here after I decided we needed to quit wasting time on meaningless activities. But you can see they've quieted down." He held his arm out in the direction of his office. We started walking.

"Define meaningless," I query. I think I know where he's going with this, but I want him to say it in his own words.

"I ask people to do certain things and they act like I want them to kill their mothers." I could see he was close to connecting the dots. That's what good coaches/consultants/counselors do. We help our clients put two and two together so they not only understand they have four, but fully appreciate what four means and where it came from. The hardest part in helping idiots connect dots is getting them to realize they need at least two dots before they can connect concepts.

Idiots have no problem connecting one dot. They'll draw single dots all day long if left without adult supervision. It makes them feel busy and useful. More importantly, they never have to deal with the complexity of contemplating how two dots relate to one another. God forbid if you ever ask them to consider triangulation. Their heads would explode.

I had to help this man find at least one more dot if I was to do him any good or help restore brain function to at least some of his staff. Despite how cynical we consultants tend to become over time, we really do want to help our clients. We come in the door with a genuine desire to leave things better for having been there, regardless of the money. The money is nice and it helps make the Volvo payments, but I can honestly tell you the desire to make things better than they were before I arrived has nothing to do with money.

By helping bosses get better, I make life easier and more fruitful for their team members. Yet, despite my optimism on the way in the door, I often leave feeling utterly defeated. I tend to like and trust people on the front end until proven otherwise. About eight out of 10 times I leave wanting to hire a hitman. As I conversed with this I-Boss, my inner voice said, *call Guido*.

Inner voices can bring good or bad news. When I was practicing mental health intervention as an intern registered with the California Board of Behavioral Sciences, my supervisor modeled true cynicism. Supervision sessions for mental health professionals are the most politically incorrect powwows imaginable. Although the imperative is to facilitate emotional growth and healing, the tension and mental exhaustion resulting from treating mental health clients can push those of us teetering on the edge the rest of the way over. We let off steam by making cynical remarks about our clients.

No psychologist will ever admit to any of this, and I never taped a supervision session, so you'll just have to take my word for it. I remember my supervisor, in describing a schizophrenic she was treating, asking rhetorically, "Why do the voices always tell them to kill, to hurt themselves, or to live under an overpass? Why don't the auditory hallucinations say, take a bath, get a job, and pay your therapist?" She got out of the business shortly after that.

While walking and talking with this I-Boss the voices inside my head were saying, *Find the nearest janitorial closet and lock yourself in before you kill him or jump out the window.* Then a second inner voice joined the conversation. You know you're in trouble when multiple inner voices appear.

Which is it? my rational inner voice demanded. *Do I kill him, kill myself, or crawl under one of these desks? If I jump out the window first, I won't kill him, and I won't have that on my conscience for the final three seconds of my life. But would I really regret killing him as I fall to my own death? Or would the final, homicidal act of a desperate man be a gift to the world he leaves behind?*

Many business executives would need to change their underwear if they ever knew what consultants are thinking about them at any given moment. "What exactly did you ask them to do?" I asked aloud, setting him up.

"I asked them to rework the mid-range plan," he said nonchalantly.

"Rework?"

"Yeah, do it over again."

"How many times had they done it before?" We reached his office, a glass-walled cell featuring a panoramic view of the entire floor, from the coffee nook to the copy room.

"I dunno, two, maybe three times."

"You didn't see any problem with that?" I asked, settling into an armchair facing his desk. The question was typical Socratic consulting/coaching, leading the horse to water. But even so, I could tell this one stood a good chance of dehydration.

"No, I didn't see any problem with it," he answered honestly as he closed the door and sat down behind his desk. I had to give him half a point for that. Sitting down without incident that is. "But they had a problem with it." He motioned toward the sea of zombies moving methodically in all directions outside the glass walls of his office. In there, with the door shut, we couldn't hear the low-pitched moaning that gave the zombie parade its edge. The lack of a soundtrack made the sight even weirder than before. More than glass partitions insulated this I-Boss from his team members. At least he saw them out there. That was a start. That was a seed. I decided to go with it.

"What makes you think they have a problem repeating the same task over and over again?" I asked, tilting my head toward the zombies.

"Look at them," he said. "You would think I asked them to carry loads of bricks up 30 flights of stairs." This guy was a few bricks short of a load himself and he was starting to make me feel really uncomfortable. Being a professional, I breathed deeply, rotated my shoulders backward to loosen up the muscles that had been steadily tightening in my chest since he emerged from the men's room. I knew it was going to take awhile for his elevator to rise 30 floors, so I resigned myself to be patient and try to remember I am paid by the day.

"Why do you think they look that way?" I continued, trying to point him toward the second dot that he needed to form an association.

"I guess they would rather just be goofing off," said he.

No dot.

"Goofing off?"

"You know."

"I do?"

"Wasting time."

"Oh," said I. "If left to their own devices, your team members would just waste time?"

"Yeah," he sighed. "What can you do?"

You can stop thinking like an imbecile.

I didn't actually say that. I just thought it. I can't speak for other coaches, counselors, and consultants, but I have terrifying dreams that my microphone switch will one day malfunction and I'll say aloud what I'm actually thinking. These dreams feel eerily similar to naked dreams.

"What were they doing when you asked them to stop and rework the mid-range plan for the third or fourth time?"

"I dunno," he said, getting a bit irritated. "Why the third degree?" Clients can get snippy with consultants if pushed too far. They're aware of who works for whom. I decided to press on anyway. I owed it to those formerly hard-working, formerly dedicated, former human beings on the other side of the glass.

"This is important," I said. "Try and focus." Instead of raising his eyebrows at the condescending comment, he actually leaned forward and listened more intently. Cluelessness can have a silver lining. "Were they doing something you assigned to them when you asked them to drop what they were doing and rework the mid-range plan?" I was highlighting dots left and right. Still he couldn't seem to draw a line between any of them.

"Probably," he said, leaning back in his chair. "What does that have to do with anything?" My horse had not only reached the water, he was standing in it. And still he refused to drink. I abandoned Socrates and took out my invisible Magic Marker.

"It works like this," I began. It makes me feel like such a failure when an obvious line of questioning doesn't move a client toward enlightenment. Teach a person how to connect the dots and there is hope. Connect the dots for a person and he's still and idiot. "When you ask your team members to do something, that thing becomes a priority. They will jump into the task with intentions of doing a good job." I was referring to early career people before a long line of I-Bosses snuffed out their passions and turned them into hopeless cynics. "When you interrupt their work to shift their efforts to a new task, that diminishes the importance of what they're already doing."

"So..?"

"So, every time you ask them to do something and then ask them to abandon that task, they become increasingly cynical about the real importance of either task."

"Cynical...?"

"It's like the boy who cried 'wolf'," I explained in hopes that a child's tale would resonate with him.

"Why did the boy cry 'wolf'?"

"It's not *why* he cried 'wolf'," I said without moving my jaw. "The point is that the boy cried 'wolf' when there wasn't a wolf."

"That was stupid," he scoffed.

"Yes," I blurted out, barely containing my enthusiasm at the hint of a breakthrough. "It was stupid to cry 'wolf' when there was no wolf. Do you know why?"

"It was stupid because there was no wolf."

"True," I said. "Can you drill down deeper and think of a bigger problem his actions might cause?"

He hesitated for a long moment and pinched the bridge of his nose as he tried hard to conjure an answer. I waited. "I don't know," he sighed amidst a gush of air from his lungs as if a balloon had been untied. Slapping his open palms on his desk to signify his growing frustration he added, "This is stupid."

I could see that his meter had expired. Giving someone an answer as opposed to helping him discover the answer violates centuries of Chinese wisdom, but I needed to catch a plane. "When the boy first cried 'wolf', everybody took him seriously and ran or hid. But, there never was a wolf. Finally, they became cynical. Then, when a real wolf appeared and the boy cried 'wolf', they didn't heed his warning."

"Are you saying that I cry 'wolf'?"

I touched the end of my nose with one finger and pointing at him with the other.

"Are you're saying when I give my people something to do, I should let them finish it?" I repeated the gesture. Just when I was starting to think his elevator was out of order, it was moving again. "But what will I do?"

"Do?" I asked.

"If I give them assignments or let them choose their own assignments...won't that get boring?"

"Boring for whom?"

"For me."

Just when I thought that I was leading him, he led me right into the heart of the matter. Although I credited him with opening an understanding previously hidden from me, I didn't offer to reduce my fee. But now at least he had two dots to work with.

"Wow," I said. "What an epiphany!"

"Epipha...?" he said blankly.

"Never mind," I continued. "Boredom has you switching gears on everyone and frying their brains."

"Do you think so?"

"There's your answer."

"Where's my answer?"

"If you were engaged in the ongoing mission of the department, you wouldn't be bored and keep interrupting what people are trying to finish."

"Engaged in the ongoing mission?" he asked. "Wouldn't that be micromanaging? I went to a seminar once and they told us not to micromanage people."

"It's a little late for that," I said aloud. That pushed the envelope, but I sped ahead before he could react. "Who reads the mid-range plan?"

"The executive committee, I guess."

"Has anybody ever come back to you and asked for an explanation of variances from the mid-range plan?"

"No," he said thoughtfully. "Once they're finished and presented, they go up on the shelf and never get opened again."

"Except when you get bored?"

"Yeah, I figure it couldn't hurt to do a little tweaking."

"Okay, let's connect the dots," I came right out and said. "You know the mid-range plan is an exercise in futility. Your team members know the mid-range plan is an exercise in futility. Yet, you ask them to keep revisiting it."

"Not a smart thing now that you put it that way."

"Right," I affirm. "That is micromanaging in the worst sense of the term. You're looking at your department as a bee hive that exists to amuse you."

"I wouldn't say that," he protested.

"You don't have to say it, I just did." I was emboldened by the rush that consultants get when we're on a roll. "What if I were to say you can macro-manage by becoming a trailblazer and clearing a path through the bureaucratic jungle so your people can be more productive?"

"Really?"

"Really. You will be entertained, even challenged. And your people will come back to life and do amazing things."

"When can I start blazing trails?"

"You already have," said I.

The story I just told you is a fantasy. Real I-Bosses don't get it that quickly. I always miss my flights. But they can get it, given sufficient guidance and encouragement. I've seen some radical turnarounds in my time. I've even been the catalyst for many of them. More commonly, however, I-Bosses are influenced by other I-Bosses, in which case bad behavior only gets worse, and the body count in their departments grows to staggering proportions.

The Fourth Step:
"We must inventory our own idiotic behavior."

This kind of thing keeps me humble. When I'm drawing on every ounce of creativity and influence I possess to teach some sorry son-of-a-goat I-Boss how to connect dots, I need to be mindful of where I came from and how difficult it was for me. As I said at the top of the chapter, sometimes flying into a righteously indignant rage just feels right, even when it's wrong. To paraphrase Sigmund Freud, sometimes an idiot is just an idiot.

Apart from the question of where idiots come from, if you are serious about trying to successfully work for one, it's important to understand how idiots wind up in leadership positions. Just as idiots didn't intentionally set out to become idiots, neither did most Idiot Bosses intentionally set out to become bosses. It's important not to confuse I-Bosses with God, Machiavellian, Masochistic, Sadistic, Paranoid, Buddy, or even Good Bosses.

That Loud Sucking Sound

To reduce the cockamamie thing to its lowest common denominator, Idiot Bosses leave a vacuum where intelligence, vision, and wisdom should be. The natural universe abhors the vacuum and begins sucking hard to fill it. If intelligence, vision, and wisdom are wandering by at that moment, the story will have a happy ending. But when's the last time that happened? Usually, some random, meaningless, irrelevant idea gets sucked into the vacuum.

An idiot might initially become a boss for any number of reasons. He might be the only available candidate because everyone else in the department has jumped out of windows or is cowering in a janitorial closet. Perhaps, he found a proposal on the floor, picked it up, and was looking at it when someone higher on the food chain walked by. The higher-up thought it was the idiot's creation and promoted him. Sometimes idiots apply for a promotion because it looks like fun and accidentally appear competent long enough to get the job. By the time their true character emerges, it's too late.

Don't you wish you could vote on your next boss? You can vote with your feet the way my WED counterpart at Disneyland did when our department was co-opted by the Machiavellian. But wouldn't it have been nice if they had asked us first? Fat chance. I'm suspicious of the democratic process anyway. The concept of democratically elected office is supposed be self-cleansing and purge itself of incompetence, complacency, and corruption. In practice, the first order of business for elected officials is to short-circuit the democratic process and make their jobs as secure and lucrative as the unionized bureaucrats who run federal, state, and local government.

What "sucking up" really means

When an I-Boss is promoted, especially near the top, the sucking can be felt throughout the organization. All I-Bosses move up one notch, leaving a vacuum (and more suction) behind each one. Even though there is only one hole to fill on the organization chart, there are many more idiots in your future. The vacuum that idiots in high places create is replicated at every level. It's a type of automated, systemic inbreeding and the bloodline becomes more anemic with every reshuffle.

The grand matriarch of a wealthy family on Lookout Mountain, Tennessee once welcomed a new bride into the family who came from outside the ancestry. Instead of turning up a haughty nostril toward the commoner, the matriarch welcomed her by saying, "We need some new blood in this family. There are enough babbling idiots on this mountain already."

Unfortunately, idiots are only idiots by comparison. Only non-idiots can point out they are idiots. Therefore, the people who make idiots feel the least like idiots are other idiots. Guess with whom idiots choose to surround themselves. The higher and more powerful the I-Boss, the greater his ability to pad his staff with additional idiots.

The Peter Principle is correct in that persons can be and are regularly promoted beyond their level of competence. What Larry Peter, founder of the Peter Principle, assumed happened next was wrong. Idiots don't stop rising in the organization once they are promoted beyond their level of competency. Since when has competence been a prerequisite for executive office? Incompetence, especially in the area of human motivation and understanding, can be a first-class ticket to the executive suite.

The only things keeping some I-Bosses out of higher office are God, Machiavellian, and Sadistic Bosses who can outsmart, outmuscle, or steal away the position while the idiot is in the restroom. Just when you thought it couldn't get any worse, you get rid of the idiots by plugging their spots with God, Machiavellian, and Sadistic Bosses.

Once Ignited, the Fire Spreads

Even if an I-Boss is created by accident or misunderstanding, it is no accident that idiots are promoted. It's one of the more unpleasant aspects of human nature rearing its ugly head. The principle bearing the name of the late Larry Peter only explains a portion of this phenomenon. Even though increasing one's cognitive capacity is a tall order, it is possible for persons promoted beyond their level of competency to nonetheless recognize their dilemma and work to increase their abilities or, at least, seek assistance from more competent persons. In the case of Idiot Bosses, there is sparse evidence they were ever competent to begin with and don't have a clue they need to be.

Like me, many idiots get into positions of leadership for the wrong reasons: by accident, luck of the draw, or they were just walking nearby when the sucking started. The point is, they, like me, might eventually discover there is much more to leadership than meets the unenlightened eye. But once you're there, the thought of doing the honorable thing and resigning doesn't enter your mind. Instead, Idiot Bosses, like their counterparts in professional politics, start to tap dance as fast as they can and things deteriorate.

Institutionalizing Incompetence

If you think there are more idiots than any other kind of boss, you're right, especially in large organizations where idiot aggregation is most common. For those to whom competency has never been a factor, is it any wonder they are least threatened by (and most of the time downright comfortable around) other idiots?

Having no real competency of their own, I-Bosses are impressed by the things others claim to have accomplished, and might innocently believe they did accomplish, but probably had nothing whatsoever to do with. Being essentially clueless, they take the person's word for it, promote him, and voilà, another I-Boss is born. I-Bosses begetting other I-Bosses, and the cascading suction resulting from the promotion of high-level I-Bosses produces the dreaded mushroom effect.

There are both micro- and macro-mushroom effects. When idiots discover they are not capable of doing what their jobs require, they look for someone else to do it. They don't want to give up the perks and prestige of their positions. Such is the inherent flaw in classical, bureaucratic, hierarchical organizations. The only way to get more is to move higher. Enlightened organizational designers don't attach the concept of *more* to the concept of *higher*. They find innovative ways to reward productivity without institutionalizing incompetence.

The mushroom effect

The micro-mushroom effect is usually a departmental issue. A lower-level I-Boss does not have the budget or authority to create and fill unjustified positions and becomes an insufferable aggravation to his team members the way the zombie king did. A Peter Principle candidate who has been promoted beyond her competency might not be aware she is incompetent to lead other human beings in activities she managed to muddle through before as a peon.

What about the truly competent person who is promoted into management based on her skill and ability? This is another example of inherent flaws in bureaucratic, hierarchical organizations. (Can you tell I don't like them?) For a skilled and competent person, moving into management is her only way to earn more money and acquire more power. The reason for the promotion, however, has nothing to do with perks for the promoted.

To the managers and executives higher up the food chain, promoting the person with super skills and abilities is a way to generalize her performance. If she is extremely good at something, she can make everyone else good at it. Or so the logic goes. Such reasoning is, in a word, stupid. Leading other people, which requires guiding their professional growth and development as well as motivating them, calls for a highly specialized skill set and servant's personality, neither one of which the new manager probably ever had or wanted to have.

Making widgets, writing code, cold calling, or crunching numbers are important functions. You wouldn't ask a wizard at widget making to stop making widgets and start cold calling, unless you're an idiot. Only an idiot would ask a code warrior to take customer service calls. That's one factor that contributed to the demise of dot-coms. You wouldn't ask an accountant to head up the engineering department or an engineer to head up accounting—despite the fact both are linear thinkers and live to calculate and extrapolate.

Anyone with half a brain realizes that people who have demonstrated tremendous competence in a specialized skill and have, in all likelihood, spent most of their adult life mastering it, thrive when doing whatever it is they're so good at. All common sense notwithstanding, the most common promotional practice in hierarchical organizations is to separate people from the tasks they love and put them in charge of less talented people doing those things.

Traditional promotions in hierarchical organizations require new bosses to teach pigs to sing. The newly promoted boss, being a rare species of singing pig, only annoys the common pork, which has no desire or intention to sing. The net result of the whole caper is a herd of annoyed pigs and a resentful former singing pig with no opportunity to vocalize.

Promote based on natural talent

Facilitating the personal and professional growth and development of others is something some people have a natural ability and desire to do. These folks are as naturally suited to leadership as number crunchers are to accounting. The trailblazer concept of clearing the way so others have the space, resources, and oxygen necessary for optimal operation comes naturally to servant leaders. Like their specialized, competent counterparts, they have a natural tendency to continue learning and refining the skills they are naturally suited for and the learning never stops.

If organizational chieftains really want to dominate their respective industries, they will position their gifted leaders in positions of leadership and let them blaze trails for the super-competent widget makers, code warriors, cold callers, and number crunchers. But this is the rarest of exceptions. The general rule holds that top executives place widget makers, code warriors, cold callers, and number crunchers in positions responsible for the professional growth and development of other people. Wrong, wrong, wrong.

The widget makers, code warriors, cold callers, and number crunchers no longer get to do the things they love. They are forced to deal with issues of human motivation and the basic problems of day-to-day living—other people's problems. You are left with a bunch of angry bosses, who are by no means idiots. Terrible leaders, yes. Idiots, no. And now they're being paid a lot of money. They're not going to step down. Maybe one in a million will. Most will exchange their happiness and vocational fulfillment for the cash and benefits. They are being held hostage in the hierarchy.

The mushroom cap includes everyone who is being paid, but is not contributing much of anything. The stem contains the harder working people supporting the crowd in the cap. Eighty percent of the work is done in the stem while those in the cap receive 80 percent of the payroll and benefits.

The cap of the mushroom spreads as non-leaders in leadership positions surround themselves with people to insulate them from the problems people bring to their doorstep daily. The cap of the mushroom also spreads as Idiot Bosses surround themselves with people who make them feel comfortable in their stupidity. The next time you read in *The Wall Street Journal* that someone has received a big promotion in a large organization, lower the paper and listen. That loud sucking sound is the cap of the corporate mushroom expanding along with the caps of lots of little mushrooms throughout the organization.

Timber!

The stem of a mushroom can only support so much weight before it buckles and the whole thing topples over. We've all seen how organizations can be created to exploit changes in technology or government regulations. In the wrong hands these organizations are built, made prosperous, and even celebrated, all the while being bled dry by the executives at the top of the hierarchy. Many top executives and public administrators have a license to steal as surely as James Bond has a license to kill. After the guts of these organizations are transferred into the top executives' bank accounts and the husks blow away in the wind, an outraged public cries out for justice.

Too late. The horse is already out of the barn. Even legitimate large and small organizations that play by the rules often barely survive the incompetence of their leadership. The dedicated hard work of the unsung heroes in the mushroom stem keeps it all going. They hold up all of that weight. But the cap of the mushroom can still grow too large for even the hardest working people to support. How many corporate mushrooms have you seen topple in your lifetime? As the ancient Chinese proverb says: If we do not change our direction, we are likely to end up where we are headed.

Think of an enormous operation such as a major airline. No single person is in charge of operating the complex web of activities and responsibilities. Thousands of flights a day, arriving and departing safely, full of people and cargo, all operated by tens of thousands of individuals who take on whatever leadership responsibility is necessary to get the job done.

What if those people decided they were going to do only what they were instructed to do minute-by-minute? What if they decided not to come to work unless someone called and woke them up in the morning? What if they didn't return from lunch until someone went and escorted them back? It sounds silly until you think about the collective conscience of all those people and how a leadership spirit, larger than all of the individuals combined, ties them all together with a single spirit of accomplishment.

Sprinkle Idiot Bosses throughout the organization and the burden that dedicated individuals carry on their shoulders to make things run correctly becomes heavier. Give top executives lucrative bonuses at the same time as asking wage and benefit concessions from the workers supporting the stem of the mushroom and you just killed morale and caused the people who make the organization run to lose any motivation. Giving obscene financial rewards to top executives before they demonstrate they can lead the organization in corresponding growth only makes sense to an idiot. Giving obscene financial rewards to top executives after they've led their organization to the brink of bankruptcy only makes sense to a thief.

The Right People, the Right Reasons, the Right Things

Even though I-Bosses are inevitable, they don't need to be terminal. If you work for one, try to understand his shortcomings and make him feel less threatened. You might actually slow the growth of the idiot population. The only place a mushroom cap can grow indefinitely is in government, where the solution is to keep expanding the stem. The public sector doesn't need to make a profit, nor does it need to provide competitive goods and services.

We can observe other nations around the world where virtually everyone is part of the mushroom stem. In that case, it's advisable to be in the political class that occupies the cap and not the stem. When the entire private sector is sucked into the stem, as in the former Soviet Union, then the cap shrinks. Enormous stem, tiny little cap. Ultimately, the stem can't support its own weight and topples over. The Soviet experiment didn't last from one end of the 20th century to the other. When Mother Nature grows a mushroom, the stem is always in proper proportion with the cap.

If you are reading this book, chances are good that you're part of the mushroom stem and not the cap. My cap is off to you. Be strong, but also be smart. Even the strongest stem can't hold up a mushroom cap that has grown too big and heavy. Working smart helps shrink the size of the mushroom cap. If it's not possible to shrink it, you can hopefully slow its growth until you can get out from underneath it.

Work your Fourth Step. Continually update the inventory of your motivations and methods. Don't do things for the wrong reasons the way I did. If you have been, change your priorities and approach. Continuing down the same road will only waste your time and create a herd of angry pigs. Stand back and look at your organization. You'll see how and why those I-Bosses got where they are. Look at the less-than-intelligent things you have done along the way. We're all part of the idiot world—some bigger parts than others.

Idiots will always beget more idiots. By understanding the dynamics of idiot aggregation and procreation, you can break the cycle when it's your turn on top. Be patient and encouraging with your I-Boss. How would you like to be sucked into a corporate vacuum cleaner?

5

Banishing Talent

The congressional resolution proposing an early warning system for idiots among the general population was shot down in committee as politically incorrect. That makes me suspicious. The only people who don't see a need to issue idiot alerts are idiots. That's because they don't see themselves as a threat to operational efficiency in the workplace or the health and psychological well-being of their team members.

What many idiots do see as a threat to their own health and psychological well-being is competency. Idiots often perceive competent and talented people as threats, not because they have anything against accomplishment, but because their bosses might expect them to actually accomplish something. Machiavellians are shrewd enough to lay claim to your accomplishments and present them up the food chain as their own. Idiots would rather just keep talent out of it.

In your Idiot Boss's twisted logic, if nobody's doing anything worthwhile, he won't be expected to accomplish anything worthwhile. If there are no talented people in the immediate vicinity, his chances of flying below upper management's radar are improved. The best way to make sure no one in the department demonstrates talent is to banish it altogether.

The Fifth Step:
"Admit to my Higher Power, to myself, and to others the nature of my wrongs."

I'm beginning to see why 12-step programs have such a high success rate. They don't let you get away with anything. Denial is dead among the 12 steppers. But it seems like all I've been doing so far is confessing my stupidity to you and to my Higher Power—who knows what I'm going to say before I say it—so, why bother confessing? It's the "admit to myself" part I struggle with. My ego doesn't want to deal with the fact I've sat on both sides of the idiot desk.

I'm beginning to realize when my frustration boils to overflowing and I rail against the idiots in the universe that I'm not accepting the full measure of my own past, present, or future cluelessness. As they say in the program: If you can spot it, you've got it. We can most easily recognize the problems in others we have in ourselves. As an employee, I've often felt my talents and abilities were overlooked or ignored. As a prerecovery I-Boss, I'm sure I must have overlooked or ignored far more talent than I ever had to offer.

If you suspect your boss is not recognizing your talent, remember many idiots wouldn't know talent if it bit them on the toe. If your talent is being intentionally, premeditatedly, systematically, and methodically ignored or hidden under a bushel, your boss is probably not an idiot. Banishing talent is a common and vicious practice among God and Paranoid Bosses.

Banishing talent is a blow to any organization. It can cost companies dearly in lost efficiency, effectiveness, productivity, and profitability. None of this is of any great concern to Gods, Paranoids, and Idiots. They see talent as a threat to their control and the attainment of their objectives. Paranoids spell threat with a capital T. For some reason, these bosses haven't developed the Machiavellian's brass constitution, which allows you to exert tremendous effort, and exercise immense talent, only to have your boss snatch away the glory.

It's not fair. But since when did fair count for anything in business? If you truly want to make the most out of working for an Idiot Boss or worse, be advised to remove the word *fairness* from your vocabulary. If you don't go so far as to remove it, you must at least reduce your expectations. I have wasted years and countless professional opportunities throwing hissy fits over what I interpreted as unfair treatment. Even if the treatment was genuinely unfair, becoming obstinate and defiant produced nothing except increased frustration.

The Circle of Fairness

The universe has a way of evening things out. Sometimes things go my way. I don't know why, they just do. If you're like me, when things go your way, you don't complain. It's human nature to make a federal case when things seem unfair, while making a silent, mental note when things go our way or we receive what we consider justice.

When my team gets shellacked at volleyball or basketball, I can be caustically and cryptically vocal about the unfair team selection or how the referee made questionable calls. I might even limp a little and blame my gout. In other words, I'm a sore loser. When my team shellacs the opposition, I'm a gracious winner.

When I feel empowered, I am pleasant and magnanimous. When I feel cheated or powerless, I can snarl like a badger. How about you? When your demons out-shout your better angels, is it because you feel you've been treated unfairly? If so, join the club. If we but trust our Higher Powers to bring the good times back around in due time, we might be less aggravated in difficult times. There will be fairness to balance the unfairness.

An unfortunate yet effective way to control others and recruit them to your way of thinking is to play on their sense of unfairness. Confirm their feelings that they are being treated unfairly and you have their votes, donations, loyalty, or whatever. You're not doing anyone a favor by playing the fairness card any more than you want to be manipulated that way. The most valuable use we can make of this awareness is to recognize feelings of disenfranchisement in others at work. If someone is snarling like a badger or grumbling like a belly full of yesterday's pepperoni pizza, they're probably being treated unfairly.

Maybe they're not. More important than the reality of their treatment is the fact they feel that way. If you know others feel as if they're being treated unfairly, aren't you going treat them with a little empathy and sensitivity? You will if you don't want your head pinched off. Moreover, you can't achieve happiness or contentment in your work environment (or any environment) if you feel your life can be summed up in two words: raw deal. Getting over it and accepting that life is cyclical, even though the cycle sometimes seems to rotate slowly, will make you more pleasant to be around. More importantly, you'll enjoy being around yourself more. Try it. Climb out of that bitter cesspool, look back at the others still slopping around in it, and say to yourself, "There, but for the grace of a small attitude adjustment, go I."

Head Bashing

As hard as it is to believe sometimes, bosses are human beings. Their consistently aggravating behavior might make you think there is a diabolical doctor somewhere programming Stepford Bosses and shipping them into companies across the country. To fight against or think you can change your boss's essential nature is like believing you can change human nature. Nevertheless, many people go to work each day thinking they can hold back the tides of idiocy without drowning.

For those brave, stubborn, and self-righteous souls, I suggest you pause about 50 feet from the front of your building, ask a coworker to hold the door open, get a running start, attain full speed, lower your head, and smash into the edge of the open door. When you regain consciousness, go inside and enjoy the rest of your day. Follow that routine every day for six months and you might damage the door enough for maintenance to replace it.

Ramming the door makes as much sense as trying to change someone else, especially your boss. Even if you succeed in getting to him, they'll just haul him away and pull the shrink wrap off another Idiot Boss from the Stepford doctor. They'll always be able to manufacture another door or another Stepford Boss. How many times will you regain consciousness? Resenting the unfair way of the workplace hurts you more than it hurts them. I might remind you how toxic resentment is 100 times before you finish reading this book because it took me 1,000 head-banging lessons to even begin accepting the concept.

Communicate Your Way to Serenity

You can't change bad bosses, but you can change the way you approach and deal with them, which can change how you feel about yourself, them, and life in general. If you intentionally and regularly keep your I-Boss informed of what you're doing, he will be less threatened. This means premeditating "chance" encounters with your I-Boss in the hallway, at the water cooler, or following him into the restroom.

Yes, I'm suggesting strategic bio-breaks. For females working for male bosses and vice versa, your options are limited. However, women can pass on information to female clerical assistants in the sanctity of the ladies' room, as can men with male assistants. Working your propaganda through the clerical assistant is often more effective than delivering it directly to the boss.

Don't make a big thing of it. Intersperse your media. Give micro-reports on your activities face-to-face. Send an occasional e-mail. Hand in a report. But be surgical with your timing. Don't toss your communiqué on top of a huge pile of reading your boss is already resenting. Don't add your e-mail to an overflowing inbox. Monitor when your boss is bored and dispatch one of your entertaining-yet-informative missives at the appropriate moment.

Don't dismiss this as pure satire. Keeping people comfortable is the secret to happy and healthy relationships. Consider the alternative. If you want to be a disnatured torment to your boss, remember to ask an associate to hold the door open for you tomorrow morning. No matter the content of your verbal, nonverbal, or written communications, the net result is to create the impression you are operating within your boss's comfort zone and even protecting it from unwelcome threats.

Use language that allows your I-Boss to take at least a portion, if not all, of the credit when reporting progress and achievements. I know he doesn't deserve it. But you're working this plan to bring more joy to your world, so let go of bitterness and resentment. They hurt you more than they hurt anyone else. In your correspondences, use phrases such as, Per your suggestion..., As we discussed in the meeting...,When studying the assignment you made, several options appeared.... Go ahead and bite the bullet with, "Your idea really worked out well."

If you don't gag, you'll experience an immediate improvement in the atmosphere around the office. Clouds will lift and the sun will shine. As much as you will be loath to admit it, you will actually feel better. So will your I-Boss. The principle is this: You can't harbor resentment when you're focused on complimenting others. It will dissipate like the noxious and toxic gas it is.

Communicate with caution

Don't be so obvious that your I-Boss and your peers perceive you as a kiss-up. If someone calls you one anyway, simply say, "I don't want to work in an atmosphere of continuous conflict. Life is too short. If keeping the boss involved and informed helps my serenity, I'm all over it." Or just offer to hold the door open for them tomorrow morning.

Also bear in mind how much keeping the boss informed and involved puts control in your corner. In the information age, information is like money in the bank. I-Bosses drive people crazy with third and fourth versions of meaningless plans and reports because they (the bosses) are bored and figure they should be doing something. Keeping your I-Boss informed and just a little bit flattered will keep him off your back. What's that worth to you?

Communication techniques are effective with Idiot, Good, God, Buddy, and possibly Paranoid Bosses where flattery can earn brownie points. Machiavellians are another breed altogether. Don't try communicating your way to serenity with a Sadistic, Masochistic, or Machiavellian Boss and then write me a cranky letter with your remaining good hand claiming I didn't warn you.

I spend a lot of time explaining to abused and bruised team members in various organizations the need to take evasive action against the seemingly unprovoked attacks, slurs, and general abuse from some of their peers and bosses. What is unprovoked to you might seem justified in someone else's demented thinking. If you are in direct competition with someone, it's more obvious and understandable how anything good you do will threaten his chances to win. Just because you're not in competition with another person, your boss for example, doesn't mean that he still doesn't feel threatened.

I wasn't challenging my Machiavellian Boss at Disneyland for control of the department I had been instrumental in creating. I admit resenting the hell out of him for stealing it. But compete with him for control, no. Besides being confrontation-phobic, I know when I'm up against a superior foe. Besides, I was making inroads in the show development area where my heart wanted to be in the first place. Despite the fact the desk-diving secretary worked over there, I was more a writer/director type than a technical supervisor. Show Development was where my primary interests could be realized, and I had designs on making a lateral move when and if the opportunity presented itself.

Nevertheless, the Machiavellian's power grab took me by surprise. A cleverer, more suspicious, or politically savvy person wouldn't have been caught off guard. If I have any reason at all to be suspicious, I generally don't get blindsided. But not being one to walk around suspicious of everyone and everything, I'm still vulnerable to sneak attack. Focusing too closely on creating reports and memorandums, as I'm still tempted to do, also kept my eyes focused down and not up where they might have seen things coming.

I'd like to say it was my innocence and attention to detail that made me vulnerable to a mugging by the person who became my Machiavellian Boss at Disneyland, but truthfully, it was just stupidity. Unfortunately, I only learn partial lessons from my experiences, and those I learn I soon forget. Never forget your competence is seen as a threat to those who are less competent or have convinced themselves anything positive for you is negative for them.

This is hard to grasp if competence in others doesn't threaten you. But to those who live in an inversely proportionate, mutually exclusive world, the fact that you're breathing means you're using their oxygen. The fact you're not competency-phobic means your guard might not be up where it needs to be.

You're open to a backhand when you least expect it. To take a punch when you have no idea it's coming can really knock you for a loop. Be aware your natural desire to do things well and to contribute your unique talents and abilities to the achievement of organizational objectives is likely to get you knocked on your prat.

To paraphrase another Chinese proverb: "If you understand—things are the way they are. If you don't understand—things are the way they are." To recovering idiots, the proverb refers to the stuff we can't change. Why bother to lose sleep, grow gray hair, or pop your aorta over stuff you can't change anyway?

Shamu Management

My Machiavellian Disneyland boss was no idiot. He was as shrewd as they come. He might have felt my demonstrated competence was a threat because he assumed that everyone thought in terms of conquest and constant competition, as did he, and everyone was trying to be king of the hill, as he was trying to be. That's how he secretly managed to get himself secretly appointed to head a department he had no role in creating, and no background from which to supervise. Machiavellians distrust everyone but only have the power to exact vengeance on those below him on the food chain. Ken Blanchard has a possible explanation.

In Ken's speeches, he sometimes describes behavior modification in animals like Shamu the killer whale at Sea World in San Diego. He talks about how the Sea World trainers start every session with the animals by simply jumping in and swimming with them. He points out that people are often like animals and need to be constantly reassured you're not going to hurt them before they will trust and stop acting defensively. Although you can earn the trust of many people through consistent, non-threatening behavior over time, some people will never trust you. If their motives are not pure, it's likely they'll never fully believe your motives are pure either.

Even if competence is not an overt threat, competency will cause some incompetent people to feel seasick. An I-Boss doesn't have to know what's causing nausea to realize he is nauseous. The trick is to package your competency in ways that will benefit you and not threaten your boss.

It's a Cruel World, But a Great Life

I would like to believe that competency in the workplace is routinely rewarded. But my experience and observations have been otherwise. If you have been rewarded at work for your talent and competency, you've been blessed with enlightened leadership. Be grateful and throw your enthusiastic support behind any culture that recognizes and rewards excellence. On the other hand, there is nothing to be gained from getting frustrated and beating your head against a wall every time competency is punished. Punishment for competent behavior is not always part of a conspiracy. Sometimes, bosses just don't know any better.

Competency is ignored more than it is overtly punished. Having no competency to speak of, most Idiot Bosses can't be expected to recognize it in their employees. At the end of the day, competency gets you nothing with Idiot Bosses, except perhaps banished from their inner circle for making them feel uncomfortable. That's the root of competency-based punishment or neglect—the fact that it makes certain people uncomfortable.

Competency, Creativity, and Change

True competency is usually accompanied by creativity. Competency and creativity are foreign concepts to most idiots. To I-Bosses, there are fixed and rigid ways to do things based on nothing more than the way they learned to do things. When one is not sure of oneself, there can be comfort in rigidity.

Change and uncertainty are like Kryptonite to idiots. Rigid people avoid change because they don't understand it. True competency leads to change and resists rigidity. Many people seek rigidity in their lives as a substitute for competency. Just give them a framework in which to operate, a strict set of rules, and they will operate with confidence. The next time your I-Boss explains something by saying, "Because that's how we do things around here," you'll know he is not being flip. He really likes to have fixed policies and procedures to fall back on, whether or not they make sense.

Security that emanates from structure is a childhood developmental phase. You remember when your mom used to say, "Because I said so," and that was enough. You turned that around and used it on a younger brother or sister saying, "Because mom said so," and expected it to be enough. What did it feel like the first time you saw Mom or Dad doing something completely uncharacteristic of the behavior you grew to expect from them? I'll bet it shook your world.

I-Bosses are developmentally arrested in that phase of childhood where things are done the way they are done because that's the way they are done. They find security, not in the competency they don't have, but in the rulebook. True competency and creativity can be rewards in themselves. To creative and competent people, change is a welcome and often stimulating challenge.

Building calluses

Like Shamu, we intentionally do things to make ourselves feel comfortable and intentionally avoid things that make us feel uncomfortable. Hence, the concentric rings around incompetence. While this protective layering insulates incompetent bosses from potential discomfort, it also pushes competency farther and farther from the epicenter of decision-making in organizations.

Sometimes the concentric rings of incompetence are formed intentionally, sometimes unintentionally. With each new I-Boss and the insulating personnel he gathers around him, another ring is formed. It was a painful moment in my professional life when I discovered I was one of the people my boss was insulating himself against.

A boss who needed insulation from me was Bill, my partner in an electronic publishing firm I became involved in after leaving Disneyland. He was a powerful businessperson I met before I resigned my position at Disney and, when the opportunity arose to become involved with the independent audio/video production company, I called him for advice.

The more we talked about the opportunity, the more he saw dollar signs and invited himself to join the party. I didn't balk at his enthusiasm. For one thing, he had the capital to help finance the aspirations I had for the fledging business. He was successful in the construction engineering field and I figured I could learn a thing or two from him, which I did.

I noticed Waldenbooks had recently begun selling books-on-tape. Formerly, only a product for the vision-impaired, they were now being commercially marketed to the general public. We became the second company in the country to publish what were then known as Waldentapes. Bill was the best of mentors and the worst of mentors. I learned more about business from him than any other person in my life. I learned important principles for successful operation of an enterprise. I learned if something costs X to manufacture, you must charge X times three at a minimum to cover hidden costs and turn a profit. I also learned how to torture people.

Big Bill believed in management by intimidation. I call him "Big," not because he was big and tall, like Steve and Doug at Disneyland, but because he had a large presence. It quickly became apparent how he had earned his fortune in the construction industry. When a bunch of contractors gather on a job site (in Big Bill's case, skyscrapers, major hotels, hospitals, and university buildings) decisions must be made about necessary alterations to original plans, how to proceed with the variances, and whose fault it is. The inevitable disputes and conflicts must be resolved quickly. In the construction business, negotiations on the job site aren't conducted as judicial processes or mediation sessions. They are conducted more like a brawl in an alley.

Bill could out-brawl them all. Imagine being belligerent enough to make construction contractors, those guys who drive the big gas-guzzling SUVs and monster trucks, throw up their hands and walk away saying, "Have it your way." I saw it happen many times, after which he liked to go drink hard liquor and debrief his victory. For one like me who hates confrontation, my relationship with Big Bill was conflicted from the start.

The ambience in the literary publishing industry is different from the construction industry. There is gentility about publishing Bill never even tried to understand or honor. Thankfully, the sissies in the publishing business repulsed him and he stayed out of the end of our business that involved negotiating intellectual properties and anything else that might tarnish his reputation as a two-fisted businessman. He left all of that up to me.

As senior partner, he had an office in our facility, but he operated mostly out of his engineering firm offices and his Mercedes. He appeared around the publishing company several times a week to check up on us or to amuse himself. We never knew from one appearance to the next what kind of mood he would be in. He fluctuated between overt and covert intimidation.

He might come in one day and go off on how there was a box of tissues in everybody's office and he would be damned if he was going to pay for everyone to blow their noses. On other days, he would come in happy-go-lucky and greet everyone with a big smile. "Hey, easy money," he would say to our graphic artist. "When are you going to get to work and stop stealing my money?" he chuckled at the guys sweating out in the warehouse. He had a great sense of humor.

Although they never took a vote, I'm sure our staff preferred the seagull approach. Seagull management, as Ken Blanchard describes it, occurs when a manager comes into an office, flies around, flaps his wings with great commotion, craps on everybody's head, and then flies out. Rather than feel the sting of Big Bill's underhanded humor, designed to remind you who works for whom, I know I'd prefer somebody to come at me with his foul attitude clearly visible on his sleeve.

Constantly reminding staff members of who works for whom, even with a smile, is a power play. The unmistakable message is, I'm the big dog, you're the little dog. I'm strong. You're weak. I'm important. You're not. I'm irreplaceable. You're easily replaceable. You could make a case, technically speaking, that all of those statements are true. But they're only true in a context of hierarchical relationships. As much as people like Big Bill think this attitude will make them a lot more money, they fail to accept that those who practice a more equi-table and appreciative approach to people in their employ will make a lot more money.

For all the good Big Bill did for me, for all of the doors he opened for me, for all the opportunities he made available to me, he still left me impaled on the horns of a dilemma. By the time I left Disney, I was a disciple of Danny Cox and the principle that team members get better right after the leader does. My motto had become: lead the way you like to be led. Whatever characteristics I wanted from my team members, be it hard work, high energy, innovation, creativity, loyalty, efficiency, or high performance, it was up to me to model every be-havior before I could credibly expect it from others.

Damage Control

My management philosophy was the complete opposite of Big Bill's, and he felt compelled to take me under his wing and teach me how to treat employees. They were never loyal, according to him. They were efficient because the punishment for inefficiency was se-vere, as in the tissue incident. They worked hard because you paid them to work hard. Bill was convinced that, despite their paychecks, people only worked hard when he was looking in their direction.

I couldn't convince him otherwise. When I pointed out that our present staff was half the size of the staff I took charge of initially, and they were producing four times the revenues, he attributed the increased produc-tivity to his surprise visits and autocratic management style. Our staff was generating revenues of close to $250,000 per person. To me, their superior performance was in spite of his influence, not because of it.

I spent time after each flight of the seagull encouraging various team members and refocusing their efforts. We had a molecular orga-nizational design and every work pod orbited around the manage-ment core. Each person was a leader in his or her own area. Granted, we were a small company, but the principles of autonomy worked well and our people responded and performed just the way organization behavioral specialists predict people with a sense of ownership and autonomy will perform.

I managed up the food chain and down the food chain, doing my best to keep Bill happy and to keep our team members happy and productive. That meant dropping whatever I was doing when he showed up. After he made his rounds greeting and insulting our team members, he signaled to me it was time to have coffee at Coco's down the street. We could have sat, talked, and drank coffee in my office or his office, but that was against his rules.

Bill believed in leaving the premises to discuss company business. According to his philosophy, employees will eavesdrop and become privy to information they have no business knowing (99 percent of which nobody cared to know anyway) if you stay in the office. Thinking back, the stuff we talked about off-site was mostly information emanating from our team members anyway.

Bill was into psychological warfare. Another reason he left the office to have coffee was to create the illusion we were discussing our team members beyond their earshot. This was supposed to make them fear for their jobs and therefore work more diligently.

Big Bill was The Man and I reconciled myself to being a good soldier and charging up the hill when he said charge. In the publishing industry, he didn't even know which way to point the canons. We succeeded in spite of him. When I say succeeded, we grew fast and developed a tremendous reputation in our field. When we sold the company 40 months after the day Bill and I bought it, his piece of the pie was more than five times his total investment—net.

Charging up the hill at his command usually involved doing anything with little or no impact on our organizational objectives. Thank goodness he didn't like to bother with strategic planning. I would have been up to my tailpipe in mid-range plans. I felt all along he should have been more appreciative of my efforts on our collective behalf. And I whined to friends, family, and anyone who would listen. Many people can identify with the tremendous resentment I harbored for Bill.

My role in my own misery

I had the mother of all epiphanies thanks to the unrelated efforts of Bill and a friend in the mental health field. I was getting my first master's degree, the one in Marriage and Family Therapy, and one of my supervisors grew weary of hearing me complain about my business partner. One day, as I was launching into the vicissitudes of working with him for the 100th time, my friend said, "When are you going to stop worrying about him and start dealing with your role in this relational friction?"

"My role?"

"He knows you resent him and that makes him uncomfortable around you."

"Okay," I said. "I'll admit that I resent the hell out of him. He doesn't appreciate a damn thing I do even though I'm doing everything I possibly can for the business. I'm making him a lot of money."

"He's still uncomfortable."

"Let him be uncomfortable," I shot back. She didn't have to say anything. She just patiently waited for me to stew in my own stupidity for a few moments. "All right," I mumbled. "And your point is...?"

"You can't hide resentment. No matter how hard you try, it seeps into everything you say and do."

"He comments about my sarcasm all the time," I confessed.

"Are you sarcastic?"

"All the time."

She hit me in my wheelhouse. I couldn't deny that I had enormous resentment toward Big Bill, just like I had for my Machiavellian Boss at Disneyland. No wonder neither one of these guys was comfortable around me. No wonder they took everything I did as an assault and my every comment as a veiled insult. Whether they acted fairly or unfairly, competently or incompetently, appropriately or inappropriately, I was just as much to blame for the tension as they were. Whenever I was around them, it didn't matter what words came out of my mouth. I was always in an adversarial posture.

Put the Boundary Where It Belongs

As true as it all was, I didn't want to hear it. I've learned in the years since that it is not what my consulting clients want to hear either. It's a difficult pill to swallow. What about your situation? Upon closer examination, are you being punished for your talent and competency or are you poisoning the atmosphere around you as I did? Most likely it's a combination of both and you only have control over your part in it.

If others make you boil, your attitude might be helping increase the flame on their burner. I feel a little goody-goody, frou-frou asking the rhetorical question: Can't we all just get along? Yes we can, but not always on our own terms. Truly getting along with bosses and coworkers is rarely on our terms. Draw the line where you need to protect yourself and your best interests, but when the line is drawn to protect your ego and to prove you're right, it's time to redraw the line.

We can all get along if we'll accept that life and work are never perfect and there are times and places to settle for less in the moment to gain more in the long term. There are also times not to compromise. Deciding which is which is up to you. How serene you can be despite your I-Boss is your call. How much you allow his inevitable stupidity to rob you of valuable time and energy is your decision. You might not be in control of what your I-Boss says or does, but you are in control of your attitude.

Deciding to admit your role in the chaos and discomfort caused by your I-Boss is a start. When I realized and accepted that I contributed to Bill's bad attitude, the tension between us immediately eased off. When my attitude improved, so did his. You and I have tremendous power to alter the climate in which we work, regardless of our I-Boss's incompetence or his fear of our competence.

We can and should do good work. We can and should take pride in what we do. That causes us to focus on accomplishment rather than focusing on the burden someone else is placing on us. And we can present our good work to the I-Boss not as a threat, but as our contribution to the overall efforts of the team.

If you want to live a happier, more fulfilling life, live by the words of Aunt Eller. You remember Aunt Eller, Miss Laurie's adult supervision in the Rogers and Hammerstein musical *Oklahoma!* Judd Fry, the ranch hand with designs on Miss Laurie and a vendetta against Curly, her betrothed, dampens the newly nuptualized couple's spirits by trying to burn them alive on their wedding day. In the film version, after a narrow escape, good old Aunt Eller comforted her niece by saying something like, "You must look at the good things in life and the bad things in life and say 'well, all right then' to both."

I've never heard it said better. Look at the good things at work and the bad things at work and make peace with both. Like the Chinese proverb I mentioned earlier says, life will be what it is, whether you understand or not. That's why we recovering idiots pray for serenity to accept what we can't change, the courage to change what we can, and the wisdom to know the difference.

You have no control over your Idiot Boss. Your control is limited to how you think and what you say and do. The good news is the way you think and what you say and do can improve the way your I-Boss treats you. As you become less threatening to your I-Boss, his respect for your talent and competencies will increase. Who needs control when a little bit of influence can cause such a major improvement in how others look at you?

6

Success In Spite
of Stupidity

The Sixth Step:
"I'm entirely ready for God to remove my stupidity."

Success and stupidity don't mix. Your boss's stupidity is only half your problem. Your own stupidity can easily complete the disaster. With the help of my Higher Power, I'm counting on my recovery process to give me a chance to rise above my own intellectual challenges. Although my Idiot Boss's mental shortcomings remain beyond my control, I can anticipate his thinking and behavior and proceed accordingly.

Throughout my career, I have done things I shouldn't have done, not done things I should have done, said things I shouldn't have said, and not said things that could have made things better. If wishes were Winnebagos, the homeless would pay exorbitant insurance premiums. I must choose every day not to waste precious time and energy dwelling on mistakes I've made in the past, wishing I could go back and try again. That would be dumb. What's done is done. But to delete the past from my memory and make the same mistakes again would be dumber.

The problems that once bothered me most, as an Idiot Boss or Idiot Employee, were of my own devising. All the while, the keys to my happiness and serenity were in my pocket. The keys to your happiness and serenity are in your pocket right now. I resisted as long as I did because I didn't want to give up my antiquated notions of how life should be. Not that my vision of how life should be was completely misguided. It was the belief I could somehow will it to perfection that wasted enormous amounts of time and energy.

Stop Pursuing Perfection

Professional growth, like personal growth, is a process of refinement. As they say at recovery meetings, it's about the process—not perfection. Honoring the process is more important than achieving perfection. Even if you achieve perfection, others in your organization (starting with your boss) will get their hands on your work, screw it up, and you'll wind up aggravated, agitated, and alienated all over again. Letting go of the notion you can somehow achieve perfection will be one of the most liberating experiences of your life.

The first thing a key to serenity does is unlock the leg irons called "pursuit of perfection." The second thing it does is crank up your creative engine. Once your old notions of how to achieve perfection in yourself and others are discarded, you must replace them with something else. If not, you'll simply fall back on your next worst idea. If you don't reinvent yourself, at least retread your tires.

One way of replacing the stupidity of expecting perfection with something better is to observe ways other people do things. By observing the behavior of others, you can plagiarize behaviors that appear to work well for them, avoiding those making them look like morons. I recommend adopting thought processes of successful people, although thoughts are much harder to observe than actions.

Being Right Is Stupid

My obsession with fairness and perfection launched me on a self-defeating mission to prove I was right about everything. In my stupidity, I never stopped to consider if losing what I was ostensibly working for was worth someone telling me I was right. I battled tooth and nail to be right. Doing the right thing was a secondary concern and doing things right mattered little in my quest to be right.

All people want to think they're right, which means not everyone who thinks he or she is right can actually be right. Step back and reflect on your long-term plan. What is your ideal big picture? Which is more important, achieving your long-term goals or being right? Once you stop insisting on being right and granting the honor to someone else, barriers start falling, you'll feel energized, and wind will fill your sails.

As long as you are engaged in a tug-of-war with someone else over who is right, your focus and energy can't be applied to goal achievement—

unless your only goal is to be right. Try it the next time you lock horns with someone over something that won't alter the course of the universe. Simply agree with the blockhead and say, "You're right, the lay-offs won't affect morale." Of course they will. But if they're inevitable and beyond your control, what good is arguing about it?

A much better use of your time and energy is to make plans for how to deal with the demoralization rightsizing will create. Save yourself and others who are spared the axe. You will all be working twice as hard. Maintaining a productive and, hopefully, rewarding work environment will be a bigger challenge than before. Don't waste time arguing about the obvious, especially to people too stupid to see the obvious. You have more important fish to fry.

If it's your boss or someone higher on the corporate food chain, what do you think you're going to gain by convincing her she's wrong? If intentionally aggravating someone with influence over your working conditions, job security, and future prospects is your formula for success, I don't want to read the book you plan to write in the leisure hours after you're canned. Making others feel good is so easy it's ridiculous not to. Just say, "You're right, hurricanes rotate clockwise in the northern hemisphere."

Who cares? Allowing someone else to be right doesn't make you wrong. Abdicating the throne of "right" to someone immature enough to think it will matter 10 minutes, 10 years, or 10 centuries from now is the big thing to do. It's an especially grand gesture when you have immutable proof the other person is wrong.

Since I've stopped battling over being right, I've come to enjoy letting people who are wrong about something think they're right. I quietly hold a private smug fest. Best of all, I'm no longer tripping myself on the way to the finish line. I also sit back, watch the winner bask in the glory of rightness, and think to myself: *Did I look that imbecilic when I insisted on being right?*

How the Smart (and Lucky) Succeed

The greatest successes in my life have not come as the result of a well-structured strategy. Despite best-laid plans, success seems to rely mostly on the proper alignment of planets in the universe otherwise known as luck. You and I don't have the power to align planets much less predict when it will happen. All we can do is have our ducks in a row when the universe decides it's our turn. We can't create luck, but we can be prepared to take advantage of it when it pays a visit.

The last thing you want to be caught doing when the planets align is to be acting stupid. One of the greatest tragedies in life is to not be ready when your number is chosen. You can't win the lottery if you don't have a ticket. Self-help motivation books are good for helping prepare for that moment.

Books written by or purporting to reveal the thinking of successful people contain nuggets of truth. But the truths apply to the authors' unique circumstances, which usually include a run of luck. I think books promising fail-proof paths to wealth are mostly self-aggrandizing accounts of how rich people want the world to believe they succeeded. And they want the world to believe they did it all on their own.

For instance, take my golf game. I'm a lousy golfer in spite of all the books I've read on the subject. On that rare occasion when I hit a towering drive off the tee or sink a long serpentine putt, I maintain my composure, calmly lean against my putter, and wait for the others to finish. It's embarrassing to jump up and down in a juvenile celebration over a putt or drive only to have someone top my feat.

If no one does any better, I can act cool and confident as if luck had noting to do with it. If others buy your myth that major achievements come purely from natural talent or inspired intelligence, your legacy is assured. Maintaining the myth works best with people who don't know you or, in my case, how badly I play golf.

Fortunately, chances at success come more often than winning lottery numbers. Even if you stupidly blow an opportunity, chances are good that another will come along. But how many? Don't ever accuse me of recommending you banish yourself to the sidelines just because you missed an opportunity or two. Mega successes happen for a number of reasons. Making a large fortune is easier when you start with a small one, as in the case of Donald Trump or Howard Hughes. The best we can hope for is to start where we are and improve on our blessings.

Making a huge fortune can also be a matter of doing something smart while standing in the right place at the right time, as in the case of Bill Gates. He was not the first person IBM approached to develop a disc operating system. He was the first person to deliver what they asked for. What would Bill be doing now if the first person IBM approached had come through? Although Bill Gates responded to IBM with sufficient ingenuity and effort to satisfy their needs, he had no control over what the first person asked would do. Gates didn't line up the planets. But he rolled up his sleeves and opened up the door when opportunity knocked.

The best we can do is keep ourselves in a state of readiness for anticipated and unanticipated opportunities. Then give ourselves a break. You and I can't create miracles. Just because your I-Boss stumbled into his lucky break doesn't mean the same opportunity will fall into your lap. Nevertheless, positive thinking can help. Thinking positively won't align the planets. It helps align you with the planets.

Benjamin Franklin said, "Early to bed and early to rise makes a [person] healthy, wealthy, and wise," or words to that effect. I say, luck will get you the last three without bothering with the first two. But you can't count on luck. So, lay down with the sun and rise with the chickens. That's all you have control over.

I still recommend studying the lives of successful people even if their claims of self-actualized success are sometimes overstated. Paying special attention to the things they did leading up to their big breaks will expose the most valuable information. There is more to learn from how they intentionally or inadvertently positioned themselves for planetary alignment than from what finally transpired.

Mr. Cellophane, or the invisible executive

In some cases, the best way to succeed in spite of your Idiot Boss is to hide. How can he drive you to distraction if he doesn't know you're there? If you think I'm kidding, you would be surprised at how many presidents and CEOs ended up in their top jobs simply because they were the last people standing.

"Our CEO just went to prison," an anxious board member exclaims. "Who can we get to replace him?"

"How about Wilson?" another board member suggests,

"Under indictment," the in-house counsel vetoes.

"There's always Harold."

The other board members turn to see the face that belongs to the calm voice. "He's been with the company 30 years," the HR Director continues.

"Criminal record?" the Chairman inquires.

"Clean as a whistle," the in-house counsel confirms.

"Then let's get on this," the Chairman commands with renewed confidence. "Get the PR people started on a press release, get the tailor from Barney's in here to measure him for some new suits."

What was the secret of Harold's incredible ascent to the executive suite? He stayed out of sight for three decades. In organizations where competence is ignored or even punished, the fastest way to get yourself fired is to be good at something. Following that through to its illogical conclusion, one way to increase your corporate longevity is to draw as little attention as possible.

Doing important and worthwhile things usually draws attention to you and can threaten others. Small fish that threaten big fish are soon gobbled up, or at least bit in half. Schools of little fish resistant to change can gobble up bigger fish that threaten time-honored cultural paradigms. Making waves doesn't promote corporate longevity. If long-term job security is your goal, swimming under the waves is one way to do it.

Doing bad things or making highly visible demonstrations of your incompetence won't help your cause any more than doing good things— although dumb things don't tend to threaten people. But doing highly publicized dumb things will get your name on the "next-to-be-sacrificed" list, in which case you have until the other shoe drops to clean out your desk.

The real Harold

I knew a real-life Harold who worked for a firm in New York City. Although he never made CEO, he was a master at invisibility to all but the payroll department for more than 30 years. He caught a 5:15 Metro North train to his home in Connecticut every night, no matter what. A major meeting could be raging with huge deadlines looming and, at 5 p.m. sharp, Harold's seat was empty. Most people wouldn't have the guts to get up and walk out like that, but nobody knew why he was in the meeting to begin with. So, nobody missed him when he left.

Carrying on a conversation with Harold was difficult. After a minute or two, I'd find myself distracted by the paint color on the walls or the condition of the office plants. The only way I knew he retired was by visiting that office one day and finding a copy room where Harold's cubicle had been.

Faking Your Own Firing

Harold's cellophane existence intrigued me because I spent my life trying to be as visible as possible, which explains much of the trouble I've experienced. Had I attempted to preserve my anonymity, especially at strategic career junctures, I would have taken less incoming fire. If keeping a low profile is the longevity tactic you choose, the following cloaking techniques can help you survive in hostile environments:

- Be aware you can generate conversation, even when you're not present. If you do good things, people will talk about you. If you do bad things, people will talk about you more. If you become a pawn in a social chess match, you will be talked about. If you are king or queen in a social chess match, you will be talked about much more. If you align yourself with the blue office faction, your fellow faction members will be aware of your presence or absence. If you align with the green office faction, the blue faction members will still monitor your comings and goings in order to calculate a firing solution.

- Don't align yourself with any faction if you want to remain invisible. If you don't align with a faction, yet remain visible, you will be everyone's active target. Never give anyone incentive to give you a second thought in your presence, much less your absence. Don't become vital to anyone. Don't become a liability to anyone, except perhaps stockholders' equity.

- Generating paperwork will get you noticed. Never generating paperwork is a way to fly below the office radar. In the cyber age, the same thing applies to e-mail. If you never send e-mail, you'll never place a demand on anyone to respond. If you never reply to the e-mail you receive, you'll eventually be forgotten. To remain invisible, get your name deleted from as many lists as possible. It goes without saying that the less your name appears anywhere, the lower your visibility.

- If you must attend meetings, don't speak. Don't even ask anyone to pass the donuts. If you are asked to say something, never offer a new idea or challenge anyone else's ideas.

Boss-generated ideas are particularly sacred. Even a pinprick at the sanctity of their incoherent reasoning can threaten job security.

- If people poke their heads into your office or cubicle and ask what you're doing, say you're generating reports. No one wants to read reports, so they'll leave you alone and never follow up. No one wants to help write reports either, so they'll avoid you like the plague.

Those who think these are not serious suggestions or accurate observations have never worked in a large bureaucracy in the public or private sector. How many times have you been frustrated by someone behind an airline ticket counter, a customer service desk, at the IRS, at your credit card, local telephone, or cable TV company who refuses to act boldly and decisively to resolve your problem? How grateful are you on that rare occasion when a service representative does?

It's not that timid plodders are necessarily uncaring, bad people. They are simply keeping their heads down. Remember when president Ronald Regan was shot? As they wheeled him into the operating room, he looked up at Nancy and said, "Honey, I forgot to duck." Timid, pension-bound professionals are in a constant state of "duck," even when no one is shooting at them.

There are countless people literally putting in time until they can retire with their maximum pension, go get a real job, and buy timeshare in Bend, Oregon. Many of these water-treaders don't mind keeping busy with company business as long as they aren't asked to break a sweat. To career bureaucrats, asking for work is asking for trouble. In a bureaucratic environment, if word gets out that you are the least bit aggressive at taking on and finishing tasks, you'll return from a bio-break one day to find everyone's work on your desk. I'm not here to criticize these folks. If becoming a non-entity and preserving your anonymity is how you choose to survive in the workplace, now you know how.

Consider your options

Be realistic when considering what you want to accomplish in your workdays. Most people reading this book are doers by nature and have found themselves frustrated by bosses who impede progress and accomplishment. Before you crawl under your desk and withdraw from the rat race, answer some basic questions:

- Do you want to be active or idle?
- If you want to be active, do you want to just keep busy or do something meaningful?
- Does *meaningful* mean advancing your career and earning potential, or cataloguing rare fungi?
- If you want to earn more and be more involved, are you willing to become a smart blip on the corporate radar screen?

Unprepared blips are continuously frustrated and disappointed because blips on the organizational radar screen usually become targets. You might simply be a target for those who want to shirk their responsibilities and dump them onto the first person who will accept them. Becoming a target can also mean serving as a scapegoat for someone else's lack of performance. If you intentionally want to become a more active and visible player at work, be aware of and prepared for the potential downside of visibility.

Many people are highly skilled at internal and external planning for their organizations, yet rarely apply those same planning skills to their own careers and working conditions. Surviving Idiot Bosses can be enhanced by planning your way into more rewarding activities. It's not hard to stay ahead of Idiot Bosses, so if you're not trying to hide in the janitorial closet until retirement, put your planning skills to work for yourself.

- Consider what you want to become involved in. Look ahead and listen to the company propaganda for activities and initiatives that the department is likely to be gearing up for in the near future. Identify those things you want to be involved in and offer to do preliminary research and legwork.
- Consider who is likely to be involved with the new initiatives and decide if these are the people with whom you want to share a foxhole. Look at who will likely be the team leader and consider how shiny this person's star is within the organization. Someone you personally enjoy a great deal might not be very popular up the food chain, in which case you could have a decision to make—having comfort now or keeping future options open.

- Consider the importance of the new activities and initiatives in the context of long-range organizational objectives. It might be fun to resod the corporate softball field, but will redesigning work processes put you in a more lucrative limelight?

- Consider what you are best suited for. Don't try to take charge of an aerospace engineering project if your background is in advertising or public relations. It's always in your best interest to align your professional responsibilities that resonate with your natural strengths and competencies.

- Consider how others see you. Although your unique strengths and competencies might be right for a project or corporate initiative, do others recognize you as a leader? You could maneuver your Idiot Boss into assigning you a project, which technically legitimizes your power. But if your peers don't perceive you as a competent leader, they will sabotage and subvert your efforts, leaving you wishing you had stayed under your desk.

- Consider how much time and effort you're willing to exert to overcome obstacles in your path, what amount of abuse you're willing to absorb from detractors, and whether the potential rewards are equal to the sacrifice. I slightly misstated the point earlier when I said I would have taken less incoming fire by keeping a lower profile throughout my career. The problem isn't coming under fire. The problem is not being properly trained for combat operations.

Surviving Your Performance Review

Invisibility has its rewards. Transparency in the workplace can lead to job security, as it did for cellophane Harold, or even promotion. Most people nonetheless prefer a stimulating challenge and the opportunity to excel. I believe professional people have a natural inclination to perform well. Why, then, is the performance review such a dreaded experience? Theoretically, management should be eager to regularly examine the organizational population and review their performance in terms of who is contributing. Yet, you would be amazed at how vigorously some managers avoid reviews. Good bosses are eager to give performance reviews to praise performance and encourage growth. Sadists enjoy giving performance reviews for the opposite reasons and thereby render them useless for their intended purpose.

Ostensively, the performance review is to determine promotion and raise eligibility. In reality, most organizations go through the performance review process at least once a year after much pushing, prodding, and threatened litigation from the Human Resource Department, which is only trying to cover the company's derriere in the event of a grievance or wrongful termination suit. As a general rule, giving performance reviews is a no-win situation. In the competent leadership vacuum common to most organizations, I would prefer serving as a human shield before I would recommend issuing performance reviews.

To give you a raise, most boss types must deny money to someone else. The company will claim in court that a highly effective and completely objective system is used to determine who receives and does not receive pay increases. Truthfully, the raises are doled out to the boss's favorite people. It's difficult to prove, although people sometimes win handsome settlements. If you want to get your hands on the money sooner and save legal fees, become one of the boss's favorite people by preemptively using the techniques listed under the various boss types.

By design, performance reviews require a manager to sit on the throne of judgment. I didn't apply for Solomon's job and don't want it. If a manager gives an honest appraisal, the team member might feel slighted or even attacked. If the manager inflates a review to protect the team member's fragile ego, the boss might feel guilty for subverting the system, rendering it meaningless. With the possible exception of the masochist, all of us like to think we're more valuable than we really are. (I have yet to work for a company that can't survive my departure.) When bosses go through the performance review motions, what constitutes a good employee to them and what constitutes a good employee in the real world are often two different things.

If top executives are genuinely concerned with organizational productivity and performance, they should have team members do performance reviews on their bosses. To organizations already doing so, I extend a heartfelt "attaperson." To the others I say: Wake up, morons. Bad bosses have 1,000 times more destructive potential than ineffective team members. If you can't find the courage to have team members review their bosses, at least use 360-degree feedback for performance reviews. It's more valid, reliable, and objective than the manager-generated performance review.

Performance review horror

Performance is reviewed every day in organizations where open communication is encouraged and information flows freely among all team members. My worst performance review came from a particularly mean-spirited manager whom I will always believe had it in for me for graduating from college and using words in excess of two syllables. I remember thinking to myself as my manager yakked in the background: *Are we talking about the same person here? All this time I thought I was doing a good job. Does he think I work long hours because I have nothing better to do? If I'm this bad why did he wait so long to tell me?* He wrote that I needed improvement in quantity of work, quality of work, work habits, and especially communication—then he demanded that I sign it. Based on that performance review, I'm surprised security didn't escort me from the building in handcuffs.

Don't allow poor performance reviews to wound your ego. They are a more reliable indicator of the boss's mood and ability to deal with people issues than they are accurate reflections of performance. If your boss discusses goals, objectives, habits, and behaviors on performance-review day, and no other day, the performance review process lacks any kind of credibility as far as I'm concerned.

For those who still suffer under the oppressive yoke of their boss's performance reviews, the least I can do is offer some pointers. Performance reviews mean different things to different boss types. Depending on your boss's type, you can slide through unharmed or emerge from your performance review bloodied and bruised. Regardless of the challenge awaiting you, it's best to go in with your eyes open.

According to recent data from the career development office at The College of St. Catherine, professionals over the age of 35 change jobs on average every three years and workers under the age of 35 can expect to change jobs every 18 months. Yikes. That's a lot of Idiot Bosses to deal with. Changing jobs anywhere near that frequently means you're likely to get your share of other boss types, too.

You need to be prepared for them all. Reflect on what I've already told you about the various boss types, their likes and dislikes, and their underpinning career paradigms. You must present yourself in the best possible light to your boss 12 months a year, not just 30 days before performance reviews. Violate the particular protocol of divergent boss personalities at your own peril. A bad performance review will shatter your serenity. Even if you manage to preserve a semblance of happiness and contentment in the workplace following a poor performance review, your long-term job satisfaction will be shaken.

The God Boss Review

God Bosses enjoy the performance review process because it gives them the opportunity to let you know how much you have pleased or displeased them during the preceding year. To a God Boss, a good employee genuflects. As long as the team member being reviewed spends sufficient time on bended knee worshiping the God Boss and presents suitable tithes and offerings, the review will be positive, regardless of whether or not anything is getting accomplished in the department.

To prepare for a performance review with a God Boss, choose your wardrobe carefully. Sackcloth and sandals might be appropriate. Perhaps a prayer shawl for the men and a Khimar for the ladies. Your clothing should reflect humility and submissiveness. God Bosses take themselves very seriously. The more ceremony you engage in the better. Burning incense and chanting his name are nice touches. Be careful though. Pay attention and determine what will be an adequate demonstration of your devotion without going over the top. God Bosses don't appreciate being mocked.

For your best shot at getting a raise from a God Boss, use terms like "your greatness," "your majesty," and "your lordship," throughout the year. It all sounds blasphemous because it is, but do you want the raise or not? And don't worry about the true God feeling mocked. The sight of the whole thing probably has Him on the floor. No matter how literally you take your God Boss, always refer to his accomplishments, his glory, and his mighty power when talking business or golf. Go with the flow on this one; anyone who thinks he's God could be dangerous. Whatever he says or does, act eternally grateful.

Prepare all year long for a God Boss by:

- Articulating how appreciative you are for the opportunity to serve in his department in emails and other appropriate correspondences.
- Thanking him for his help and guidance on projects.
- Offering to do him favors or small services.
- Bringing him small gifts, even if they are humorous tokens and trinkets.
- Mentioning to his peers how his accomplishments have driven the department forward.
- Acknowledging his leadership in written reports and evaluations of projects.

Before you write these suggestions off as frivolous, consider doing these things, within reason, for 12 months. If your diagnosis is correct and your boss thinks he's God, what kind of performance review do you think you'll receive?

Don't worry about real productivity. You accomplish that for your own satisfaction and to earn the respect of your peers. A God Boss will evaluate and qualify you for promotions and raises based on how faithful a disciple he thinks you are. I guarantee, if he perceives you as a detractor or ungrateful, no amount of real productivity, efficiency, or cost savings will bring you into his good graces at performance review time.

The Machiavellian Boss Review

To Machiavellian Bosses, staff members who step aside in the hall when she passes, turn and walk in the other direction when she glares, and routinely put the Machiavellian's name on superior work the staff members complete will receive high marks on a performance review. A high mark on a Machiavellian's performance review is a C+ because she doesn't want anyone outside her domain to see high performance ratings and come looking for people to promote. Whether or not the staffers have done anything to promote the achievement of organizational goals and objectives, promoting the career ambitions of the Machiavellian translates into job security.

Prepare for your performance review with a Machiavellian Boss by reviewing everything you have done for the company and make sure you didn't receive credit for it. If you did receive credit, go into the performance review and immediately apologize for the mistake and promise it will never happen again. Act as if you're at a loss to explain how your name became attached to something the Machiavellian was obviously responsible for. If you're written up in the company newsletter for some achievement, demand a retraction in the following issue.

Men should keep several suits and ties in the office to ensure color coordination with the Machiavellian. Women must dress to compliment rather than compete with the Machiavellian. If she comments about the similarity of your wardrobe, tell her she sets the fashion trends and emphasize how you watch her closely for guidance. Furthermore, tell her whatever she wears, drives, eats, or reads should be required for the entire organizational population.

Understand that everything the Machiavellian tells you regarding your performance is twisted through the lens of how it either promotes or impedes her career. Nod and agree to everything. Don't get into an "I'm right and you're wrong" thumb wrestling match with a Machiavellian if you want to go home with two thumbs.

There is but one goal in the Machiavellian's department and that's the ascending career of the Machiavellian Boss. Make sure everything you say and do reflects that agenda. Raises are next to impossible to wrench out of a Machiavellian unless you have really convinced her your purpose for living is to help her attain the top spot for which she is predestined.

Prepare all year long for a Machiavellian Boss performance review by:

- Articulating how her work is deserving of much more acclaim from higher up using e-mails and other appropriate correspondences.
- Thanking her for allowing you to work on her behalf.
- Volunteering to take on special projects that promote her agenda and enhance her image.
- Selecting wardrobe and decorating your workspace in ways that suggest allegiance.
- Mentioning to her peers how her accomplishments have driven the department forward.

- Acknowledging the superiority of her leadership in written reports and evaluations of projects.

Consider doing these things, within reason, for 12 months. If your diagnosis is correct and your boss is truly Machiavellian, you will receive the best marks possible on your performance review.

Concern yourself with productivity as a way of accomplishing something you can give her credit for. You can still be productive as a means of self-satisfaction and to earn the respect of your peers. However, a Machiavellian Boss will evaluate and qualify you for promotion, and raises based on how convinced she is that you support her and do not compete with her. I guarantee, if she perceives you as a threat or competitor, no amount of real productivity, efficiency, or cost savings will bring you into her good graces at performance review time.

The Masochistic Boss Review

Masochists use the performance review to prove what miserable failures they are. If they were better bosses, they reason, you would be a better employee. That is true, but not for the reasons they're citing. Masochists think everything they touch turns to ca-ca and they don't stop to think about how that might insult you. Don't take it personally. You didn't have anything to do with creating the masochist's condition, and there is nothing he can say or do to turn you into fertilizer.

Wearing something drab might help because it won't draw attention to clothing. If you wear something bright and cheery, he will probably notice and go into a downward spiral about what a lousy dresser he is. He is a terrible dresser, but do you really want to sit and listen to all that? I'd rather have him tell me I need improvement in quantity of work, quality of work, work habits, and communication.

Do not carry sharp objects into the masochist's office. Hot coffee is not advisable. You never know when the urge might strike him to snatch it out of your hand and pour it into his own lap. Sit with your eyes down and ever so slightly nod your head in agreement when he describes the futility of his life. Say nothing. Offer no solutions. Bear with it as long as you can. You might consider having someone call you 20 minutes after entering the masochist's office with a fabricated family emergency providing adequate justification to excuse yourself.

You might be able to get a raise from a Masochistic Boss if you can convince him it will damage his budget enough to draw a reprimand from his boss. If he doesn't figure that out on his own, it's up to you to mention it. As you rush out to visit your brother in the intensive care unit, pause at the door, turn, and say, "I suppose a raise is out of the question because it would really bring your boss down hard on you... ." Then run. The raise should be approved by the time you get back.

Prepare all year long for a Masochistic Boss performance review by:

- Articulating how he struggles under an excessive workload that no human being should be expected to manage—use body language and expressions that slightly mimic the slumped shoulders and hopeless countenance on his face.

- Pointing out, in e-mails and face-to-face conversations, reasons why projects and initiatives imposed on the Masochistic Boss's department are doomed from the start. Let him know how sorry you are that he has been put in this untenable situation.

- Volunteering to take on special projects and extra workload from time to time gives you the opportunity to produce worthwhile work. However, don't rush into the boss's office rejoicing in the accomplishment.

- Being prepared to celebrate secretly with your peers. When and if your Masochistic Boss acknowledges the success you realized, remain solemn, sigh, and say, "Yeah, boss, we really got lucky on that one. Don't you wish we could be so lucky all the time?"

- Making wardrobe and workspace decorating choices in ways that avoid exhibiting a dramatic contrast in self-image between you and your Masochistic Boss—he should not feel minimized just being around you.

- Avoiding overt reassurance with your Masochistic Boss— when things go terribly wrong, don't tell him it wasn't his fault. Say instead that it could have happened to anybody or that anybody could have made a similar mistake, miscalculation, or misunderstanding.

Consider doing these things, within reason, for 12 months. If your diagnosis is correct and your boss is a true masochist, you will receive the best marks possible on your performance review. Like all bosses, masochists will evaluate and qualify you for promotion and raises based on how convinced they are that you understand and sympathize with their dilemmas. Don't avoid productivity altogether; you and your peers still want to achieve a sense of accomplishment. Just don't celebrate it as reward for a job well done in front of your Masochistic Boss. At all times, keep your own interests in perspective. Despite the skilled ways you play to your Masochistic Boss, you don't want to be an individual martyr working for a martyred individual.

The Sadistic Boss Review

The performance review is a Sadistic Boss's dream. A legal, sanctioned, and even required annual session of torture is almost too good to be true. The Sadistic Boss can hardly contain herself as her employees absorb the psychological punishment, wail in torment, grimace in pain, tear their hair out by the fistful, and are forced to come back at least once a year for more. Sadistic Bosses claim beatings and the psychological suffering they inflict are related to the achievement of performance goals and organizational objectives. Yet, nobody knows better than her long-suffering employees that she gets off on causing immense pain to the safest, and most vulnerable and available targets.

If you want to get a raise from your Sadistic Boss, claim any increase in your income will cause you painful tax consequences. Emphasize the word *painful*. It's not her money to begin with and, if it can cause you anguish, it's worth padding the budget.

Setting up your Sadistic Boss for a good performance review throughout the year requires some acting on your part. Learn to moan convincingly. You should throw in an anguished cry and plaintive wail now and then. These can be prerecorded and played back on your workstation speakers. As long as your Sadistic Boss thinks the sounds coming from your cubicle are the result of her painfully punitive workload, she'll like having you around.

Dress as if you sleep in your clothes. If she comments, say flatly that you haven't slept since she gave you the Mid-range plan to re-write again. Wear clothes that are too large so she'll think that you don't have time to eat. If you're a good makeup artist, make your face a bit more sallow, apply some bags under your eyes, and hollow out your cheeks. Pile your office or cubicle with stacks of papers and reports from floor to ceiling. Leave only enough room for one person to get in and out. If she thinks you're slaving in there (cue the moans and wails), she'll leave you alone and go hunt down someone who looks rested and well fed.

Prepare all year long for a sadistic performance review by:

- Articulating at every opportunity how you struggle under an excessive workload—never cross the line and act angry toward your Sadistic Boss over the excessive work issue. Instead, act defeated and worn down. I don't know about you, but I naturally launch into a litany of how much is on my plate when someone asks, "How are you?"

- Using body language and expressions that support the grim descriptions you offer of your circumstances—this also comes naturally to me. I feel so overwhelmed with my many and varied tasks at any given time that I don't have to fake an overworked and underpaid countenance. I don't know exactly why my heavy burden makes a Sadistic Boss feel good, but I know enough to give her credit for my struggles, even if she's not responsible. Attribute a kidney stone to her work demands. There is a possible seed of truth in it, but not likely. However, knowing that you're struggling under an excessive workload while suffering from a kidney stone will enlarge her sense of satisfaction.

- In e-mails and face-to-face conversations, pointing out reasons why projects and initiatives imposed by your Sadistic Boss are tremendous encumbrances, even if they're not. It's a sort of dance you do with a sadist. She's happy with the appearance that her power is sufficient to cause you discomfort and you don't mind throwing out that impression if it, in fact, smoothes things out for you in the real world.

- Never volunteering to take on special projects and extra workload—that's taking away her power to control and abuse you. You must maintain the illusion, whether it is an illusion or not, that anything she tells you to do could be the straw that breaks your back.

- Being prepared to celebrate secretly with your peers. When and if your Sadistic Boss acknowledges the success you realized, remain solemn, sigh, and say, "Yeah, boss, that project took so much time we got backed up on everything else." If she believes you, she might not immediately load you up with additional work.

- Making wardrobe and workspace decorating choices in ways that avoid exhibiting a lighthearted, carefree existence. Your work area should be piled high with accumulated stuff, whether it has anything to do with your current project or not. A wardrobe motif? In two words: salt mines.

Consider doing these things, within reason, for 12 months. If your diagnosis is correct and your boss is a sadist, you will receive the best marks possible on your performance review. As before, don't avoid productivity altogether; you and your peers still want to achieve a sense of accomplishment. Just don't expect a job well done to be welcomed with time off to catch your breath. The silver lining on the sadist's dark cloud is the fact that she needs the illusion of power as much as she needs the actual power. Sadistic Bosses don't generally need to cause real pain and suffering. If you play your role convincingly enough, a Sadistic Boss will accept your stellar performance as payment in full.

The Paranoid Boss Review

Your Paranoid Boss will give you an average performance review by marking all threes on the one-to-five scales. He'll stare at you in silence as you come in and sit down. Clutching your performance review in his hand, he'll shut the door, close the blinds, turn up the radio, and speak in a whisper in case the room is bugged. Some Paranoid Bosses might even search you for a wire.

He'll tell you the review process is nothing but a veiled attempt to trick him. But he's too smart to fall for it. He'll say he gave you all average marks so as not to raise any suspicion with HR, but he knows what you and your scheming team members are up to.

It's best not to wear all black during your performance review or at all around a Paranoid Boss. Don't whisper in the office or talk into your cuff. Don't even take your cell phone with you into the performance review. If it rings, he'll dive under his desk.

If you want a raise from a Paranoid Boss, take a deep breath, search the ceiling for hidden cameras, lean close to him and tell him he's right. Everyone is out to get him and you know who, when, what, and where. If he'll give you a raise to "cover expenses," promise to deliver a full report exposing the conspiracy and conspirators. For your safety, make him agree to transfer you out of his department one week before the report is due. Once out, you can forget the bogus report. How is he going to explain rescinding the transfer and raise?

Prepare all year long for a Paranoid Boss's performance review by:

- Keeping everything you do as visible as possible—take every opportunity to keep all activities in plain sight of your Paranoid Boss. To the extent you are able, arrange your working space so that he can observe you from his office or regular routes of travel.

- Using body language that features broad, sweeping arm gestures that suggest openness—as if to assure him that you, nor anyone else in the department, have nothing to hide.

- In e-mails and face-to-face conversations, describing how you and your fellow team members came up with your conclusions and what activities led to your results—the more you can paint a picture for a Paranoid Boss, the less he will rely on his imagination. That's where the conspiracies exist, in his fertile imagination.

- Taking on special projects as if you are working in the front window at Macy's—giving everyone involved, directly or peripherally, a brief account of the project's origins before you move on to a progress report. The contextual framework within which you place your information can lead to unsolicited comments coming back at your Paranoid Boss, indicating an open atmosphere. An open atmosphere is less threatening than the possibility of covert operations in dark corridors.

- Celebrating success openly with your peers—including your Paranoid Boss at every opportunity. Celebrate in the office as much as possible so he can't avoid seeing what you're doing and can't pretend he was excluded. Even if he doesn't join in the festivities, your message is clear. You're not hiding anything.

- Making wardrobe and workspace decorating choices in ways that provide maximum access and exposure—with as few walls and partitions as possible. When you meet with coworkers, do it in the open where the boss can see you. Do it within earshot if you can. Wave at your Paranoid Boss during these impromptu meetings and gesture for him to join you. Your work area should be piled high with accumulated stuff, whether it has anything to do with your current project or not.

Consider doing these things, within reason, for 12 months. If your diagnosis is correct and your boss is paranoid, you will receive the best marks possible on your performance review. If you have kept him updated on a daily basis, even with brief, "spontaneous" reports when there is little to report on, he can't help but feel less threatened.

If you give in to your natural urge to avoid the pain in the corner office and keep your work, office associations, and comings and goings to yourself, you're asking for trouble from a Paranoid Boss. As always, surviving and thriving in the workplace, especially under a paranoid person, places the responsibility for proactive solutions on your shoulders. Sure, it's not fair. By now you should realize that little in life and virtually nothing at work is fair. You haven't been hiding anything, so why should you jump through hoops to prove as much to your stupid boss? Because fair is what you make it, that's why.

The Buddy Boss Review

Your Buddy Boss will treasure the one-on-one time with you. When she suggests you meet once a month instead of only once a year, smile and ask if you get a raise every month. She might be so happy you want to spend time with her that she'll come up with the extra coinage. How bad could it be? Your Buddy Boss wants to interact with you constantly. There shouldn't be anything new to discuss at a performance review after being joined at the hip to your Buddy Boss all year long.

To drive your Buddy Boss into an elated frenzy, wear similar clothing and act excited as you point out how you match. What a surprise! What a wonderful coincidence! It must mean you're meant to be friends forever. When it gets too thick, go out for some oxygen. Don't try the emergency phone call about your brother in intensive care. A Buddy Boss will beat you to the hospital. Just act delighted with everything your Buddy Boss says and does and, the moment you're out of her sight, do whatever spins your crank.

Prepare all year long for a performance review from your Buddy Boss by:

- Keeping everything you do as friendly as possible—take every opportunity to make all activities seem as socially driven as possible without embarrassing yourself in front of the cynics in the company. Arrange your working space so that she can observe you from her office or regular routes of travel. The higher your literal visibility, the more opportunity to wave. That's right, wave. You can often keep her out of your space by waving across the office. That contact will be enough for her if she's just needing an acknowledgement fix.

- Using body language that features friendly, welcoming gestures that say, "It's so good to see you"—to assure her you are having pleasant thoughts. The more time that passes without reassurance, the more she will be nagged by doubt. It doesn't matter that you've been friendly, even giddy, every time she encountered you for the past 15 years; if she has received no assurance in the last 15 minutes, you might want to wave. Tell her you'll be think- ing about her (at least that project of hers) whenever you leave the office and make sure you give a visual or verbal reassurance that all is peachy each time you return.

- Using voice mail and e-mails to reassure her that she is in your thoughts—like the Sadistic Boss, your Buddy Boss doesn't need the full measure of her remedy as much as the regular appearance. A stitch in time will save nine. A brief, preemptive e-mail or voice mail, might keep your Buddy Boss out of your office long enough to get some real work done.

- Saying up front that special projects sound like fun and will give you more opportunities to report in on a regular basis—as always, you are using special projects to write your own ticket as far as workload is concerned. You can also use them to create social interactions that will please your Buddy Boss. Now that's catching two birds in one net.

- Celebrating success openly with your peers and your Buddy Boss—she will love nothing better than a reason to party. Celebrate in the office as much as possible to reduce the possibility that she'll wind up at your place. She'll join in any festivities available. It's up to you to design the festivities in such a way you can satisfy her insatiable need for social acceptance and have a life of your own. As with all other boss types, you're managing them to the extent of your influence. If you don't intentionally remain a step ahead, resign yourself to accepting whatever your boss comes up with according to his or her own devices.

- Making wardrobe and workspace decorating choices in ways that indicate maximum affection for your Buddy Boss—like naming the softball and bowling teams after her on the jerseys. Pictures on your walls, the departmental bulleting boards, and around the coffee area should display your Buddy Boss with you and every other team member you can squeeze into the frame. Like the e-mail and voice mail assurances, these pictures are a visual reassurance that your Buddy Boss is constantly on the hearts and minds of her best friends/employees.

Consider doing these things, within reason, for 12 months. If your diagnosis is correct and your boss is as emotionally needy as the day is long, you will receive the best marks possible on your performance review. If you have included her physically, via written and spoken word, as well as in visual references, she can't help but feel included. And why wouldn't you want your work environment to be as friendly as possible? It falls to you to get anything worthwhile accomplished. But what else is new?

The Idiot Boss Review

If the sample performance review in the HR manual looks identical to the review your Idiot Boss presents to you it's because he copied it straight across. Unfortunately, the sample review has average rankings across the board. I-Bosses don't understand the concept behind performance reviews any more than they understand the concept behind inflatable tires. Bosses do performance reviews, people put air in their tires, and idiots don't understand the need for either.

They know it's better to have air in the tires than not. They figure it's better to have performance reviews than not. And performance reviews are a break in the boring office routine. Even if performance issues are discussed only once a year for 30 minutes, I-Bosses welcome the diversion. Left to invent their own diversions they usually create redundant busy work resulting in zombie land.

You can actually convince your I-Boss to improve your performance review rankings if you make a game out of it. Point out how he can give you a larger raise if he elevates your rankings. Tell him how he can get a raise by suggesting the same thing to his boss. When he does and is slapped silly, he'll be too embarrassed to confess to his boss that he gave you a raise when you asked for it. Never mention the unfortunate incident again or bring up the red handprint on his cheek. If he tries to bring it up, develop instant amnesia. He'll drop it soon enough.

Throughout the year, always have your I-Boss's latest ridiculous project nearby in case he unexpectedly drops in on you. Pull the bogus papers over the real materials or football pool you're working on and fire a preemptive comment to cut off any project he's cooked up to amuse himself. Spout something about what a terrific idea it was to rewrite last year's mid-range plan and that you should have it finished for him in a month or so.

Prepare all year long for a performance review from your Idiot Boss by:

- Keeping everything you do as overstated as possible—take every opportunity to make all activities seem driven by your allegiance to the corporate philosophy, as he understands it. Without embarrassing yourself in front of your peers, arrange your working space to reflect the type of corporate empire the idiot imagines he's in charge of.

- Using body language that reflects the type of follower your Idiot Boss imagines his leadership style will attract. If he feels reengineering means treating everyone like piston rods, walk and talk like piston rods. Hopefully, he'll fancy himself a leader of self-actualized, creative, and enthusiastic people. That way you can be yourself, except for the part about giving lip service to his hair-brained ideas.

- Using voice mail and e-mails to reassure him that his vision is being realized—like the Machiavellian Boss—your Idiot Boss probably sees his role in the universe as something other than the way the universe sees him. He doesn't need the full measure of his remedy as much as the appearance that his imagination is reality.

- Explaining repeatedly how special projects are a way to accelerate his agenda (and shape your workload more the way you want it). As always, you can create special projects or reframe your existing projects to give the appearance that his agenda is comprehensive and meaningful.

- Celebrating success openly with your peers and your Idiot Boss—the key is to boast and brag that what you've accomplished is what he imagines is important. What you accomplish might (and should) be important and consistent with the overall goals and objectives of the organization. You'll even want to make sure people who matter are appropriately informed of what you've done. However, what your boss thinks was accomplished should be tailored to his world view to keep him from asking you to do it over again.

- Making wardrobe and workspace decorating choices based on the cultural mores of the empire in your Idiot Boss's imagination—like naming the softball and bowling teams "The Cheese Movers," "The Saw Sharpeners," or "The Outside the Box Bunch." What do you have to lose? Are you really that good at bowling and softball anyway?

Consider doing these things, within reason, for 12 months. If your diagnosis is correct and your boss is an idiot, you will receive the best marks possible on your performance review. If you have convincingly created the illusion that his imaginative empire is alive and well, he can't help but feel important. You should want your Idiot Boss to feel important. While it's true he's not, any doubt he has about his importance will wind up as burdensome, unnecessary, and even ridiculous work on your desk. Preemption is key to applying all of these techniques to all of these boss types.

The Good Boss Review

A Good Boss will have engaged you every day throughout the year about organizational goals, objectives, and your role in attainment. You will have nothing new to talk about at your performance review except how she is scheming to get you more money and better working conditions. If she has truly been a Good Boss, she will have orchestrated an effective and well-balanced team approach to organizational performance objectives.

Many larger organizations appropriate a fixed amount of funds to be distributed as raises in each department. This is done independently of the performance review process. The performance review is simply a means to slice up the pie. I like the 360-degree approach myself, and a Good Boss will attempt to gather and consider peer input to balance and validate her own, even if it's not the official approach of the HR department.

Your Good Boss knows productivity and loyalty are tied to a sense of ownership and a sense of ownership increases proportionately with participation. If team members can actually influence how salary and wage increases are distributed, they will feel empowered. The bond between Good Bosses and their team members is the strongest of any power disparity dyad because the boss has earned the team members' trust by sharing power.

Although Good Bosses share power, they remain ultimately responsible to the point of taking the heat when team members screw up. As leadership author and lecturer Danny Cox (*Seize the Day*) says: "If the team hits a home run, a true leader points to them and says, 'They did it.' If the wheels come off the project, a true leader says, 'I'm responsible.'" If you have a Good Boss rejoice, thank your Higher Power, be grateful, and pass it forward. A performance review from a Good Boss is probably the only one you'll feel truly good about signing.

Like Likes Like

Whether we're right or wrong, hard workers or lazy, smart or intellectually challenged, the fact remains that a boss won't give a raise to someone she doesn't like. It's human nature and I don't advise betting against it. Observe and determine what boss type you're working for and start developing your plan from there.

Reflect to your boss what makes her happy. Spend your energy making her feel comfortable. Get all you can from the cards you were dealt and only then think about more. You can ignore the nature of the beast, work diligently with a sense of integrity despite your boss, and hope she will recognize and reward you. I tried that for most of my working life to little avail. To keep frustrating myself long after I should have known better means I clung to at least some of my stupidity after I asked God to remove it.

Be real

I rarely have difficulty working with or relating to anyone after I honestly inventory myself, my motivations, and what I might intentionally or unintentionally bring to the party. Coaching, counseling, consulting, and mediating have all taught me 90 percent of the time, when conflict is based on assumptions and limited information, the conflict will evaporate once the truth is brought into the light of day for everyone to see. Conversely, when the issues dividing people are clearly articulated, it doesn't necessarily bring them closer to agreement. But everybody can see what must be overcome and can focus his or her energies on reaching compromise rather than on being right.

Conflict is rarely one-sided. In a conflicted personal or professional relationship, even if Person A is a diabolical monster, completely without redeeming virtue, Person B, at the very least, is contributing to the problem by staying in the relationship. Usually, Person B is up to more, consciously or unconsciously, than she is willing or able to admit. Consider what happens when Person B exits the problematic personal or professional situation. It reverts to being Person A's problem. That's fine until Person B hooks up personally or professionally with Person C who is remarkably similar to Person A.

Imagine the therapist's surprise when Person B comes in complaining that Person C is a diabolical monster, worse even than Person A, and she (Person B) is completely without fault in the scenario. There is a theater in Moscow named for this line of thinking. It's called the Bolshoy, which in English doesn't mean what I'm suggesting it means, but it's as close to barnyard language as you're going to get out of me without asterisks.

The buck stops with you and me

Many people have trouble listening to Dr. Laura broadcast her therapy because she immediately goes to the caller's role and responsibility in the presented problem. That's not what most people want to hear and it's the last thing they want to talk about. It's more fun to talk about how someone else is making our lives miserable. But if we're serious about having our stupidity exorcised, we must first admit we have some. Calling my bosses names, no matter how accurate, doesn't release me from my responsibility to be a skilled employee—skilled at working with my bosses.

Idiots beware

Ambitious, creative, innovative, and enthusiastic team members can still draw enough attention to be executed or run off by status quo preservationists. Many people do a good job and make tremendous contributions to the achievement of organizational goals, only to have those achievements and contributions minimized, marginalized, and maligned. Such people often buy into the mythical belief that they can take their hard work and enthusiasm to another organization where they will be better appreciated.

That rarely works. Most of the time, they find the grass no greener in the new pasture and all they have succeeded in doing is lowering their seniority. There are bad bosses everywhere. You might as well master the art of working with them right where you are. After a few such disappointing attempts to find greener pastures, some formerly enthusiastic people go numb, fall silent, melt into the woodwork, and manage to coast across the retirement finish line before anyone notices. They didn't set out to do it that way, the system merely knocked them unconscious, and that's how it turned out.

The "greener pastures" syndrome has always worked in favor of lifers. As the enthusiastic, optimistic hard workers clear themselves out in search of more promising digs, the bureaucrats have less to challenge them, organizational leaders eventually accept less from them, and we get the kind of service we've come to expect from the government agencies: overpriced and underdelivered. When planning your personal and professional strategy, make a realistic assessment of the role and influence idiots might play in your success and try not to be the biggest idiot of them all.

7

Idiotthink:
The Great Disguise

The Seventh Step:
"Please, please, God, remove my stupidity."

Sometimes the distinctions between the 12 steps for recovering idiots are subtle. In Chapter 6, I prepared myself for God to remove my stupidity. Now, I'm wondering why it takes Him so long. I'm formulating numerous plans for replacing stupidity with something useful, which is what the preparation for stupidity extraction is all about. It should be obvious that, once stupidity is removed, the resulting vacuum will suck something in. We must fill the void where stupidity once lived with something premeditated and consciously selected to avoid another, more profoundly stupid idea, notion, or behavior to be sucked in.

The plan I suggest in this chapter is the old "false identity" ploy. If you can't beat 'em, join 'em. Or make it appear as if you're joining 'em. Sometimes it's just no use fighting the system. Burn your personal fuel cells on things you have some control over and enjoy. If you're trapped in a culture of idiots with no possibility for improvement in your lifetime, you might as well blend in. Why burn yourself out? This method of job survival is different from the invisibility ploy described in Chapter 6. By adopting the appearance of an idiot, you can move up in the organization without threatening anyone.

Changing identities is not a clever maneuver to trick your I-Boss into liking you. That would be difficult to sustain over the long haul. As "honest" Abe Lincoln said, "You can fool some of the people all of the time and all of the people some of the time. But you can't fool all of the people all of the time," or words to that effect.

In the workplace, it's possible to fool some of the people all of the time. You can pretend to like your I-Boss just enough to make him comfortable around you. You might even be able to convince everyone you're on good terms with him. But some people will put you into the same category as the I-Boss and never trust or cooperate with you again.

Attempting to fool all of the people all of the time requires you to operate against your essential nature. Operating against your essential nature is like struggling against gravity. You're better off being real and finding ways to use your essential nature to your advantage. Pretending you like your I-Boss when "despise" is the more accurate term is like holding a fully inflated beach ball under the water in a swimming pool.

It's easy to do at first and can be kind of fun for a while. Then it becomes tedious. You start to wonder why it's so important to hold the ball under the water. "Oh, yeah," you remind yourself, "I'm fooling everybody by keeping my true feelings beneath the surface." As time goes by, it becomes increasingly difficult. What seemed at first like a small expenditure of energy starts to add up. Every now and then, the ball starts to slip. You catch yourself just in time to shove it back under the water again. "Whew," you think. "That was close." You almost let the cat out of the bag, so to speak.

Beach Ball Nightmares

As you read this, there are more people than you might realize wandering around your office holding big beach balls under the water. They're the ones who have funny expressions on their faces. You know the expressions I'm talking about—the look of constipation. They appear to be holding their breath a lot. The truth is they're in constant fear the beach ball will pop to the surface and their true feelings toward their I-Bosses will be exposed.

The lucky ones really are constipated. The only thing between them and relief is an effective laxative. There is no off-the-shelf laxative for unresolved malice toward your I-Boss. You must find a way to simultaneously be real and peacefully coexist with him. Stoking your conflict boilers won't bring you relief. Constant fear of exposure causes you to toss and turn all night, raises your blood pressure, and can give you ulcers. I've often bolted upright, out of a dead sleep, in a cold sweat, after dreaming my beach ball popped out of the water in the middle of a staff meeting. To make matters worse, sleep deprivation makes it even harder to concentrate on keeping the thing under water.

You know you're in trouble if your I-Boss, or even a coworker, wanders by unexpectedly and catches you off guard. "Whatcha doin' there?" your I-Boss asks. Taken by surprise, you frantically scan the office for telltale signs of your beach ball and instinctively counter-move with a response you learned in childhood. "Nothing," you say with all of the energy and innocence you can muster.

"Aw, come on now," your I-Boss cajoles. "You're up to something. You jumped when I snuck up on you."

"You snuck up on me?" Surprised indignation might turn the blame around onto the I-Boss. If he purposefully attempted to catch you in some sort of subversive or insubordinate behavior, you might be able to invoke the entrapment defense. The entrapment defense is a brilliant way to claim doing something bad isn't bad if someone catches you doing it. A.C.L.U. lawyers use it to defend criminals against the crooked and conspiratorial cops all the time. To A.C.L.U. lawyers, there are no criminals, just victims of crooked and conspiratorial cops. To sourpuss employees, there is no subversive or insubordinate behavior, only Idiot Bosses.

You've always considered yourself above such reprehensible, utterly amoral, and deleterious abuse of the legal process, until your I-Boss snuck up and surprised you. Instantly, your number-one priority is to get off the hook at any price and by any means possible, ethically or unethically—before you know if you're even on the hook. The guilty human mind is an amazing thing. Once you determine there is no smoking gun lying around where your I-Boss can see it, you start to worm your way off the hook.

"What makes think I'm up to something?" you retort with confidence returning to your voice as you realize the beach ball never reached the surface. This is remarkably similar to a mother catching her child with his hand in the cookie jar. Once the evidence is swallowed, he can deny it until the cows come home.

"You practically jumped out of your chair when I opened my mouth," your I-Boss presses. "Are you sure you weren't trying to sneak in some real work instead of working on the rewrite of our mid-range plan?"

"Yeah, that's what I was doing," you blurt out, seizing the opportunity. "Nothing gets by you, boss. I was trying to do something productive and you caught me red handed."

"Well," he says proudly, "we do what is important to me in this department and not what's important to anybody else."

"I forgot for a minute," you apologize. "But you brought it to my attention just in time."

"I'm not as dumb as I look," your I-Boss chuckles as he continues down the hallway. "You have to get up pretty early in the morning to be more awake than me."

You sit for a moment, trying to figure out what he thought he meant by that last comment. Then, as always, you just shake it off. The important thing was your Idiot Boss didn't see your beach ball. You're safe, for now. But he noticed you were hiding something, and that's troubling. Your façade is getting harder and harder to maintain.

Don't Bank on Cluelessness

I-Bosses rarely make such transparent comments, except in the fiction I write. But, they can see a beach ball if one pops up right under their nose. They might not recognize the beach ball as a simile for your loathing and resentment, at least not right away. But if they see enough beach balls popping up around the office, their suspicions will eventually be aroused.

I-Bosses don't understand the concept of hidden feelings as much as they understand you might be hiding a candy bar in your desk when you're supposed to be on a diet. That's big news to them. The feelings you might be harboring are of no great consequence to an I-Boss. But the very fact you're hiding something is enough to set off his sensors. If you insist on holding a beach ball under water or otherwise keeping your feelings under wraps, always have a candy bar in your desk that you can pull out when your I-Boss sneaks up and accuses you of hiding something.

Idiotthink

This business about nearly everyone in the office holding his beach ball under water partially explains the phenomenon called Idiotthink.

Idiotthink is remarkably similar to groupthink. Truthfully, I merely borrowed the idea from Irving Janis, author of *Groupthink*, and gave it a new coat of paint. Just because you might not have formally studied groupthink doesn't mean you haven't been exposed to the virus. Like groupthink, most people participating in idiotthink do so without realizing it.

Idiotthink occurs because nobody wants to be a patsy. W.C. Fields put it this way: "If you're in a poker game for 30 minutes and you haven't figured out who the patsy is, you're the patsy," or words to that effect. Groupthink occurs when members of a group disguise anonymity as unanimity at the expense of quality. Idiotthink occurs when nobody wants to stick his neck out and risk being criticized or ostracized.

A group of codependents can drive you insane when they try to make a decision. Nobody wants to offend anyone else or give anyone a reason to not like them. At the same time, they're all trying to control the outcome. The result can drive people bonkers.

There is safety in unanimity. That's why it's so popular. With a group decision, the blame is spread out over many people should something go wrong. Nobody wants to ruffle feathers, even in their own imagination. You already know I'm one who avoids confrontation as much as possible. But give me a big issue and I've got to do what I've got to do.

To avoid confrontation, if something happens to me, I'll shrug and tell myself not to sweat the small stuff. Let somebody else get screwed and I'm all over it. Let a staff member get bullied by an executive at a company I'm consulting and I'm likely to lose my job standing up for that person. If there is lying going on or misrepresentations being made, I'm on the case like syrup on a pancake. I'm a whistle blower by nature, providing the issue is large or significant enough.

Righteous indignation means short-term employment

Let go and let God. Don't let your lofty expectations of fairness and social justice cost you the things you really want. I've lost more than one lucrative consulting assignment because I didn't keep my mouth shut when I discovered stuff happening that ought not to happen. A case in point: A not-for-profit organization had managed to hire a shyster as president. The shyster president hired his old cronies and, before anyone knew it, a core of shyster executives were driving expensive sports cars leased by the charity, and taking bigger and bigger chunks of change in salary after convincing the board they deserved to be compensated on a par with executives in for-profit corporations.

I urged the board to fire the shysters immediately and even offered to facilitate the termination session. They simply wouldn't go there. I believe to this day their reluctance was a form of Idiotthink. They didn't want to admit they had made a horrendous mistake for fear of what their donors would think.

Ultimately, the organization's legal counsel strongly advised them to oust the crooks or face potentially devastating legal problems. Able to pin the responsibility for their actions on the advice of counsel, the board finally terminated the bogus executives. Supporters of the organization forgave the board members, something I tried to convince them would happen all along. In the end, it was clear they should have acted the moment they identified the rats they were smelling, thus saving the organization a ton of money.

This is not stone throwing. It's a warning label. Don't let your emotions run away with your common sense. I'm not suggesting you incorporate unethical or moronic behavior in your great disguise. This is a heads up about the tangled politics you'll encounter as you launch your plan to remain as real as possible as you disappear into the crowd.

A tough lesson I've learned is that every time I try to enlighten people as to subversion or outright theft in their organizations, I end up being treated like the bad guy. Idiotthinkers are messenger killers. Their mantra is: See no evil, hear no evil, and speak no evil. Idiotthinkers have a deathly fear of being embarrassed, being wrong, and of making mistakes.

I've seen top executives pal around with people they know are covertly subverting their authority and hurting the organization. The executives aren't necessarily crooks, they simply refuse to challenge inappropriate behavior. The top executives know what's going on because I told them. I don't doubt they believe the reports. Yet, they are reluctant to admit a mistake or confront the evildoer. This pretense gives the conspirators much to laugh and guffaw about when the top executives are not around.

I've seen some truly colossal screw-ups caused by Idiotthink. Consider the ironic report that came in off the Internet of the company president fired by the board for "lack of intelligent leadership" after nine months on the job. Despite his brief stint, he was paid a prenegotiated severance package of more than $25 million. I'd say it was the Idiotthinkers who lacked intelligence.

The Great Disguise Reversed

Every time the name of this book is mentioned, somebody says, "I have a great Idiot Boss story for you." I'm convinced working for Idiot Bosses is one of the most common experiences on Earth. I'm also convinced that Idiotthink is the second most common experience. Everywhere I turn, individual acts of stupidity are being eclipsed by acts of group stupidity.

Being out of touch with the pulse of an organization is characteristic of an I-Boss. For an executive to know the state of an organization and pretend he doesn't is something else again. After leaving Disney, selling the audio publishing company, and becoming an author and consultant, I walked into another spinning propeller—proving once again that no matter how much you might try to put distance between yourself and stupidity, it's never far behind.

I was hired to facilitate a Board retreat that turned weird before my very eyes. Just when I think I've seen it all, I'm suddenly blinking, mouth agape, caught off guard, staring at something I never imagined possible. I had been providing executive coaching for the president of another nonprofit company and, with his permission, I interviewed department heads and others to help develop a comprehensive "state of the organization" report. The story I uncovered was far different from what the president predicted I would discover. I won't say he was a complete idiot, but he apparently thought things were much rosier than they really were.

This president was a sweet fellow you could hardly bring yourself to hold accountable for anything. When his own people tried to tell him about problems in the organization, he buried his head in the sand. As president, he was out of his league and he knew it. But he liked the lifestyle and there was nobody bucking for his job from the inside. So, why not let things work themselves out?

Instead of asking for help, he tried to bob up and down in the troubled waters and hope problems would simply disappear without a trace. Eventually, many problems do seem to disappear, but they leave traces. Problems not dealt with in a proactive manner leave a bad taste in people's mouths and a stale odor around the office. This president was content to let sleeping dogs lie. Then he let the dogs die. Then he left their decomposing carcasses to the flies and buzzards. With the passage of time, he figured they would turn to dust, which is true, as far as it goes. Meanwhile, his entire organizational population came down with a company-wide staff infection.

Employees felt abandoned and betrayed; as if their problems didn't matter to him when, in truth, their problems might simply have overwhelmed him. No matter. He didn't address their problems. Nor did he actively seek out and reward the good things people in his organization were doing. He practiced the maxim, "No good deed goes unpunished," by not making a conscious, cultural priority out of identifying and rewarding superior performance and effort.

I don't promote recognition based on effort alone. Real rewards should be reserved for real results. In a perfect world, anything worth doing is worth doing well. But the world we live in isn't perfect. Often, anything worth doing is worth doing badly, if only to get us off our butts to do something. I could load you up with clichés like, "Nothing ventured, nothing gained." They're all basically true. At the end of the day, it is better to have tried, failed, and tried again than to have never tried at all.

Any leadership consultant will tell you that in most cases, organizational executives hire consultants not to develop leadership, but to wave a magic wand and develop followership. You could make the argument that seeking my counsel was a sign the meek and mild-mannered president wanted to grow as a leader. Usually, clients just want a silver bullet. What I continuously offered him was a chance to be coached through the difficult process of rolling his sleeves up and addressing the issues his people needed resolved.

Resistance is a familiar term to most therapists and consultants. He constantly turned the conversation toward what he referred to as the unreasonable pressure the board placed on him. I repeatedly tried to refocus him on his role in support of his team members. He continued to whine about the board's unreasonable demands. It should not have come as a surprise when he recommended I facilitate the upcoming board retreat.

Stepping right in it

I did what I usually do when I facilitate a retreat and circulated a questionnaire to all of the participants in advance to poll and rank their most pressing issues. That way we don't waste the first half of the first day determining what the group's feelings and concerns are. I wrote up the survey findings and distributed them to all participants before they left for the retreat. I did the same thing with the staff and the president. When I analyzed the data, I found the staff, Board, and the president all had a different take on the organization's most pressing issues.

It quickly became clear that the president wanted me to facilitate the retreat so I could plead his case before the board. The board members were immediately suspicious of me because I was asking questions. They began to sense that there might be evil lurking out there, evil they would feel compelled to ignore, not discuss, nor confront. Meanwhile, the team members back home were hoping I would give voice to their concerns before the board for the first time.

The discussion I facilitated quickly began to reveal a rift in the board. Some were unapologetically supportive of the president, while others openly wondered why, if he were doing as well as some Board members wanted to believe, team members would make comments like those on the survey. I steered clear of endorsing or criticizing what he was doing. I wanted the organization's problems and suggested solutions to emerge from the dialogue.

To my surprise, the more some Board members "got it" and began to talk in terms of challenges and opportunities for positive change, the more others resisted acknowledging there were any problems at all. We reached a sort of stalemate. On the morning of our final day, I knew my window of opportunity for results was closing. Instead of thinking of a continuing payday with this client, I became impatient and allowed my maniacal obsession with truth, justice, and the American way to cloud my judgment.

It was a bad economic move. It should have been easy to read the handwriting on the wall, announce the dialogue was inconclusive, and continue coaching and facilitate for this company indefinitely. But no-o-o-o. The horse was standing in the stream and I felt compelled to shove its nose into the water. I came right out and, without naming names, announced there were key players in the organization who were looking elsewhere for employment.

I tried to say it as delicately as possible, which is like dropping a bowling ball on your toe as delicately as possible. I hoped my semi-breach of confidentiality would snap certain board members out of their denial. In other words, I hoped the end would justify the means. I never cease to amaze myself at how wrong I can be. Board members loyal to the president (that is, those who hired and protected him) were outraged that I would "stab him in the back" by bringing to their attention the fact that every core executive in their organization at that moment was posting his or her resume on Monster.com.

It was Idiotthink to the 10th power, set into motion by an idiot consultant. I wish I had taped the whole thing to use in seminars to illustrate how well-intentioned people can cripple an organization's effectiveness. Just when I was starting to feel terrible about the wound I had opened in the board, things got worse. The president broke down in tears.

As God is my witness, the man started to bawl right there in the middle of the meeting. A woman stood up between the president and me as if to shield him from a violent assault. The venom in her eyes haunts me to this day. "I have lost all respect for you," she spit. When I blow it, I blow it big.

The reasonable members of the board who had at first wanted to legitimately consider the views of the staff suddenly fell into ranks behind the president. Before I knew what had happened, a roomful of people were glaring at me in deathly silence, except for the president's sobbing. Half of the board members huddled around and laid hands on the president, who sat with his head buried in his hands. The rest of the board members stood in a sort of semicircle around him waiting their turn.

In the midst of that bizarre scene, the president parted his fingers and snuck a glance at me that clearly claimed victory. Through red, puffy eyes, he shot me the old N.I.G.Y.S.O.B. look. N.I.G.Y.S.O.B. is a fateful moment known all too well to marital therapists when one spouse catches the other spouse (usually the wife catching the husband) in some untenable position. Loosely translated, N.I.G.Y.S.O.B. means, "Now I've got you, you son of a beaver," or words to that effect. As I started to inch my way toward the door and a taxi to the airport, I said a silent prayer asking for the divine intervention necessary to get out of the room alive.

I had swung the bat as hard as I could out of desperation, hoping to hit a home run. What I hit was a foul tip into the catcher's mitt. The net result of the board retreat was a new contract with a raise for the president, the team members back at headquarters were completely disenfranchised, and Dr. John lost another client. My moles in the organization kept me abreast of the ongoing exodus over the next year or so. The president remained intact and unchanged, and the most talented and hard-working team members left one by one and two by two. The company's performance and financial problems became famously worse. The board held emergency sessions, each time expressing confidence in the president. Heaven only knows what they perceived the organization's problems were.

The best intentions, the worst results

These episodes and others like them are painful reminders that Idiotthink will come up and bite you just when you think everything has been handled and people are truly committed to positive and productive change. It's a pervasive and insidious problem. When a group of well-intentioned people tries to accomplish something, their first order of business should be to check their stupidity at the door. Group denial, as in the case of the board retreat, is a difficult problem to overcome.

Communication problems can be repaired like washed-out bridges. However, people have strong reasons to deny reality. Overcoming denial can be practically impossible. To help someone admit he is engaging in denial is like reaching the first base camp on Mount Everest. It can be done, but only about one in 10 or 20 million people ever try. There are probably better odds in winning the lottery. Of those reaching base camp, even fewer ever reach the summit.

Blend Into the Crowd Without Losing Your Goals

If every person with no good reason to hold a beach ball under water would just let it go, beach balls would pop up all over the place. The office would look like the ball pit at a McDonald's playground. You can get rid of your beach ball by deflating it and throwing it away. No one needs to know except you. Just because you're blending in doesn't mean you have lost sight of your goals.

Denial is one of the most powerful defense mechanisms known to the human race because it cloaks us from facing reality. People avoid goal-setting for similar reasons. Setting goals makes a demand on performance. If you want to avoid the pressure to perform, don't set goals. If the challenge of problem-solving frightens you, deny there are any problems. However, goal-setting can be a private matter and you can adopt healthy ways to keep yourself accountable without becoming excessively punitive. Start by refocusing energy away from contempt for your Idiot Boss to personal growth and satisfaction.

We can all make our own lives easier by purging as much resentment and pent up hostility as possible toward our Idiot Bosses and replacing them with healthy alternatives. It sounds Pollyanna-ish, but it's true. Just because you are no longer in denial about your feelings doesn't mean you can't find more productive ways to relate to your I-Boss. It's never too soon to get started, and even small attempts to tune in the I-Boss frequency can pay off.

Start by facing some facts:

- Your I-Boss has more power in the office than you.
- You have more power outside the office than your I-Boss.
- Assuming you work 60 hours per week and sleep eight hours per night, you still have a net gain of two hours per week in non-work waking time. Feel the power.
- You like the paycheck although it could be better.
- You like your I-Boss, don't like your I-Boss, or could care less.
- The I-Boss can't control your thoughts or emotions. How you think and feel is up to you.
- You have the choice to stay or leave and how to set up the emotional scenario to make staying as appealing as possible.

Your Great Disguise Wardrobe

Some of the following wacky ideas have worked well for people. Try dressing outside of fashion guidelines. I-Bosses are clueless creatures. This is often reflected in wardrobe choices made by male idiots. There are occasions when female I-Bosses dress in shocking and inappropriate ways, but it's rare.

You can always tell when an I-Boss has been to the mall. Male I-Bosses can show up for work in a coordinated wardrobe the day after they go shopping and sales clerks have selected their clothes. But give them a few days to get the matched clothing intermingled with the rest of their wardrobe and color coordination is a thing of the past. Your window of opportunity to compliment the I-Boss on a co-ordinated outfit is narrow.

Don't be afraid to dress like an idiot. Unless the male I-Boss has a wife or girlfriend who asks the rhetorical question, "You're not going to wear that tie with that shirt, are you?" he will. Bizarre ties usually amuse I-Bosses and show the rest of the world you're a pillar of self-confidence. Be bold.

It's hard for people with taste to dress poorly. It usually requires some intense preplanning, both emotionally and in selecting your outfit. Take your cues from observing your I-Boss's wardrobe habits over time. You should be able to catalogue everything he is willing to wear in a week or two. Then try to mirror his wardrobe choices as closely as possible. He probably won't realize what you're doing, but he'll feel strangely more comfortable around you. Dressing in a manner reflecting your I-Boss's horrific fashion sense will make him far more receptive to your ideas and suggestions.

If a male I-Boss wears a blue sock on his left foot and a black sock on his right foot, and spots a male team member with a black sock on his left foot and a blue sock on his right foot, the I-Boss will probably compliment the team member on how sharp he looks. If your I-Boss wears a plastic pocket protector in the breast pocket of his short-sleeved oxford shirt, guess what you should be wearing. If you can't bring yourself to do it, at least compliment him on his stylish and sensible pocket protector. The condition of your shoes is also affects your I-Boss's comfort level. If he wears old beaters, keep an old pair in your file drawer.

I'm talking about males here. Females should not attempt to imitate bad wardrobe choices in male I-Bosses. In that rare case where a female I-Boss dresses strangely, female team members must walk a fine line between demonstrating a similar attitude about fashion and actually mimicking what the female I-Boss wears. Female coworkers with male I-Bosses should dress as professionally as possible. The male I-Boss might not have a clue how he looks in the big picture, but he's seen enough IBM commercials to know what the vertically mobile woman should look like. That is a potentially sexist thing to say, but sexism might be the least of your problems with an I-Boss.

Okay, I admit I'm exaggerating for effect. But who needs to feel comfortable here? If you want to be a fashion plate to enhance your dating life or simply stroke your own ego, that's your choice. But, if you're making your Idiot Boss look like a bigger idiot in comparison, calculate your net gain or loss.

All of this is important only if you want your I-Boss to be more comfortable around you. Not every bad dresser is an I-Boss and not every I-Boss is a bad dresser. Some extremely intelligent and gifted people dress like clowns while some clueless idiots dress like George Clooney. Machiavellian Bosses, many Sadistic Bosses, and God Bosses are typically good dressers. In fact, the meaner or more insane the boss, the more likely he or she will resemble a mannequin.

Some Good Bosses, most Buddy Bosses, Paranoid Bosses, Masochistic Bosses, and of course I-Bosses, are notoriously bad dressers. Intentionally dressing down around a Good Boss won't be necessary. A Good Boss sees the person, not the clothes, and will appreciate your appearance even if her own is less than ideal. Good bosses don't usually wear mismatched clothes as much as their clothes are out of date. Good bosses don't feel any urgency to dress for success. To them, success is an inside job.

Buddy Bosses might prefer you to dress well so they can have a cool friend. Paranoid Bosses will think your sloppy wardrobe is a critical statement about them and an indictment of their taste. It's tough to win with a Paranoid Boss. A Masochistic boss will turn anything you do into a source of pain and anguish, if he even notices what you're wearing. You could show up buck naked at the office and a Masochistic Boss will probably be too busy slamming a desk drawer on his knuckles to notice.

If your I-Boss's boss is a fashion hound, you have a potential problem. Try to determine how your I-Boss is affected by his boss's wardrobe habits. You'll need to calculate if you'll make your boss more comfortable by imitating him or his boss. You will want to impress your boss's boss and it never hurts to compliment those higher on the food chain as long as you remain aware of how your wardrobe choices and grooming will affect your most immediate relationships. It can be a tough call.

Hair and humor

Wardrobe is not the only fashion issue with an I-Boss. Many I-Bosses missed the memo from HR informing the staff that crew cuts went out of style in the Nixon administration. You might want to consider cutting your hair with a weed eater. Interestingly, many people pay a lot of money these days to make their hair look like it was cut with a weed eater.

You can make I-Bosses feel more comfortable around you by telling insipid jokes and stories about the time your dog barfed on the neighbor's morning newspaper. I chose this subject because many of the I-Bosses I've known are particular to barf jokes. Make sure to start laughing about three-fourths of the way through your joke or story. I-Bosses always laugh at their own jokes. Although longitudinal research on the subject is minimal, I-Bosses don't seem concerned if anyone else finds their jokes or stories funny. It appears they assume everyone will.

The most plausible explanation for why I-Bosses laugh at their own material is because they are telling the joke or story primarily for their own amusement. This is consistent with my previously stated theory that I-Bosses are usually bored. You can also resonate with your I-Boss's mood by always appearing to be in good spirits. I-Bosses are rarely tuned into the emotions of other people. Although they are capable of a wide range of emotions themselves, they don't pick up on emotional indicators from others, such as weeping, screaming, throwing furniture, and other demonstrative acts, probably instigated by the idiot's behavior.

Flag waving and drum beating

The more bizarre and incredibly stupid a superior's idea might be, the more over the top your support should be. When your I-Boss suggests the solution to your firm's filing for bankruptcy is to have all of the fire extinguishers serviced, throw down your pen and say, "Brilliant. Why didn't I think of that?" That's a good line to have at the tip of your tongue anytime you're near your I-Boss.

Go legit

One of the first ways you'll know that God has removed your stupidity is by accepting your powerlessness over your boss's stupidity. That's when you'll be able to abandon your futile struggle to control the uncontrollable. You can then begin to change the things in yourself that have kept you on the merry-go-round of madness for so long.

If swallowing your pride to advance your agenda around an I-Boss is too difficult, take the legitimate approach. Disguising yourself as one of the idiots might not be so bad, especially when you discover how much you have in common. You and your I-Boss might agree on more than you think. It will be up to you to do the research and inquiry, but the results can be positive.

A little office anthropology on your part might reveal your I-Boss likes to play golf, but never has time. You might love to play golf, but don't have the time. It's up to you to take the initiative and organize the office golf outings. Several good things can happen. You might get to play golf on company time or the company's dime. You can at least be sanctioned to spend work time organizing golf activities for team members. If you have golf in common with your I-Boss, you've opened up a new language and context in which to communicate that's actually pleasant for you both. If you don't play golf and hate to talk about it, you might at least get your I-Boss out of the office for half a day per week by encouraging and facilitating his recreation.

Any activity in which you share interests can have a positive effect and hold potential for activities or conversation—love of movies, literature, photography, fine dining, greasy spoon dining, expensive wine, cheap wine, animals, hiking, motorcycles, sports of any kind, you name it. Even if your initiative to organize avocational interests around the office doesn't include anything specifically appealing to your I-Boss, the fact that you're contributing to a relaxed and pleasant working environment will probably give you an upbeat image in his eyes.

Idiot Bosses, unlike their Machiavellian, Sadistic, Masochistic, and Paranoid counterparts, like it when everyone seems to get along and enjoy each other. Being a part of making that happen is not fake or phony, even if it started that way for you. Helping to bring out the true interests and passions of your I-Boss and fellow team members, then exerting some leadership to establish avenues to share the joy, will pay dividends for everyone, most importantly, you.

Putting on the great disguise might seem like a cheesy, manipulative ploy in the beginning. But it can be a way to test the waters and see if you really wouldn't be happier and more content at work using some imagination to expand your horizons. Using your energies to organize activities offensive or displeasing to your I-Boss will be counterproductive. The whole point of the great disguise is to set your feet on a path to workplace resonance, even if the direction is not one your instincts initially tell you to follow.

Break out. Push back your boundaries. Be crazy. Put on the disguise and make your workplace more you-friendly. What do you have to lose except long nights of tortured slumber and teeth grinding while your I-Boss sleeps like a log? You can always return to your current state if being happier and less resentful doesn't appeal to you. What are you planning to replace your stupidity with anyway?

8

A Strategic Partnership

How to Harness the Idiot's Power

It's important to understand the high-level antics of organizations because they engender the organizational atmosphere in which you work. The shenanigans taking place on Mahogany Row flow to the rest of the organizational population, sometimes in a trickle, other times like a busted dam. Much of your success in tapping your Idiot Boss's power will depend on how savvy you can become with the unwritten, unspoken, and disavowed rules of engagement that actually govern organizational life.

Let's begin with some high-level issues and work our way down. Non-idiot top executives who find themselves saddled with idiots in management positions below them on the food chain are faced with a complex problem. How do they make the company work in spite of these people? This was not such a difficult question back when everyone knew each other. In my father's day, you joined a company right out of college and stayed there until you retired. Among other things, that meant you knew people. You came up through the ranks together. If certain people were idiots, you had 40 years to figure out what to do with them, 15 years if they were recent hires.

Today, fewer and fewer executives near the top of the corporate food chain worked their way up through the ranks. Now, for-profit and not-for-profit organizations recruit most top brass from outside. They recruit much of their middle brass from outside. The single-employer career many of our parents knew has faded into history.

In today's rapidly changing and unstable corporate landscape, top executives must deal with how to organize, motivate, and lead the idiots in their workforce in such a way as to maintain a productive working environment for the non-idiots. The dynamic nature of upper management presents a series of new problems, not the least of which is what happens when the newly recruited top executive is an idiot.

Recruiting and hiring top executives is a dicey business. If you stop and think about it, why would executives who are wildly successful in their present situations want to pull up stakes, fold their tents, and move to other organizations? Why would effective leaders who've cleaned up messes, turned losses into profits, fine-tuned their present organizations until they're firing on all cylinders, and built confidence and morale to the highest levels ever, want to leave their accomplishments behind and move to an ailing organization?

We've all heard the legendary stories about empire builders who get bored after they've done it all and long to roll up their sleeves, find some raw clay, and build another empire from scratch. That happens more in the movies than in real life. It's far more common to find chief executives on the move who aren't getting much accomplished despite an incredible salary, bonus, and benefits package. Why so eager to leave? Why are their boards not more intent on keeping them?

If a top executive does for her company what Jack Welch did for General Electric, she will retire from General Electric, as did Welch. If a top executive does for a company what Michael Eisner has done for Disney, you won't see another entertainment firm hiring him away. Executives hop from one firm to the next when they're vertically blocked and the jump opens the ceiling again. What about those executives making essentially lateral moves for a compensation increase their current employers could easily match? Methinks the executive with suitcases packed is either unhappy where she is, has a family or lifestyle need to consider, or is not doing a very good job and is smart enough to get out while the getting is good.

In the latter example, it makes sense why the present employer doesn't fight to keep her. So, what does the new employer get? Someone with all of the right credentials for sure. Someone who can look and sound the role she's been hired to play. What else? Could the new firm be hiring the former employer's problems? Is it possible the unsuspecting new firm has just taken on an idiot? As an executive, I have unloaded idiots on unsuspecting employers and had idiots unloaded on me. If the truth be told, it might save everyone money just to have companies build a people-mover to shuttle idiots from one office building to the next.

Do happy people move?

Are these executives happy in their present positions? Apparently not. Are they people who are given to loyalty and revel in healthy, long-term relationships with their coworkers? Definitely not. Are they willing to wave goodbye to their team members and say, "Have a good life, I was just offered a bigger payday?" Apparently so.

In many cases, the hot,new executive was available and anxious to make the move because she failed to move the previous organization purposefully forward, was starting to worry when the non-standard accounting practices making things appear better then they were would be exposed, and knew it was just a matter of time before someone pointed out the empress had no clothes. I know one fellow who is in his fifth or sixth corporate presidency, each one lasting approximately two years before he is canned. He is disemployed from every presidency after proving himself completely incompetent. Yet, there is always another firm ready to hand him the key to the president's office.

At the first sign his new firm is on to him and his rationalizations won't hold up any longer, he calls the headhunters, lets them know he's back on the market, and winds up stepping straight out of one executive office into another without getting his feet wet. I doubt seriously if the headhunters ask, "By the way, why are you available again so soon?" Hear no evil, see no evil, and speak no evil.

Power

Many companies produce eloquent mission statements, manifestos, and mantras. Would you believe me if I told you most of them don't operate by those principles? Very few organizational value systems are primarily about serving the customer, the community, or the corporate population. It's not even primarily about money. The occupants of Mahogany Row are preoccupied with power. Power is more than mere money, it's the ability to make or influence major decisions that make or break careers, build or lose fortunes, install or overthrow governments. In Las Vegas, the executive suite would be called the high stakes room.

There are several reasons why power brokers become power brokers. By power brokers, I mean board members or anyone with the authority to negotiate high-level positions and commit significant portions of the organization's treasury, not their own. The behavior of the board members at the retreat with the weeping president was admittedly over the top. But board members everywhere are notorious for acting just as stupidly, even if they don't get quite so melodramatic.

It's human nature to want someone else to fix things. Wealthy southerners say it like this: "If you don't want to do it yourself, hire it done." Board members do that with the leadership of the organizations they govern. They hire it done. There's nothing wrong with hiring it done until they abdicate their role in leading the leader. But that's human nature, too.

As children, when we had a boo-boo, we wanted Mommy to kiss it and make it all better. As adults, when we have an ache or a pain, we want the doctor to make it go away. When our automobiles stop running perfectly, we want the service technician to make it run like new again.

As children, we didn't pay Mommy for loving ministrations. Our tears were sufficient motivation for her. As adults, with the exception of the not-for-profit president I coached to tears, crying doesn't get us very far. We expect to pay people to make our problems go away.

Plumbers and power

Plumbers know they have you between a rock and a hard place when your kitchen faucet becomes a geyser. Although they mask it well, plumbers' inner plumbers must grin from ear-to-ear when they walk into your house and see a toilet overflowing. They know you're out of your league and desperate. You'll pay nearly anything to get the problem solved. If it weren't for capitalist competition, plumbers would be among the highest paid people on Earth. Not that they aren't already, but the fact that there are other plumbers in the yellow pages helps control plumbing prices.

Plumbers don't do much on the lesser-skilled end of a plumber's list of services most people can't do for themselves. That's one thing you learn when you decide to become a do-it-yourselfer kind of person. Instead of paying a plumber to come and fish an obstruction out of your toilet, you roll up your sleeve, reach your arm way up there, and pull it out yourself. You even learn how to fix leaks, change faucets, and a host of other home improvement activities that bring you no pleasure except to save a lot of money.

Plumbers and big-money executives have more in common than large incomes. Board members with dysfunctional organizations and homeowners with overflowing toilets also have much in common. Board members are capable of making sound decisions and hiring leaders who will come into companies and build their organizational populations into highly effective, profit-generating teams. But most Board members don't look at organizational populations as potentially effective, profit-generating teams. They look at low-functioning organizations as stopped-up toilets.

Not wanting to roll up their sleeves, fish around, and dislodge whatever is stopping everything up, board members hire a new plumber. The new plumber, knowing the board of directors merely wants someone to come in and unclog the organization, charges an arm and a leg, and promises free-flowing pipes in no time. The directors, who aren't spending their own money, keep their sleeves rolled down and quickly agree to pay an arm and a leg.

The press releases announcing major corporate appointments are couched in very contemporary, corporate-sounding, positive, future-oriented language. But the release is not describing anything more sophisticated than the plumber analogy. Do the research, track the comings and goings of chief executives, chart their compensation, and match it to the performance of their companies. You'll wind up nodding your head and mumbling, "plumbers."

The free flow of accountability

Sometimes the new plumber/CEO is able to fix the problems, sometimes not. Most of the time it really doesn't matter. The new executive might be most talented at making it appear the problems are being solved and things are turning around when they're not. That's usually enough to satisfy the board. My weeping president didn't even need to convince his board that he was capable of solving problems. They seemed to be satisfied that he was trying so hard.

Board members often deny the ineffectiveness of their new executives, which makes it much easier for ineffective executives to fake it. Sometimes new executives putter around for a while, take the money, and then take a hike, without ever unstopping the toilets. You'll swear wonders never cease when you read how another board at another organization has hired the same ineffective executive, probably for more money than she left behind.

How much confidence can you really have in a top executive who negotiates a royal ransom before doing a doggoned thing, and receives her ransom whether she makes the boo-boos go away or, worse yet, causes more pain? You have to wonder what goes through board members' heads when they realize the super-executive they just hired is holding the organization hostage, just waiting to be handed the bag of gold to go away and repeat the process somewhere else.

Do the board members think, "Gee, we just made a huge mistake?" It's doubtful. More likely, the Board members say, "This problem is obviously more complex and challenging than we originally thought. We need to retain a search firm to help us identify someone better suited to making our pain go away."

This is how some boards take their avoidance and denial to another level. They escalate their ivory tower thinking and raise the stakes. They will spend even greater amounts of other people's money to locate an executive who will demand even more money before she lifts a finger, including signing bonuses negotiated by the search firm. It sounds insane, but it happens every day.

Other factors

Board members are also impatient. They look primarily to short-term financial indicators to justify their moves. Serving the long-term interests of their organizational populations comes well down the list. They will claim that external stakeholders demand the financial performance. However, most external stakeholders, as well as employees with ownership interest in the firm, are in it for the long haul. This means the people the board members are claiming to appease would prefer to see long-term growth, not knee-jerk, expensive, quick fixes. Historically, organizations that invest first and foremost in the growth and development of their team members perform better on their bottom line than those that don't.

Your Rock and Hard Place

You can look at all the impatience, denial, avoidance, and outright lying going on at the highest levels of American enterprise and become cynical and resentful. Or you can say, "Well, all right then," to all of it. Whether you fully understand it or not, it is what it is. A fellow I know recently defined "resentment" as drinking poison then waiting for the other person to die. No resentment here. No cynicism either. Just reality.

Your challenge is what to do in spite of the impatience, denial, avoidance, and outright lying going on in your organization. It's there, more in some companies than others. But it's there. And scenarios played out in the executive suite are replicated in smaller scenarios in managers' offices everywhere. To stop fighting 'em and join 'em doesn't mean adopting their values. It means learning how to operate effectively in their environment. As long as you swim in the same fishbowl, there is no avoiding the ethical construct and behaviors around you.

Drinking Poison

Forget about justice. That's God's job. I was obsessed with justice for most of my life and it nearly killed me. Only after I became a recovering idiot did I learn how my pursuit of justice was a disguise for my insistence on being right. Looking back over my serpentine career path, I can appreciate how my insistence on being right (or pursuit of justice if you prefer) caused one train wreck after another.

After I went independent, I received a call from a long-time video production/duplication vendor who had a chance at a major corporate video contract. His potential client wanted to begin with audio training programs for the sales force. My friend didn't have a lick of experience with audio programming, so we presented his prospect with a number of the more famous books-on-tape I had produced and the client immediately gave us the contract.

The deal called for me to produce the audio programming and, once the new client branched into video, I would write those programs as well. Writing, directing, and producing corporate and education film and video generated the lion's share of my income after I went independent and I had an extensive list of national and international clients. Everything worked well and I wrote the first video production the client ordered in addition to producing the monthly audio newsletters for the sales force.

A month or so later, during an audio taping session, the client mentioned he wasn't very happy with the script to his new video. That was news to me. Not that he was disappointed, but that he had ordered a new video. I confronted my old "friend" about it and he explained how he liked to keep everything in house as much as possible. After reminding him of our (verbal) agreement on handling this account, he told me that his exact words were that he would "try" to have me write the video scripts.

I reminded him how my audio productions had been the distinguishing factor that won his firm the contract to begin with and I didn't extend myself in that way in exchange for his best efforts at something. I expected him to live up to his end of the agreement, not "try" to live up to his end of the agreement. He promised he would comply with what we had agreed to, and I left feeling I had received justice and forced him to acknowledge I was right.

I learned several weeks later that by 10 a.m. on the morning following my brilliant confrontation, he had visited the client, reported that I had abandoned the project, and convinced the client he was contracting another audio producer to provide uninterrupted service despite my "unprofessional" behavior. If you've ever been in a dispute where your client is the only possible arbiter, you know what a brilliant move that was on his part. Checkmate. When the dust settled, I had lost three to four years of highly paid work. Because the agreement was verbal, I had little chance of successful litigation.

Was I bitter? Yes. Was it unfair? Absolutely. Was I outmaneuvered by a far superior gamesman? Can a bear spot a picnic cooler in Yellowstone Park? I was merely wounded by the other fellow's devious maneuver to save a little money at my expense. But I was the one who boldly marched into his office in the pursuit of justice, slit my own throat from ear to ear, and lost all of the money. I drank the poison and waited for him to die. Instead of dying, he acted swiftly and even more deviously to ensure my death.

Make Your Move—Positively

Being obsessed with justice is being all about you and your unresolved childhood fairness issues. Justice is great, fairness is wonderful, and being right is a treat. But put on your own oxygen mask first and help other people on with their masks afterward. You'll be of no use to yourself or others if you're passed out. Your first calling is to position yourself for maximum effectiveness within the organization you have chosen to work for.

Let's assume a people-centered executive has made it to the top of your company or the board managed to hire one in spite of themselves. It can happen. What does the new executive do with the idiots she inherited? It's a problem. I-Bosses seldom do enough of anything to get them in trouble with HR. Neither do they usually accomplish anything beneficial to the organization overall. But doing nothing particularly good or bad is not enough cause for termination in today's litigious labor market.

If you use some of the befriending techniques discussed in previous chapters and tap into your I-Boss's power cell in an organization led by a person-centered executive, the woman at the top might be extremely grateful. The I-Boss under the leadership of an effective executive is a potentially positive force because the top person wants to create a productive scenario in a culture of encouragement. If you contribute to that, your efforts are likely to be recognized and rewarded. You can be part of the solution the big boss wants and do yourself some political favors at the same time.

This can happen several ways. An ambitious person studies what successful people do and tries to get the same results from similar effort. A clever person studies what successful people do and then attempts to get the same results through someone else's effort. Your job is to make your I-Boss look clever. Make peace with contributing good work your I-Boss will take credit for. If you have an intelligent, person-centered big boss, she will be quick to recognize the good work coming out of the idiot's department is not being done by the I-Boss, but by his talented and hard-working team members.

If the big boss doesn't recognize this right away, drop some hints. Do this in the form of a compliment. Say to the big boss, "I sure do appreciate how my boss gives me the encouragement and support to complete these projects on time and under budget." If the big boss has half a brain, she will recognize your I-Boss didn't have anything to do with your successful efforts and was probably a millstone around your neck as you tried to swim the channel.

The big boss wants the department to run smoothly, so she will appreciate your contributions in that regard. If the big boss doesn't notice such subtleties, keep at it subtly and consistently. If she still doesn't catch the drift, you might not have the well-meaning ally you thought you did. If that's the case, and you've kept things positive by framing your comments as compliments to your I-Boss, you haven't hurt yourself or left a bad taste in anyone's mouth.

By framing all of your propaganda in a positive context, you open up the possibility that a truly intelligent big boss will begin to like having you around. That could mean a promotion. Positive people like to be around other positive people. In the best of all possible worlds, the big boss might recognize that you are being strategically positive and affirming. Seeing your advanced political shrewdness, the big boss might think, *Hm-m-m. That's the kind of person I need on my 'A' Team.*

Being positive never hurts, unless your boss is a masochist, sadist, or Machiavellian. In those cases, it's best to just disappear, literally or figuratively. Being negative doesn't help with those types either, unless you're attacking the nice people. Being a constant irritant won't put you on anybody's "A" Team. As a rule, you'll get more mileage out of hitching a positive wagon to your I-Boss's organizational power source.

Learn His Language

Regardless of the reasons why Idiot Bosses are in charge, the fact remains that they are. You can think martial arts and use their own weight and momentum as weapons against them. Or you can think more positively and learn how to best position yourself vis-à-vis your I-Boss. Start by studying what your I-Boss thinks is positive. Never assume you know. This goes beyond just studying his hobbies and interests. It drills deeper, into his spoken and unspoken languages.

Observe your Idiot Boss's routines and rituals to learn his self-comforting behaviors (and therefore weaknesses and vulnerabilities). What does he like to talk about? What kind of terms does your I-Boss use when he is being positive? "Awesome," is often heard when I-Bosses are trying to overstate something. "Incredible" is also used, even though it approaches maximum syllabic capacity for most I-Bosses. Any time the word "really" is used to precede anything, it is intended to add extra weight to the adjective, as in "really awesome."

"Great," "super," "totally," and "unbelievable" are reliable indicators that the I-Boss likes something. When he says something is "good," he is lying. Nobody says something is "good" unless he thinks it can and should be better. Saying, "We're making good progress," is a polite way of saying, "We need to do better than this or we're screwed." Learn these terms and begin associating them strategically with things you want your I-Boss to feel more positive about, such as the work you're doing.

Pay attention to your Idiot Boss's superiors and study carefully how they:

A. insult him when he's not around.

or

B. humor him when he is around.

By subtracting B from A, you will learn how useful he is to them. If they insult him whether he's present or not, don't waste your time coming to his rescue, he's toast. If I-Bosses are treated respectfully by their superiors, whether they are present or absent, you know his superiors are decent folks and will probably give you a fair shake, too. The worst place to openly criticize your I-Boss is in the presence of those who can and choose not to.

Next, pay attention to how your peers:

A. insult your Idiot Boss when he's not around.

or

B. insult him when he is around.

By subtracting B from A you will learn how cognizant he is of reality. Most I-Bosses don't know when they are the brunt of jokes. In these cases, the budding sadists around the office have a field day with poor, unsuspecting I-Bosses. It's always a good idea to avoid the cynical I-Boss bashing, no matter how tempting it is. Should the I-Boss ever be in a situation to help you, it's advisable to keep an upbeat face on your relationship. More than that, you don't want to be observed bashing your I-Boss by his or her superiors. That will not score points for any possible plans they have to enhance your future prospects.

When the big boss is not friendly

I took the easy scenario first, the one in which the top executive is enlightened, friendly, and supportive of dedicated, hard-working people. As you might have guessed from the bleak picture I painted of hiring practices atop many organizations, you're more likely to encounter a top executive who sees you as little more than a piston rod in the big engine of life—if she sees you at all. In these cases, your I-Boss is not going to receive much personal coaching and nurturing attention either.

It's sink or swim for everyone. Because terminating employees is such a tricky business, many executives allow the bottom of the pool to fill with the bodies of those who sank and hire new bodies to replace them. You can exercise your prerogative to become disgusted, get angry, feel disenfranchised, and resent the heck out of the new administration. Or you can put your newly acquired skills to good use and exploit the situation to your advantage.

As I mentioned before, everyone has an agenda, even new top executives with ice water in their veins. Put your research and inquiry spectacles on and find what the big boss most desires and determine if your Idiot Boss can fit into that scheme. It's dangerous for you to make an end run, even on an I-Boss. He may not get upset, but those above him will see someone out of their box. The keepers of hierarchical power charts like everybody to stay behind their bosses in neat, straight lines. Exiting your silo is likely to get you in trouble as well as your I-Boss who will also be asked to explain why you were in the hall without a pass.

Try to engineer schemes and plans that will resonate with the bigger boss's ambitions and feed them to your I-Boss for presentation. He might not understand what it is you want him to do, so the operation must be approached delicately. If you can put together good stuff and make sure it makes its way into your I-Boss's office, you can then "leak" word to those higher up that your I-Boss has some exciting new stuff coming along.

You can mention "in passing" to the big boss's clerical assistant, "Ever since your boss came, my boss has been acting like a new man. He even has three plans for trimming costs and increasing production based on your boss's last speech to the stockholders," or words to that affect. Add, "These must be exciting times around the executive suite." The clerical assistant will feel important and you might have set the wheels in motion for your I-Boss to receive an invitation to Mahogany Row.

He won't want to go alone because he knows he can't explain your plans. This is a great opportunity to assure him of his capabilities, pump up his ego, and offer to go with him to back him up. Comfort, support, and encouragement will get you much farther with your I-Boss than resentment and cynicism. Properly planned and executed, strategies like these will make you seem indispensable to your I-Boss. You can't control when the opportunity will arise from which you will benefit, but you can be positioned to take advantage of it when it does.

Building a partnership with your I-Boss requires you to take the initiative and do all the work. The research, strategizing, planning, and patient execution of each step are all on your shoulders. But this is the closest thing to control you'll ever have. If you care enough to invest in your career in spite of the idiots in your path, you must take this approach.

Facing criticism

The cynical and negative people in your area will resent you for no longer joining them in bashing the I-Boss. They might downright distrust you for actually initiating contact with him. That's okay. This is your opportunity to point out how the work you're doing is moving the organization, or at least your small part of it, in a worthwhile direction. The alternative is to continue going around in circles, which is characteristic of an I-Boss-led department, or worse, rewriting the mid-range plan again.

What you're doing is taking the lead in setting the department's agenda based in part on what you've discovered the big boss's agenda to be. More importantly, you're shaping the agenda based on what you believe is important. You do this tastefully, of course, all the while making your I-Boss think it's his idea. This is all made possible by your newly developed management skill set.

Handled properly, you could even become a champion for your coworkers. Unless they are terribly misguided, which is always a possibility, they would prefer to set their working agenda rather than haplessly jumping and fetching with every changing whim from the I-Boss.

If you can forge a strategic partnership with your I-Boss in which you can actually influence departmental priorities, you will be your co-workers' new best friend.

Who Are You Really?

Where and when did you stand at your crossroads and etch your worldview on the inside of your forehead? Where did you make the decisions that now inform your attitudes about fairness and meaning in the workplace? Many people never wax nostalgic for the days when their personal context was framed and their professional foundation was laid. Yet, that's where your current attitudes toward work and play, duty and destiny, and family vs. career are anchored.

Developmental arrestment means unfinished business. If we don't successfully complete our developmental phases, we won't fully mature. More specifically, people who do not successfully complete their developmental phases can develop nasty habits rooted in their unfinished business. Those nasty habits will drive others insane (in the non-clinical sense).

It's never too late to finish unfinished business, and the world will be forever grateful. It is thus a good idea to poke around and learn what really makes you tick. Once that's done, you will know how to become an asset rather than a liability, a friend rather than a foe, and a truly strategic partner to your Idiot Boss. Like everything else, you go through this exercise because he won't.

Stuck in Adolescent Rebellion

Engaging in denial and avoidance of real issues, which is the cultural paradigm of far too many working environments, creates a population living in a state of ignorant dysfunction. Lacking the knowledge or courage to adopt a better plan, many of us resist and even refuse to replace denial and avoidance with healthier thinking and behavior. Among the first things middle-aged idiots realize when entering recovery is that they're stuck in adolescent rebellion.

To become unstuck, we must first realize and accept we're developmentally arrested in a stage when a child's mind occupied an emerging adult body. It's childish to believe that the answer to every problem or discomfort is to blame authority, no matter how our bodies have aged. Back then we blamed our parents, teachers, the police, and the president. Now, we've either forgiven or stopped talking to our parents, still blame the president, and project responsibility for the rest of our grievances on our bosses.

Now for the bad news: Your Idiot Boss won't accept your responsibility to get unstuck. Not because he has a highly actualized respect for relational boundaries (he's still an idiot). Your I-Boss wouldn't know what you're talking about if you brought the subject up. Just as well. You shouldn't be shopping around to find a host for a parasitic sense of responsibility anyway, no matter how available and enticing a host your Idiot Boss is.

To paint with an admittedly wide brush, most of us who call ourselves Baby Boomers, and many of our offspring, are stuck in adolescent rebellion. Being developmentally arrested in the adolescent rebellion stage explains many of the internal problems organizations face today. For me, becoming a campus radical was a good way to flex newly acquired freedoms. The first thing I did with my freedom as a college freshman living away from home was to stop doing things I wouldn't have done if my parents hadn't made me—like going to class. Classes at 8 a.m. were a real drag, so I quit going. It was cool. Nobody came and woke me up. Nobody called me on the telephone or banged on the door and told me to get out of bed and go to class. It seemed like a workable arrangement until my grades came in.

Being on academic probation after my first semester threatened my new freedoms, I decided to start demonstrating more academic responsibility as a means of protecting my new freedom. I began to appreciate the interdependency between work, sacrifice, recreation, and abundance. We enter adolescence still expecting the labor and sacrifice of others to sustain our recreation and abundance. Then, abandoning logic altogether, we rebel against the authority figures who have invested the labor and sacrifice to get us where we are. While still in the throes of adolescent rebellion, we haven't yet given up the notion that somebody else is responsible for our happiness and well-being. Therefore, as adolescent reasoning goes, it is someone else's fault if we're not feeling as happy and well cared for as we can imagine we should be. Sound like your office?

Smelling the coffee

The experience of working for an idiot might have inspired you to buy this book. Hopefully you'll finish it with a strong sense that you're really working for yourself, and that how content or contentious you are is up to you. I remember the first time I stood at the crossroads of adolescent rebellion and maturity. I say, "the first time," because my self-aggrandizing imagination has brought me back to that crossroads 1,000 times since.

My roommate at Wartburg College, Hector, was in school on a full-ride scholarship from Mom and Dad. I was there on a half-ride, working all kinds of jobs to save money, only to clean out my checking account with one stroke of my pen on tuition day. Even paying half of my way through college gave me a sense of moral superiority over Hector. As far as I was concerned, my right to protest campus administration policies was bought and paid for and his wasn't, unless he was voting proxy for his folks.

Nevertheless, Hector was loud and proud. Have you noticed how disgruntled folks around the workplace are the loudest and seem shameless in voicing their grievances? Like many of the people I've worked with over the years, Hector didn't make any distinction between what he wanted and what belonged to someone else. During the Hector phase of my life it was still cool to smoke and I kept a carton in my dormitory dresser drawer. The bottom drawer of my dresser held bargain brand sodas I bought at the supermarket to avoid paying higher prices at the vending machines.

Hector brazenly helped himself to my cigarettes right in front of me. The least he could have done was wait until I turned my back before he walked over, opened the top drawer on my dresser, and snagged a pack of smokes. Never being a big one for confrontation, I nevertheless told Hector to buy his own damn cigarettes.

Addressing the issue directly, as with working associates, is a sound practice. But don't be surprised if laying down a boundary doesn't merely send them through another door. For those still stuck in adolescent rebellion, there is no vice in riding on someone else's initiative. If access is denied here, simply approach from over there.

I was pleasantly surprised and emboldened when Hector took my advice and started buying his own tobacco products. In a clever ploy to ensure I never stole back cigarettes from him, he bought non-filtered Pall Malls, which no human would ever set a match to. He came right out and bragged about buying the horrendous things so nobody would bum them. How often around the office do people refuse to accept treatment from others they don't hesitate to engage in themselves?

Just as I was beginning to think I had helped Hector make a break-through, I noticed my stash of sodas was diminishing much faster than I was drinking them. Being pleased he wasn't helping himself to my cigarettes anymore, I resisted the notion he might be drinking the sodas. But as the stash continued to dwindle, I faced the choice of confronting him again or just subsidizing his soda consumption. Still pumped by my recent behavior modification success with the ciga-rette snatching, I confronted him only to find out he wasn't drinking my sodas.

He was selling them to raise the money to buy his cigarettes. In my attempt to instill a sense of personal responsibility in Hector, my best-laid plans had backfired. I had barely closed the door before he found a window to crawl through.

Beware your associates

You don't need to be an active practitioner of adolescent rebel-lion to be sucked into its back draft. Have you ever found yourself involved in a grievance meeting at work, wonder how you got there, and wished you weren't there? Watching television coverage of cam-pus radicals acting out at places like Columbia and Berkeley, I was hanging out with a bunch of Hector's intellectual, elitist friends in the student union one night trying to conjure a way to bring our placid little campus into the fray. They were itching for something to feel righteously indignant about.

One thing led to another, and it was decided to pick a fight with the campus administration. Over what, we didn't know. So, we just started complaining about life in general and slowly spiraled in on a galvanizing issue; a habit we would all carry into our careers and work-places. Although none of the minority students on campus were among us that night, we decided the college wasn't awarding enough full-ride scholarships to underprivileged students.

In an uncharacteristic display of charisma, which in retrospect appears to be a case of drawing the short straw, I was appointed spokes-person for the group. I reluctantly accepted the role and led the three dozen or so students on a one-block parade over to the dean of student's house at two in the morning. It had taken us that long to decide what we wanted to protest.

Surrounded by angry students, I knocked on the front door. A light came on inside, the door opened a crack, and the dean's wife peeked out. That's when a light started to grow brighter inside my head. Seeing that little woman with curlers in her hair, clutching the front of her bathrobe against the night air made me think to myself, "What are you doing, John?" But it was too late. I was across the Rubicon. I had nearly 40 spoiled, upper-middle-class college students looking to me for leadership. When you find yourself embarrassed by your actions or to be associated with a popular movement at work, that's your cue to exit. Your fellow protesters will whine and complain, but it's better to leave as soon as your recognize your embarrassment than to wade in deeper still.

When I should have been in bed with my alarm clock set to make an 8 a.m. class, I stood instead on the dean's front stoop and announced our grievance, demanding we be allowed to address the administration. He agreed to assemble a delegation to hear us out the following afternoon at 1 p.m. in the Student Union. If he had been smart, he would have scheduled it for 8 a.m. None of us would have been there and the meeting would have lasted 60 seconds.

As the panel of administrators sat down the following day, a mob of bleary-eyed students began to gather in front of them, sitting on the floor, draped over furniture, and leaning against the walls. To my surprise, the ranking administrator turned to me and asked if I would act as moderator. He correctly suspected the dialogue might quickly become unruly and unproductive. As a class president and duly elected mob leader, he thought I might have some measure of influence over the group.

Before the gripe session even began, I felt an urge to apologize. I realized that gaining more scholarships for minority students could have been better accomplished through channels, if only we had the maturity, discipline, and passion to follow that route. As it was, we were just rebellious adolescents acting out, not genuinely fighting for a worthwhile cause.

Our mob of students at Wartburg College had no clue what patient discipline in pursuit of a greater cause meant. We couldn't even spell *sacrifice*. Whatever the true merits of freedom and justice, the agenda for most of those kids was to be as noisy and disruptive as possible. Acting up and causing general disorder is the adolescent manifestation of a 2-year-old's foot-stomping tantrum. In spite of my best efforts to maintain order, the meeting became noisy and unruly. Hector seized the opportunity to become shrill, rude, and disrespectful to the administrators. He savored every minute of it, only pausing long enough to light another Pal Mall.

Suddenly, my entitlement issues reemerged. I felt if anybody had a right to rail on the campus administration it should be people who paid all or part of their own tuition in cash or sweat. Yet, the loudest and most caustic voices came from Hector and others who, to my knowledge, had no personal investment whatsoever in the college except to be there. It's been my experience in the workplace that those who have most earned the right to gripe are usually the least likely to.

That chaotic, angry session with the campus administrators was a transformational experience for me. When was yours? How many have you had? I admit I didn't learn as much from each transformational opportunity in my life as I could and should have. But, speaking for myself, the harder the head, the more bumps it takes to get one's attention. When you take up a cause, which might be standing up for the principles you believe are important in the workplace, I hope anyone looking into your eyes will see the real deal, and not an over-aged adolescent tantrum.

Then and Now

It amazes me how many Hectors I still encounter in organizations all over the country. They exist at all levels. Sometimes they're union stewards, sometimes they're vice presidents. Like anyone else, the more power they wield, the more damage they can do. Despite how righteous I felt about protesting campus administration policies because I paid tuition, I had to back off and let go of that resentment. There are Hectors everywhere, people who don't put into the system, but claim the right to complain about it, and make demands on it.

If I resent everyone who I don't feel has earned the right to do what they do, say what they say, and receive what they receive, I'll become immobilized by my own anger and sense of injustice. Then who suffers? If you have earned the right to express yourself through enormous contributions you've made, I applaud you. But guess what? Others who've made no such contributions are going to make themselves heard anyway, and they will be recognized. Get used to it. Better yet, for your own sanity, get over it. Shift your focus to ways you can contribute still more. That's being true to your nature. Blaming your I-Boss is not.

Although many people do little to earn respect, nobody deserves to be treated disrespectfully. Like my chronically tardy technician at Disneyland, we need to be reminded from time to time that we contribute to the corporate cause because doing our part is part of the grand scheme, the scheme that benefits lots of people. Dealing with I-Bosses might cause you to bite your lip, so take a deep breath, count to 10, and let it out slowly. But getting over it doesn't mean giving up. There is no reason to accept your lot without proactively doing something about it.

If you choose to remain passive, blindly accept what your I-Boss hands you, then gripe about it, I must assume that griping lights your wick. Meanwhile, you're not truly helping yourself or anyone around you. You've read too far and have too much information now to merely accept an I-Boss relationship strictly on his terms. You're not stepping up and becoming more involved for his sake, unless you choose to. You're doing it for yourself and those around you who are willing to share your attitude.

The Eighth Step:
"Make a list of all persons I might have harmed with my stupidity and prepare to make amends to them all."

Does anybody have the white pages for the Western Hemisphere? At first glance, these recovery steps seem to be pulling me in the opposite direction from my emerging coexistence with my I-Boss. However, as my understanding grows, it all weaves itself together in a sort of cosmic tapestry. The stupidity I've been describing so far didn't just hurt me, it also made life difficult for others. Don't you wish your I-Boss had such an epiphany? Will you choose "me for the sake of me" or "me first, who wants to follow"? The steps helped me learn the difference.

I used to dwell on the injustice of office politics. Things I felt were unfair could keep me up for nights at a time. The board of directors/ weeping president nonsense made me an insomniac for the longest time. Before that, there were times I felt it was my moral obligation to expose my I-Boss as a moron. But none of my complaining hurt my I-Boss. And none of it helped me.

As much as I feel compelled to expose things for the way they really are and force the hand of justice, I've learned it's more important to keep our composure. Discretion truly is the better part of valor. Positioning ourselves properly relative to our I-Bosses requires constant positioning radar. If we stay between the navigational beacons, we will not only survive life with an I-Boss, we can thrive.

Because we can't change our I-Bosses directly, examining how we might have foisted I-Boss-like injury and inconvenience upon others will help us to keep perspective and develop a strategy to survive and prosper, in spite of our situation. Making a list of people to whom we should make amends—even if we don't actually make them—is a smelling salts eye opener. If you genuinely want to transform your attitude toward your Idiot Boss and develop a strategic (albeit understated) partnership with him, start by becoming the kind of partner you would want to have.

9

Idiotspeak: How to Talk to Your Idiot Boss

The Ninth Step:
"Make amends to all of the persons I might have harmed with my stupidity, except when contacting them might place my life in jeopardy."

Quoting the classic country song, "Take This Job and Shove It," even to an Idiot Boss who might not know exactly what it means, is not a career-enhancing behavior. If you want to be relieved of the burdens working for an idiot can place on you, if you want to be liberated from the oppressive guilt of hating your I-Boss, if you would like to restore the energy and enthusiasm you once brought to work, I have some good news and some bad news. The good news is you can change your entire relationship with your I-Boss. The bad news is you need to make some amends in your I-Boss's direction.

Not to worry; he will probably never realize what you're doing unless you come right out and say, "I'm sorry, I thought you were an idiot." Just applying the methods and techniques I've been mentioning from chapter to chapter will make him feel better around you and better in general. Accordingly, he'll start treating you much better once your strategy is executed.

Making amends to your I-Boss, to make him feel better, has much to do with language. If the words we choose to use or omit from a conversation speak volumes about who we are and our attitudes and beliefs, then our actions speak encyclopedias. Research conducted by UCLA psychology professor emeritus Albert Mehrabian determined that words account for 7 percent of a face-to-face message. Vocal inflection accounts for 38 percent, and facial expression accounts for 55 percent.

Dr. Mehrabian's analysis didn't mention Italian arm gestures or freeway rush hour hand gestures when words are unnecessary, but his point is pretty well made. It's not the words you say, it's how you say them. If you scowl while telling your I-Boss you're about to throw his computer monitor out the window, he'll dive under his desk. If you say the same thing with a smile, he'll open the window for you.

Body language is hard to mistake. The desk-diving secretary at Disneyland made a clear and concise statement with her acrobatics. Big Mike, the Disneyland union boss, wasn't the least bit ambiguous when he slammed me against the wall. Trouble was, it was my body he was talking with.

Content

You can't make a proper amend unless you understand the basic components of communication. What you say or don't say and what you do or don't do says it all. That's how it is with your Idiot Boss. You can either make your relationship with your I-Boss work for or against you by what you choose to communicate and how you choose to communicate it. I've already advised you to listen carefully when your I-Boss speaks. What does he choose to talk about: work or hockey?

If he likes to talk about hockey, you'll just annoy him if you try to steer the puck toward work-related issues. You can cleverly maneuver around this impasse by using hockey metaphors when describing the work issues you find important. Speak in terms of "taking the gloves off," reaching organizational objectives by scoring "goals," putting problems in the "penalty box," and making corporate history by turning a "hat trick."

I don't know what it means either. But if my I-Boss was a hockey fan, you'd better believe I'd know what a hat trick is, and I would have hockey magazines on my desk, a hockey stick standing in the corner of my cubicle, a puck as a paperweight, and a picture of Mario Lemieux on my screen saver. (Men can have pictures of other men on their screensavers as long as they're toothless athletes who play contact sports.)

Wayne Gretsky reportedly said, "I don't skate to where the puck is, I skate to where the puck is going to be," or words to that effect. That's a great line if your I-Boss is a hockey fan. If he's a basketball fan, use your imagination and reframe the quote, assigning it to whoever his favorite player is. Be careful not to mix your metaphors and expose your true ignorance by saying, "Michael Jordan said, 'I don't shoot where the basket is. I shoot where the basket is going to be.'" Enter hockey quotations or whatever his favorite topic is into your search engine and watch future conversations with your I-Boss ripple across your monitor.

If you want to win over the hearts and minds of other people in the office, especially your Idiot Boss, help them live out their fantasies—within reason. What extracurricular activities does your I-Boss engage in away from work or at work? If he likes to dress up as an Arab Sheik, I advise you to get your hands on a robe and sandals and drink tea while sitting cross-legged on a Persian rug. Incredibly wealthy people in the Middle East do it every day. So do old hippies in Portland, Oregon. The difference is mostly in the value of the rug. If your I-Boss fancies himself Rudolph Valentino, don't show up dressed like a Portland hippy.

I won't go so far as to invoke the "Teach a Pig to Sing" analogy, but you'll live a happier, healthier, more productive life if you develop methods and techniques to visit your I-Boss's world when appropriate rather than trying to get him to visit yours. If your Idiot Boss has frustrated you to the point of distraction, you've probably done the same thing to him. You've probably been spending excessive time and energy trying to get him to think and act like you act or at least act in ways you want him to act. That will wear anybody out.

Make an amend to your I-Boss by resolving not to pull him into your interests and favorite activities. Don't admit you've tried and failed. And you will fail if you try to go that route. Your I-Boss will make you crazy enough to run off and join an indigenous tribe long before you'll have any measurable affect on his interests or decision-making. Make it a personal task to prioritize his interests as you engage in social architecture around the office.

Idiotspeak

Idiotspeak is like learning a foreign language. Berlitz has yet to offer tapes on Idiotspeak, but they can't be far from it. Idiotspeak is not hard to learn. For example, Idiot Bosses are particularly fond of quoting the latest business best-seller or popular song. "We're going to zap this department into shape." "Nobody's going to teach elephants to dance on my watch. Do you know how much elephants eat?" Who let the dogs out?" And of course, "We're going to reengineer those seven principles."

Communicate your way to happiness

Idiot Bosses truly want to communicate with their employees because it makes them feel like they've been invited to their own birthday party. Unfortunately, of all the interpersonal skills they lack, Idiot Bosses are most lacking in effective communications. Communicating requires a meeting of the minds at some level. That leaves it up to you because your boss has no clue at what level you operate. Making your I-Boss feel like every day is his or her birthday can pay big benefits.

The Internet has made it much easier to engage in idiotspeak. Listen carefully to his pontifications and identify the books he's quoting. Search them down, either by author or by title, order a copy, then leave it lying conspicuously on your desk. Better yet, carry it around with you—to meetings, to lunch, to the restroom, read it while you wait for him to putt on the golf course. Refer to the book often using his name in the sentence.

"That suggestion you made this morning reminded me of Ken Blanchard's *One Minute Manager*, Floyd." Hearing his name mentioned in the same sentence as an author he idolizes will bring on the warm fuzzies, and the credit will go to you. Try to mention these things in emails to minimize your kissing up in front of your peers. I know we've already prepared a heartfelt response for them, but why dangle a red cape in front of them unnecessarily?

If you choose to improve your relationship with your I-Boss rather than to constantly challenge him or engage him in a battle of attrition, communication will be your best tool. And knowing your I-Boss's choice of literature is a big part of it. If he doesn't leave any books or magazines lying around the office, it could be because he doesn't read.

In that case, note key terms and phrases he uses in conversation, enter the terms on Google.com, and see what comes back. You might be able to turn your I-Boss on to a few Websites that will interest him. This is another good way to get your I-Boss distracted long enough for you to get some real work done. The stickier the Websites you recommend to your I-Boss, the more quality time you will buy yourself.

Remember, if you're not resonating with his or her interests and obsessions, you could be annoying your I-Boss. Making amends to the I-Boss doesn't mean truly being contrite for wrongs you've done, as would be the case with family members or someone you truly care about. It means using the amends model to help keep a functional sense of humility in play for your own good. When you are allowed to operate freely, you do good things, right? This is about positioning yourself vis-à-vis your I-Boss so you can operate freely and do good things.

Another way to use language to ensure your I-Boss is comfortable around you is to send circuitous messages, otherwise known as the classic third-party compliment made famous by leadership expert Danny Cox. The third-party compliment is simple. Instead of complimenting your I-Boss to his face, which might be too over the top even for an I-Boss, compliment your I-Boss to someone who is likely to tote the tale back.

If your I-Boss has a clumsy and obvious system of moles through-out the department, it's as easy as shooting ducks in a barrel. Just speak in glowing terms about the I-Boss where the mole can overhear you. Bathroom stalls provide good covert operations opportunities. If you know the mole is in the next stall, act like you're talking on your cell phone and extol your I-Boss's latest triumph. Mention how proud you are to work for such a genius.

If the mole catches up with you at the sinks, wash your hands and act as if nothing happened. If the mole brings up the overheard conversation, act embarrassed and say you sometimes just can't contain your enthusiasm. If you feel the door has been swung wide open, go ahead and lay a compliment on the mole. Mention how you heard your I-Boss saying something complimentary about the mole. The mole won't tell the I-Boss about the compliment you claimed the I-Boss made, but the mole will deliver an account of your phony cell phone conversation back to the I-Boss as proof of mole-worthiness.

If the mole is a true idiot, he might thank the I-Boss for the compliment you made up. Your I-Boss might be truly confused and say, "Gee, did I say that?" Or he might try to save face and say, "Well-deserved praise, Mole." Of course, the rare I-Boss might be sharp enough to realize he never said any such thing because he considers the mole a bigger idiot than he is. In that case, you might have raised unintended suspicion on the part of your I-Boss. You must use finesse when sending compliments via messengers.

When there are no obvious moles, you can still send compliments to your I-Boss. Compliments about your I-Boss made to his superiors are likely to get back to him. This is a more direct use of the third-party compliment. People like to pass on good news. When something positive is said about a boss of any kind, other bosses like to pretend a trend has begun. If Boss A hears one of Boss B's team members saying something good about Boss B, Boss A will make it a priority to mention it to Boss B in hopes that Boss B will have similar good news to share.

You don't have to be as obvious as to tell your I-Boss's secretary directly, as I suggested earlier, although this can be effective if the script is sufficiently believable. Positive statements about your I-Boss made within earshot of his clerical assistant will surely make their way to the ears you intended. Keep your radar moving and when the assistant is nearby, launch a compliment about the boss. This might require a few attempts before the secretary believes you, so try to vary your locations and delivery.

To make sure the clerical assistant will find you credible, spend some time observing and making notes on the secretary's associations, habits, and behaviors. Adapt the third-party compliment to the secretary. Reporting to the assistant that the I-Boss has paid him a compliment will put you on the assistant's "A" list and ensure you will be portrayed in a positive light whenever the secretary has input or influence on the I-Boss's decision-making process, which is always.

The purest form of Cox's third-party compliment is intended to make people feel good about one another without communicating directly. To help quell a dispute or smooth ruffled feathers and promote increase cooperation and collaboration, a good boss will purposefully tell Person A that Person B said something positive about

Person A. It is manipulation pure and simple. But in the right hands, it is an effective tool in the cause of truth, justice, and the American way.

Forcing the Issue

If you're too impatient to allow the third-party compliment to run its course, you can be more direct. If you suspect someone around the office is desperate to score points with the I-Boss, that person just became your personal messenger for positive and affirming messages. Say positive things about your I-Boss in the kiss up's presence because he will no doubt take the information straight to the I-Boss as a ploy to gain entry to the I-Boss's inner circle. Anyone who wants to gain access to an I-Boss's inner circle for anything but mercenary reasons is likely to be an even bigger idiot.

If you don't have a willing and able kiss up available, you might need to take the bull by the horns and be the messenger yourself. Tell your I-Boss that you overheard his boss saying complementary things about him. Everybody wants to think they are respected and admired. You didn't plant that need for acceptance in the human psyche. There is no need to feel guilty if you make use of it to bring about a positive outcome.

The increased regard your I-Boss will have for you as a result of your embellishment on the truth will make it easier for you to do more fulfilling work. Where is the vice in that? I only used the word "embellishment" because the tale you're toting to your I-Boss is partially true. In all likelihood, your I-Boss's boss makes many comments about your I-Boss. Turning them into positive messages before they reach your I-Boss's ears is just your way of being God's little helper.

His humor is your humor

Smile and nod knowingly whenever your I-Boss laughs, even if you weren't paying attention to his or her joke or story. The true definition of terror is to be caught daydreaming when your I-Boss is talking, especially if he is telling a joke or making what he thinks is an earth-shattering point. If you wake from a sound sleep to hear your chuckling I-Boss asking you if you thought his remark was funny, grin and say, "Gee, boss, I don't know how we manage to get any work done with you around."

Be careful not to say it if your I-Boss was making a serious earth-shattering point. Look around the room before you answer and see if anyone else is faking a laugh at what your I-Boss just said. If others are rolling their eyes, your I-Boss was probably trying to be funny. If everyone else is dead serious and is looking at you through piercing eyes as if to say, "Danger, Will Robinson," then you say, "Working under you, boss, helps me keep my career in perspective."

Your I-Boss will think you're paying him a compliment. He won't pick up on the sarcasm and realize his comments serve as a constant reminder that you are wasting your youth and energy working for an idiot. In this day and age, when providing for yourself and the needs of your family are paramount and not always easy in an employers' market, you might want to consider putting away your resentment and be more appreciative of the employment opportunities you have, even if it requires suffering fools with a smile plastered on your face. In times of uncertain economics, Idiotspeak can serve you well as a second language. Learn it. Speak it. Use it well.

You Can't Avoid Gossip

We know better than to believe gossip, much less pass it on, but many people do. Gossiping is a natural inclination for many and a tremendous temptation for almost everyone, be it genetic or conditioned behavior.

Whether we gossip because we're sadists or we just want to scratch a dysfunctional itch and make everybody else feel as bad as we feel, gossip doesn't help anyone; not the gossiper and especially not the gossipee. Skilled Idiotspeak doesn't include gossip because the most effective messages are positive, even if they are calculated.

The third-party compliment, as Danny Cox teaches it, is not gossip. When gossiping, you tell Person A that Person B said something critical about Person A with the intention of causing a rift, hurting Person A's feelings, creating general hostility, or all of the above. A true third-party compliment will spread positive vibes by playing to the inherent desire for appreciation. People are eager to put forth their best effort when they feel recognized, respected, and appreciated.

People will gossip for a variety of reasons, none of which are positive or productive. People resort to pettiness because they lack the imagination or reinforcement to believe they can play at a higher level.

When people believe they are doomed to a lifetime of hard labor in the salt mines, they feel no compunction about taking others down with them. The gossiper's thinking is similar to a convict with three life sentences without possibility of parole—to be served sequentially. There's not much more to lose.

Some people deal with pain, disappointment, and discouragement by doing everything they can to cause pain, disappointment, and discouragement to others. In a workplace setting, effort, loyalty, and results are supposed to count for something. Nobody knows better than a gossiper that all of those qualities can be washed away with the ingestion of a little false information into the equation. You have probably been victimized more than once by falsehoods that diminished or eliminated the good will your positive efforts should have produced. I have.

Others, especially Machiavellians and sadists, use gossip as anything from a surgical instrument to slice the jugular veins of their opponents and victims to weapons of mass destruction. Whether gossip is used for amusement, payback, or premeditated injury, it can be a destructive force. Worse, it is unavoidable.

There is no way to avoid gossip entirely. You might as well try to walk between the raindrops during a cloudburst. There will always be bored slackers, injured egos, and calculating career climbers. If you become as low profile and forgettable as Harold the invisible executive, chances are good nobody will exert the effort to gossip about you. As long as you remain a contributing member of your team, you can expect to be slimed sooner or later.

To deal effectively with gossipers and protect yourself as much as possible from the destructive effects of gossip, you need to fashion a gossip-proof slicker out of your own propaganda. Nothing guarantees complete protection against gossip any more than drinking diet soda guarantees you'll lose weight. But hiding in a closet won't get it done. Gossip can bend around corners, crawl under doors, travel through cyberspace, and penetrate the thickest walls.

The trench coat approach

Depending on how much gossip you deal with at work, you might need a bio-hazard suit. Creating a barrier to protect yourself from words is best done with actions. If you try and shield yourself with anti-gossip (mere words) you are at the mercy of a superior foe. Gossipers are much better wordsmiths than you. I ordinarily reserve the moniker "wordsmith" for eloquent endeavors such as writing books about idiots. In truth, skilled gossipers have forgotten more about the power of language than I'll ever know.

Doing positive things, meaning things your boss finds impressive, will counteract a ton of negative words—unless you keep your good deeds a secret. This is yet another good reason to make your activities and accomplishments as visible as possible, in the context your boss finds most pleasing. If a Machiavellian knows you've accomplished something worthwhile and have attached her name to it in such a way as to advance her career, she'll value you. People can say what they will about you, but as long as the Machiavellian thinks you're propping her up, the gossip will fall on deaf ears.

The same goes for all boss types. If you've done a good job of convincing them you're providing what they want, gossip flung in your direction will roll off your back. At least it won't injure you where your boss is concerned. If you are a faithful servant to a God Boss, an anguished victim to a Sadistic Boss, an enabler of punishment for a Masochistic Boss, a mole to confirm the conspiracy for a Paranoid Boss, best friend to a Buddy Boss, and a mirror for an Idiot Boss's inflated self-image, you are reasonably indemnified against the damage gossip can cause.

You must keep up the effort. Maneuvering your way into the good graces of your boss through properly publicized positive actions is only as good as your last action. Gossip is not only as ubiquitous as the air you breathe, it is relentless. It will never back off and, as soon as you participate, it will nail you. If you've allowed your gossip insurance to lapse, it will be too late to bring up all of the premiums you've paid in the past with positive actions. Keep your gossip insurance current.

The reverse osmosis approach

In yet another application of the third-party compliment, a little intelligence doesn't hurt. Not the kind of intelligence you lose when the doctor drops you on your head as an infant, but the espionage, cloak and dagger stuff. You know there is gossip going on out there, so try to monitor it. This doesn't mean becoming a gossiper yourself. It means becoming a good listener. I took pride for many years that I didn't engage in workplace gossip and paid no attention to it until it bit me on the backside.

Pay attention to who huddles at the water cooler and who makes subtle hand gestures at meetings. Who walks to the parking lot together and, most of all, who goes to lunch together. What informal network of people e-mails each other constantly? Do major rumors ripple north to south, south to north, east to west, or west to east in your office? Who is in the office when gossiping seems the most active, and who is conspicuously absent when it seems to die down?

By identifying the sources of gossip in the office, you know from whom you need protection. Most importantly, you'll know who to compliment to your boss. If you are complimenting the gossips to your boss on a regular basis, when some gossip hits the fan, your boss will take it with a grain of salt. You want your boss to say, "How can it be that so-and-so says such derogatory things about my loyal employee, especially when my loyal employee is constantly complimenting so-and-so? What's wrong with this picture?" Of course your boss can always figure you're a gullible idiot. But that's a chance you must take.

The Office Bully

Adult work environments, including white-collar offices, are often as susceptible to pranksters and bullies as the schoolyard. Gossip is an effective weapon in the arsenal of Sadistic Bosses or others who are emotionally injured. Sadists are entertained by observing pain in others. It's like the blood thirst of those who enjoy dogfights or cockfights. They could wander around and hope to see two dogs fight or two roosters rip into one another. But they're too impatient. So, they breed dogs and roosters to do combat, then stage the matches.

If your boss uses intimidation tactics, you have a choice to make. If it's a Machiavellian, God, Sadistic, or Paranoid Boss, standing up to him might only bring down more fire and brimstone on your head. Like my obsession with justice and being right, your proud defiance might hurt you more than it's worth. Career advancement is more about who has the power than who is right. Bullies don't have any power except that which you give them. Bosses have functional authority over you. There's a big difference.

If the office bully is a boss, shrugging your shoulders, grinning, and bearing it will probably better serve your long-term prospects.

If the bully is a peer, take him off at the knees. I don't recommend doing anything that will leave a mark or trace evidence. But you need to let the bully know you're not intimidated.

A good stare-down is sometimes enough. Bullies eventually blink. If you need heavier artillery, leave a copy of *How to Work for an Idiot* lying on his desk where the boss is sure to see it while the bully is out to lunch. Once the bully is convinced you're more dangerous than he is, he'll be off to find another, more cooperative victim.

Never brag or boast about defeating bullies. Don't go whining to an I-Boss, or any boss, about the bully. Bosses who lack skills to resolve conflict will just bury their heads and the bully will be emboldened. Meanwhile the boss will label you a complainer. Bosses who like blood sports will egg the conflict on for their amusement. Good Bosses are so tuned in to their team members, they will sense a problem quickly and deal with it long before you end up fighting a lonely battle.

Me and my big mouth

This is the ultimate example of how manipulative and downright deadly gossip-based workplace games can be. One evening, Big Bill's wife stepped into the doorway of my office at the audio/video publishing company we were turning around after I left Disney. She was a smart and successful businessperson in her own right and partnered with Big Bill in all of his construction engineering companies. She spent time each week in our offices keeping the finances straight. From time to time, she asked non-financial questions about our fledgling enterprise. I was happy to use her as a messenger on important matters to reinforce what I told Bill directly.

One of the employees we inherited from the previous administration was a true mother hen. April took care of everybody emotionally by pecking around in their personal affairs. In the old culture, before Big Bill and I acquired the company, her office was always in session as she listened to the troubles employees brought from home or encountered around the office. She stroked and made them feel all better. I preach and teach human-centered management practices, but April was codependency to the 10th power. When Bill and I took over the company, it was more of a coffee klatch than a thriving business.

One of our first orders of business was to get the little company operating like a business, and, if for nothing else, to stop losing $250 thousand annually as they were when Big Bill and I took over the reins. Except for Bill's tirades, we remained a friendly business even as we became profitable. As we reshaped the culture (me through coaching and education, Big Bill with a baseball bat), April felt hurt by the diminishing need for her "Come tell mama all about it" approach to management.

In the tomb-like quiet that descends on a deserted office building after hours, Mrs. Bill appeared at the door to my office, leaned against my doorframe, and asked my opinion about April. She wanted to know how I thought we could ease the tension between April and Big Bill. I acknowledged all the ways April was useful, smoothing ruffled feathers after Bill terrorized the place with one of his motivational visits.

On the other hand, April's codependency was like a drag chute on our productivity. I told Mrs. Bill how frustrated I was with my unsuccessful attempts to counsel April into behaviors and management practices better suited for a high-performance team atmosphere. It had long been apparent to me that April was only interested in mothering people. Contributing to an efficient, productive business, if she cared about it at all, was low on her list of priorities. Mrs. Bill seemed to agree with everything I said, which struck me as odd because of her apparently kindred relationship with April.

After Mrs. Bill left, I stood up, shut off the lights in my office, and walked toward the lobby, passing April's office on the way, which was right next to mine. If you've ever walked into a door, collided in full stride so forcefully that you practically knocked yourself unconscious, you know how I felt when I saw April sitting at her desk, having overheard the conversation that just took place. I would have rather walked into a door. Seeing her sitting there, staring straight ahead, face red as a beet, I was instantly engulfed in a storm of emotions—surprise mixed with shock and anger mixed with embarrassment.

Everything I had just said to Mrs. Bill replayed in my head. She had stood in the doorway of my office, leading me through a litany of complaints I had about April and her future with our company, all within full sight of April less than 10 feet away. Although I felt betrayed and set up, I elected not to confront the situation and did what any red-blooded coward would do. I continued out the door as if nothing had happened and drove home.

The next morning I walked into April's office and told her I was sorry she heard those things in the manner she heard them, but I stood by everything I said as we had discussed the issues in the past. I didn't challenge her as to why she and Mrs. Bill set up the embarrassing scenario the night before. I was afraid to know. April left shortly thereafter and took a job with one of our suppliers.

I never discussed the episode with Big Bill or his wife. So utterly flabbergasted was I that I didn't know where to begin such a conversation, and had no clue what good could come of it. In fact, I rarely spoke to Mrs. Bill after that, except when absolutely necessary. So much for my open-door mentality—I felt slimed. I might be the only person in history who ever had the third-party compliment turned into a self-incriminating third-party criticism completely without my knowledge. I let my guard down and, in doing so, engaged in some of the worst Idiotspeak in human history.

Remember these tips to avoid gossip:

- Keep your radar active to determine who is congregating for potential gossip sessions.
- Make a mental note of who could benefit from your diminished status.
- When in doubt, don't speak your mind. Use discretion.
- Don't get suckered into criticizing other people, no matter how tempting it is.
- Politely ask the person who seems so interested in your opinion about someone else to explain why the information is so important.
- If she won't talk, but insist you do—don't.
- If she blasts the other party, simply say it's too bad she feels that way.
- Suggest that she contact an intermediary from HR to work out the problem.
- Keep your comments positive. There's nothing to be gained from bad-mouthing a coworker.
- Use the third-party compliment. It works.

Shamu on Trust

No matter how you choose to communicate with your Idiot Boss or anyone else on your team, make sure there is a subtext to your message that says, "I'm your friend. I'm not going to hurt you. If push comes to shove, I'll take a bullet for you." You want your I-Boss and your peers to consider you a stand-up person. The only way you're going to convince them to trust you is to jump in the tank, swim with them, and speak their language. Most of all, consistently demonstrate your willingness to admit and make amends for your mistakes. That will send the unmistakable message: big person here.

10
Idiot-eat:

Using Meals to Advance Your Career

Always reconnoiter restaurants carefully when you come in. If you spot your I-Boss eating at a table with associates, position yourself with your back to him, but try to stay within earshot. This is always a hoot because the person trying to schmooze the boss knows you can hear what's going on. This is also why you carefully index the key points your I-Boss makes back at the office. You can proclaim to your table companions how these very ideas will revolutionize the industry. Proclaim, that is, just loud enough for your I-Boss to hear. With you quoting your I-Boss chapter and verse, he won't hear a word the person at the table with him is saying.

Maneuver yourself at parties and receptions to do the same thing. Always position yourself so your I-Boss will "overhear" you singing his praises. If praising your I-Boss in these social situations is too on the nose, praise his ideas. Say to your cocktail companions, "I don't remember who said such-and-such, but it's a fabulous idea." Your I-Boss will probably excuse himself from his present conversation and join your group to take credit.

Parties and receptions are also good opportunities to work over moles and kiss-ups, planting valuable messages in their puny brains to carry back to your I-Boss. They might not get many social opportunities outside of these parties, so make them feel welcome, even if it's not your party. Your I-Boss will be pleased if he observes from across the room you treating his moles well.

Don't Order the Crab

When dining with persons who can cash your ticket, try not to embarrass anyone at the table. God, Machiavellian, and many Sadistic Bosses usually have advanced table graces. I was trying to increase the amount of consulting I was doing with a certain television network some time ago and was invited to dinner with a very senior vice president who was known for his impeccable taste in fine dining and fine wines. He prided himself on proper etiquette. The fact he expensed thousands of dollars every month on fancy meals and obscene gratuities made him popular with many a maître d' in major cities around the world.

We were dining at a swank west-side eatery in Los Angeles with several members of his office entourage. I know enough about fine dining to start with the outside silverware and work in, but not much else. Still a power meal neophyte, I paid no attention to what he or anyone else ordered. With the network picking up the tab, I ordered the "market price" crab.

The wine was in the range of $100 per bottle, which I found out too late gets you tipsy much faster than the $24.99 stuff I'm used to. When the main course was finally served, I was feeling happy and confident despite my diminished capacity to execute the intricate procedures required to crack crab shells and extract the meat. My tongue was probably stuck out of the corner of my mouth as I struggled to get a grip on a large crab leg with the silver nutcracker.

The VP's entourage was hanging on his every word when I finally cracked open the shell sending mucus-colored crab juice spraying across the table. Fortunately, most of it missed his face, landing instead on his $3,000 Italian suit. The splatter pattern spared no one on his side of the table. The women and men of his entourage shrieked in unison. True to his stature, the VP sat serenely as a gaggle of waiters blotted him with white napkins.

I haven't worked for that network since. Business meals, receptions, and parties are not recreational activities to an ambitious person who knows how to work the room. They are privileged opportunities to conduct reconnaissance, build alliances—unholy or otherwise—and strategically position yourself for success. Never forget that food can be your best friend or your worst enemy. Eat slowly, chew carefully, and swallow before taking another bite.

The Tenth Step:
"Continue to take personal inventory and, when I'm wrong, promptly admit it."

Following the television network dinner debacle, I wrote down "table etiquette needs work" on my self-inventory. I'm glad the 12 steps leave a little wiggle room to conduct remedial work. If I had to get it right the first time, on a strict schedule, I'd probably be a relapse statistic. To continue taking personal inventory is a good idea because the more layers of the onion I peel away, the more I seem to discover.

The more I probe my personal idiot issues, the more I understand Idiot Bosses and how to deal with them. The personal inventory exercise is particularly helpful in the context of my career because I am forming a picture of how boneheadedness in my personal affairs is mirrored by boneheadedness in my professional affairs. Idiot Bosses are idiots at home, too.

If I remain seized up with anger and resentment toward Idiot Bosses, I'll keep trying to peel their onions instead of my own. Chopping their onions is a more appropriate way to put it. No, hacking them to itty-bitty pieces with a machete is the honest way to put it. But as we agreed chapters ago, that kind of bitterness and revenge seeking only spoils our day, not theirs.

Working the Meal

A one-on-one meal is a rich opportunity to tell your I-Boss everything he wants to hear without being labeled a turkey around the office. Just make sure the waiter is not a recently downsized colleague who still has your associates' e-mail addresses. I could have and perhaps should have used the offsite coffee meetings at Coco's to butter up Big Bill. But I had that demon resentment gnawing away inside me and I didn't take advantage of my opportunities. Back then I lived a one-dimensional victimhood in which everything I did was right and everything Bill did was wrong. In that twisted mindset, everything I did was virtuous and everything he did was evil. I never stopped to consider that he was a human being, too, trying to sort out his mess of a life as I was trying to sort out mine, and probably having the same amount of success, no more, no less.

Besides being unproductive, such narrow thinking was tedious. I'm the one who lost sleep at night tabulating and comparing my virtuous deeds to his evil ones. I was miserable while he, for the most part and most of the time, appeared happy. In his eruptive moments, he blew up at everyone and everything. The poor man was incapable of storing up hostility, resentment, and rage, and letting it eat at him day and night, the way I could.

Looking at the bright side, Big Bill always picked up the tab at Coco's. If you've been resisting lunch invitations from your I-Boss, try accepting once in a while. He might pay for it. Disneyland was my first real management job with an expense account. True to my tradition of missing opportunities, I didn't understand how expense accounts could be used as wealth-building tools until it was too late. Shortly after I became a "suit," a memo was circulated admonishing executives to stop taking each other out to lunch and expensing it. I had never imagined doing such a thing.

My timing leaves something to be desired. Not that I'm a Boy Scout, above stretching the privileges of position within reason, it just hadn't occurred to me. When the memo hit, I remember thinking to myself, "Gee, I could have been going out to lunch at expensive restaurants around Orange County instead of eating in the commissary every day?"

Your I-Boss might be willing to take you to lunch and expense it because he's brash enough to do it. Planets often align themselves in ways that benefit I-Bosses, so much so I sometimes suspect God has a special place in his heart for idiots. Maybe Idiot Bosses truly are His little boo-boos and He feels sorry for them. Your I-Boss's boss might expense her lunches with peers and subordinates and doesn't want to rock the boat by enforcing a prohibition on it. Perhaps nobody up the food chain has established a policy to forbid it or bothers to enforce existing policy against such things.

At Disneyland, I doubt the top executives ever stopped expensing their lunches. They probably just enforced the policy on middle management where I lived. Your I-Boss might unwittingly get by with expensing lunches because someone in accounting is robbing the company blind and allowing some fudging on expense accounts as a smoke screen.

Whatever the reason, if your I-Boss pays for lunch, enjoy it and shut up. Even if your I-Boss insists on going Dutch treat, it could be worse. He might be a regular prankster and think it's a cute trick to ask you to lunch and then stick you with the bill. The latter is more likely to occur with a Sadistic or a God Boss who considers your picking up the tab a form of tithing.

Big Bill always paid when we went out for coffee or a meal. It was another way for him to remind me that I owed him. Besides resenting his innuendo, I didn't feel the need to get out of our employees' ear-shot because I didn't have anything to hide from them. If anything, I was too open and loose-lipped with company information as I discovered the night Mrs. Bill and April bushwhacked me.

Making the most from business meals begins with following a few simple rules:

- Understand what a business meal means to your boss. Some think meals are work time, others think they're opportunities to talk about everything but work. Whichever the case, your boss sets the agenda, not you.

- Are business meals a cover for your boss's desire to slam back a few before returning to the office? If so, use the designated driver or doctor's orders excuses to not join in the drinking. If the boss has alcohol problems, he might be under secret-yet-serious scrutiny by higher ups. You don't want to be entangled in the net that might be set out for your boss.

- If your boss is a drinker, that's his business. As long as he's not endangering your life or his own, let it go. You probably just know enough of the story to be dangerous.

- Don't battle over the bill other than to impress your boss that you're a team player. Even if you don't want to feel beholden, who pays the check does nothing to alter who the boss is. If your boss wants to play the big shot, what possible benefit can you derive from spoiling his moment? Save your money.

- Don't turn down your boss's invitation to dine with him. Claiming that you have too much work to do only works with sadists and they probably won't ask you anyway. They'll do everything they can to keep you from eating.

If your boss asks you to lunch, go. Your company is obviously more important to him than the work you're doing. Resist setting your priorities ahead of his.

■ Make the most out of the opportunity to make your points to the boss while he's a captive audience. Or use the time to listen and learn. Every time bosses open their mouths, they are bound to provide you with valuable information about what makes them tick and what pulls their triggers. Knowledge is power.

Working Through the Meal

I worked for one group vice president who never stopped for lunch and didn't approve of anyone else taking a midday break. Fortunately, his office was in New York City and I was based in California. George was tall and intimidating. He smoked long cigars and left the office promptly at 5 p.m. to slam down hard liquor at any one of New York's finer restaurants, sometimes pausing long enough to eat dinner. I don't recall if he picked up the tab when I was with him or if I expensed the meal because I was the one traveling. Lunch, however, was a moot point.

George believed breaking for lunch wasted time and energy, and it was difficult to focus people after a "lunch two-hour" as it was called around the New York offices. George wouldn't even tolerate the disruption of having lunch brought in. I can recall a boardroom full of George's unit general managers, of which I was one, starving, turning pale, weakening by the moment, suffering low blood-sugar hallucinations, with stomachs growling in concert with one another.

Finally, someone summoned the courage to speak up. "George," the GM said in a quivering voice, "do you think we can break for lunch?" The rest of us exchanged cautious glances as George sat back in his green leather chair and took a puff on his long cigar.

"If you need to," he said with a sigh, "go ahead. But I'm going to keep working."

That was that. George was being a kind boss, allowing his sniveling, spineless, weak, milk toast general managers to go eat, "if they needed to." The only option to prove we were not sniveling, spineless, weak, milk toast general managers was to stick it out until 5 p.m. and then go gorge ourselves like the starving animals we were. After boot camp with Big Bill, I was able to function well with Cigar George.

I was able to apply Big Bill lessons to George. It wasn't that I developed calluses to protect myself from belligerent men in powerful positions; I truly learned to empathize and see them as human beings who were just as susceptible to stupidity as I was, but too mean and seized up in their own stuff to discuss it. Once you stop resenting and playing the victim, it is amazing how comments, behaviors, and attitudes that would otherwise have driven you into hiding dissipate into thin air.

Vacation Requests

I'm much more willing to meet offsite these days. I've even found that meeting offsite has some practical applications, especially in dealing with I-Bosses. If your I-Boss gives you grief about requesting your vacation time the way George gave people grief about going to lunch, take him offsite.

During your meal together, lead your I-Boss into a conversation about his vacation. Milk it for all it's worth. Encourage him, *beg him* not to leave out a single detail. Pay attention to the adjectives he uses to describe the landscape, the wind, the waves, the smell of fresh pine forests, whatever. If he says two weeks just didn't seem long enough, make a mental note. After he has worked himself into a euphoric state, tell him you want to take the same amount of time he did, go where he went, and, using his adjectives, have the same experience he had. Once the time off is granted, go where you want to go.

His nostalgia, combined with that full-tummy feeling, will be the best possible moment for you to ask. Nothing back at the office can match it. Hopefully, you're eating alone with him. But if that's not possible, take your shot anyway. You just gave your peers a lesson well worth the price of admission. Being away from the office tends to make people forget deadlines, pressure, and problems of all kinds. Get him to commit before you finish dessert.

Food works well with all boss types. Even masochists and paranoids feel cheerier with a blood-sugar rush. Asking a God Boss for your vacation over an off-site meal, especially if you're paying for it, increases the probability of success. His kingdom will be a little less familiar. His omnipotence will seem a little less omnipotent. Overall, he's more vulnerable. Back at the office, you'll need to do much more penance to get the dates you want. Picking up the tab might be enough to put him over the edge.

Machiavellian Bosses can be handled similarly to I-Bosses vis-à-vis the restaurant vacation request. Using his descriptions, tell him you think the head of the company should require all employees to take vacations exactly like his. Promise him you'll tell everyone at your vacation destination that your boss [so-and-so] sent you. He'll be most cooperative if he thinks your vacation will help expand his sphere of influence.

Sadistic Bosses are a complex challenge when it comes to vacation requests. In a restaurant situation, poke at your food but don't eat. Lay your fork down and sigh. When she smiles that serpent-like smile and asks what's wrong, tell her you have vacation time coming and you just hate to go on vacation.

She'll be suspicious at first, but stay with the program. Explain that all you ever do on vacations is worry about the work back at the office. No matter where you go, you can't get your mind off the pile on your desk. Describe how you always fret about the money you spent traveling to an exotic place only to sit on a sun-swept beach in complete misery. Plead with her not to make you go. Tell her if she forces you to take vacation time, you'll insist on taking work with you. Slam-dunk.

Tell your Masochistic Boss you'll take lots of pictures and tell him every detail of the fun you had as soon as you get back. You'll even call in and let him listen to the surf once in a while to help him die of envy. Mention how you'll leave travel brochures on your desk while you're gone and download a picture of paradise for a screensaver so he can be miserable every day you're away. He might even extend your time off.

Asking a Buddy Boss for vacation time is dangerous. She'll readily grant you the time off. But she'll want to come with you. Offer to organize an office vacation slide show party when you return. She might go for that. If she still insists on accompanying you, hang tough. Try telling her you're meeting a stranger from an Internet chat room, your mother is coming along, or there's a typhoid warning where you're going.

If nothing dissuades her, you might need to include her in your travel plans. But all is not lost. Insist on booking the tickets and accommodations. Blaming it all on the travel agency after the fact, send her to another continent while you wing your way to an undisclosed destination.

A Paranoid Boss will suspect you are going to use your time off to further the global conspiracy against him. Win his temporary trust over lunch by offering to test his food. If he still resists granting time off because you're involved in a plot, invite him to go along. You might need to actually purchase a companion ticket and hand it to him. Make sure it's fully refundable if you want to get your money back when he refuses to go.

A one-on-one lunch with a Paranoid Boss is best for a vacation request for the same blood-sugar advantage as with the others. His confidence might be elevated just enough for the companion ticket to work. Promise to give him your complete itinerary and telephone numbers of the places where you'll be staying, including the local American Consulates.

Lean over the table slightly and whisper that you'll carry a sealed envelope on your person at all times containing the names of all the conspirators to be mailed to him in the event of your untimely death. If you live through your vacation and don't mysteriously lose the envelope, you'll present it to him upon your return. Hopefully, he'll buy into enough of your nonsense to grant you the time off before he figures out that the only way you would know if his lunch was safe to taste is if you were part of the conspiracy to poison him.

A Good Boss will need no such manipulation. She'll bug you to make sure you take all the time you have coming because she's truly concerned with your personal and professional health and well-being. When you return, she'll probably take you to lunch to hear all about your time away. Don't forget the pictures.

I-Boss Bonding Specifics

Schmoozing over coffee, drinks, and meals is part of Western culture, especially business culture. Use these opportunities to bond with your I-Boss in ways that will make life easier for you back at the office. Remember to talk about what the I-Boss wants to talk about. Laugh at the I-Boss's jokes and funny stories, even if it's fifth time you've heard the one about how his dog vomited on his neighbor's newspaper. Your I-Boss is in search of an audience. He wants to be heard.

Your jokes, funny stories, or great ideas about how the office should be run are not on his agenda. You need to respond to the image he sees in his foggy mirror. The last thing you want to do is clean his looking glass. However, mealtime is another terrific opportunity for you to play detective and study the image he sees in his foggy mirror. Then dress your ideas and suggestions up to appear equally foggy. In other words, make them appear to be his ideas and suggestions or at least make them appear as they would in his mirror, not yours.

Whenever humanly possible, order from the menu what your I-Boss orders. Eat at the same pace at which your I-Boss eats so you'll finish your meal at the same time he finishes. With your I-Boss talking so much, you'll need to be patient. Don't shovel food into your mouth while he's talking. Wait and take a bite when he does. Draw your fork or spoon toward your mouth in a mirrored motion to his.

Maintain this culinary discipline to make him unconsciously feel as if you're an extension of him. When your I-Boss pauses to take a bite, you'll be biting, too, and won't be tempted to add anything to the conversation. Let there be silence. He will break it soon enough. As you chew your food, your Idiot Boss will be talking with his mouth full. Concentrating on eye contact will help you fight back the nausea.

Idiot Bosses reveal some of their innermost thoughts while they are chewing. If your I-Boss gets some food stuck on his face or between his teeth, politely point to that spot on your face or teeth. If he gets the message and removes the food, great. If not, forget it. You did your best. When he gets down to serious business philosophy, track his line of thinking, as difficult as that might be. Be an active listener. Maintain eye contact, nod frequently, and repeat key words and phrases aloud while nodding your head. "Uh, huh. Think out of the box!" "...the big dog on the street." "...your cheese." "...to infinity and beyond."

Be careful not to outshine your I-Boss's dexterity with the silverware. If he eats peas with a knife, you eat peas with a knife. If he eats salad with a spoon, you eat salad with a spoon. If he stirs coffee with his spoon handle, do the same, even if you haven't used your spoon for your salad. If this means holding your fork in such a way that it protrudes from the end of your fist, get used to it. You want your I-Boss to be comfortable and unthreatened around you. His sense of ease and familiarity will pay dividends.

If you're spotted at the restaurant by your peers, acknowledge everyone graciously. You can always claim you were there under duress or pleading for better department-wide working conditions. If coworkers approach your table and ask how things are going, seize the opportunity, chuckle, and say, "Our boss was just telling me about the time his dog hurled chunks all over the *Sunday Times*." Horrified expressions will come over their faces and they will back away from the table slowly. Your I-Boss will appreciate what a good listener you are and you'll have your peers' sympathy for the rest of your life.

Raising the Steaks

When your I-Boss invites you to lunch with an important client or someone higher up the corporate food chain, you must split the difference. When the big cheese isn't looking, but your I-Boss is, imitate the I-Boss. When you think you can get away with it, imitate the big cheese. It's likely your I-Boss will hog the conversation, including his dog-vomit story that gets 'em every time. You have helped create that delusion, but nobody else needs to know that.

Fade into the woodwork at these multi-tier gatherings, observe, and learn. A drama will be played out in front of your eyes that could possibly reveal why the big boss tolerates your Idiot Boss, and it won't be for his jokes and funny stories. While your I-Boss entertains, you and the kahuna can chew your food. Your I-Boss isn't playing to you anymore.

This gives you an opportunity to raise your level of table manners to match the person highest on the food chain. Laugh only when and if the big kahuna or client laughs. If the client or mega-boss doesn't laugh at your I-Boss's humor, make eye contact with your I-Boss and wink as if to say, "You're really funny, boss. What does this schmuck know?"

Save Your I-Boss's Bacon

Meals are social events. If ever there is an opportunity to demonstrate how adept you are in the social graces, mealtime is your chance to shine. You can be a Miss Manners graduate with a specialization in silverware usage, memorize wine lists and cross-reference them to historical rainfall totals in various regions of France and the Rhine Valley—and still blow it if you forget who's boss. Your shining comes from helping your I-Boss shine, not in outshining him.

Your vastly superior knowledge of fine dining can score points with your Idiot Boss when you use that knowledge to spare him embarrassment. If you don't have vast knowledge of table etiquette, go online, to the library, or to charm school and get some. Even Idiot Bosses don't seem to mind gentle reminders about which fork to use for what. "I love a crisp salad," you croon on the way to the restaurant where you and your I-Boss will meet a big muckety-muck for a meal, "...which I eat with the little fork way on the outside, of course."

Your Idiot Boss will look at you and repeat, "Of course," as if he knew all along.

"Unless, of course, they offer me a chilled fork," you continue.

"Of course," your I-Boss agrees. "Chilled is always better."

He won't admit it, but your boss is willing, even anxious, to take cues from you regarding table manners. That is unless he's a completely clueless idiot, in which case it's every diner for herself. In the event he is open to suggestions, make them. The more dependent you can make him regarding socially acceptable behavior, the more he owes you. If, as I've said, knowledge is power, then knowing your way around a meal served with white gloves is awesome power.

Put your superior intelligence-gathering skills to work and find out about the muckety-muck's proclivities. Usually, a big kahuna's secretary will gladly divulge, when asked, what his favorite wine is, whether he prefers well-done steak or tartar, and anything else that will help you make his dining experience pleasurable. Then turn around and let your I-Boss know what you found out. Hopefully, he's bright enough to realize how to use such information to his advantage. Even better, he'll appreciate that you are a font of career-enhancing data.

When cross-cultural issues present themselves, you have an opening wide enough to drive a truck through. You've always urged your Idiot Boss not to slip off his shoes under the dinner table. Now you can enlighten him on all kinds of foot etiquette, from removing his shoes at a fine Japanese restaurant (you might want to carry an extra pair of socks in case his toe is sticking out of his) to never showing the sole of his shoe to a Korean. Cultural mores from anywhere on the planet are easily researchable on the World Wide Web. All you need do is stay ahead of the game, anticipate any faux pas your I-Boss is likely to commit, do your research, and coach him. In all likelihood, he'll appreciate your efforts.

Suffer Fools Kindly

In defense of Idiot Bosses, not all employees are Einsteins by any stretch of the imagination. In many organizations, the game of who's the biggest idiot never ends. The head of a university department asked me to become an adjunct faculty member as we sat in a swanky (and pricey) coffee shop. I was drinking one of those 35 cents-per-ounce Mango-Banana-Guava Surprise health drinks and he had an iced coffee concoction of some kind.

My health drink came in a small plastic bottle with a hermetically sealed yellow plastic screw-off top. Why a health-oriented product so obviously part of the hippy-dippy, granola-eating, intellectually elite university village culture is sold in a container with a half-life of six million years is beyond me. Nonetheless, I eased my conscience with the thought that, if my empty Mango-Banana-Guava Surprise container is still bothering anyone six million years from now, they will no doubt possess the technology to turn it into rocket fuel.

My new boss was pointing out the courses I'd be teaching in the university catalogue when I reached out, picked up the drink in front of me, and started sucking refreshment through the straw. I instantly realized I hadn't been drinking my Mango-Banana-Guava Surprise through a straw. I had wrestled the yellow lid off and was guzzling it like John Wayne at Miss Clara's Virginia City Saloon and Pleasure Palace.

The straw in my mouth belonged to my new boss's frozen coffee concoction, as did the frozen coffee concoction I was swallowing. In one seamless motion, I deftly placed the frozen coffee concoction back on the table between us and snatched the plastic Mango-Banana-Guava Surprise bottle as if I had been holding it all along. If he noticed, he didn't say anything—even when he picked up his frozen coffee concoction a few moments later and started sipping through the communal straw.

I matched his motion by taking a swig from my six-million-year plastic bottle. It was one of those moments you wish you could rewind and erase like a commercial on videotape. If he saw what I did and played along with my charade, he was either in desperate need of adjunct faculty members or he was willing to accept the idiot in all of us.

I figure, if he is willing to accept the stupidity I bring to the relationship, it's only fair for me to cut him similar slack. If we little folks muster enough courage to put our work environment complaints under a microscope, we might just see the troublesome attitudes and behaviors we project on our bosses have our own fingerprints all over them. Admit it and note it on the inventory.

When it's our turn at boss, we need to accept that folks will drink through our straws now and then. Fortunately for me, he turned out to be a Good Boss. So, I'll never really know if he wasn't paying attention, or if he graciously spared the idiot who drank some of his 35 cents-per-ounce frozen coffee concoction and pretended nothing happened.

11

Idiocy: Theoretical, Theological, and Biological Roots

If idiots didn't exist, would we create them?

The Eleventh Step:
"Through prayer and meditation, I seek to increase contact with God, as I interpret Him, praying for knowledge of His will and the courage to carry it out."

The original (and wordier) 12th step refers to God, "...as we understand Him." Isn't that like saying we make up our own image to worship and hit Him up for help? God, as I picture Him, looks and sounds like Henry Kissinger to the 100th power, although He probably doesn't need glasses or a Harvard Ph.D.

Twelve-step recovery programs inspired by Bill W., as marvelous and life-changing as they are, nevertheless presaged political correctness. How tired God must become with our human hedging, "...as we understand Him." We're incapable of understanding Him. He's God, we're not.

"Kids," he sighs rhetorically, resting His white-bearded chin in the palm of His almighty hand, "what's to understand? I am who I am. I gave you a 10-step program for successful living. Now you need 12? Oy Gevalt!"

I believe God has a will and a plan far more advanced and potentially positive than anything I can devise. The secret is to get in touch with His will and His plan for how we should spend our time and energy. And I don't think it includes resentment and frustration.

He didn't send Moses down the mountain toting two heavy stone tablets containing 10 suggestions. For that He could have given Moses a Palm Pilot.

I want a God who is beyond my understanding. Someone so omnipresent His protection means something, so omnipotent His plan is a guaranteed success if followed, and so omniscient that nothing will surprise Him. How boring it must have been for God to watch *Let's Make a Deal* when He already knew what Monte Hall was hiding behind each door and curtain. There is no hiding around corners or in closets from an omnipresent God. He's everywhere I am and everywhere everybody else is at the same time.

Many of my colleagues in the academy, the club you join when you earn a Ph.D, mock the notion that a whale swallowed Jonah. They feel only gullible fools could believe in such fairy tales. Theologian Charles Swindoll said the God he believes in could have made Jonah swallow the whale if He'd wanted to play it that way. I'll believe in that God, thank you. And I don't understand Him. I don't know many people who truly understand themselves, much less the One who created them.

God's Grace and Your I-Boss

I've heard God's grace defined as blessings I don't deserve and His mercy defined as sparing me the punishment I do. Whatever blessings He extends to me, He also extends to my I-Boss. That's the amazing thing about grace. If you elevate your perspective high enough, you will no longer see smart people vs. dumb people, you'll just see people. I believe a divine Creator made (1) an environment that will forgive most any ecological disaster, (2) carbon-based bodies that heal themselves of most ailments despite how much we abuse them, and (3) minds that can reflect on the human condition—past, present, and future—and make improvements.

Maybe Idiot Bosses are not a mistake after all. Perhaps God made Idiot Bosses to keep us honest and humble. Is it possible that I-Bosses are not the freaks of evolution we initially perceive them to be? Do we need I-Bosses in our lives and we're just too proud to admit it? Who else can we blame for our continual career frustrations? Do we hate our Idiot Bosses because they deserve it or because they can't defend themselves? Are we the bullies and our I-Bosses the 98-pound weaklings?

Are I-Bosses part of the same food chain that includes the rest of us? If one person's floor is another person's ceiling, is one person's I-Boss another person's hero? Although we sometimes go off on our customers, at the end of the day, we are all somebody else's customer? Am I asking too many questions? What do you think?

I have sometimes invented Idiot Bosses in my life to evade capture and punishment for my own transgressions. Scapegoats are easier to find than solutions. Why spend energy planning for a better future when I can spend it all whining about the present and the past? We create idiots so we can stand on someone's shoulders to keep our heads above the flood of stupidity to which we all contribute. The stories about idiots are legion. They clog up cyberspace like hairs in the shower drain. Despite the reports, I'm not so sure these people are all idiots. They might merely be idiots of convenience that we trump up to make ourselves feel better.

Among my esteemed colleagues is a great teacher and a terrible golfer, all rolled into one, a distinction I reserved for myself until we met. He is a scientist and I am a philosopher. His discipline is exact science. Behavioral science, despite its moniker, is an art form. In the precise world in which he operates, fools are easily quantifiable and he snipes at them without a second thought. My friend sent me a collection of actual answers to test questions submitted to science and health teachers by students. These might have appeared in your cyber flotsam at some point:

1. H_2O is hot water and CO_2 is cold water.
2. When you smell an odorless gas, it is probably carbon monoxide.
3. Water is composed of two gins, Oxygen and Hydrogen. Oxygen is pure gin. Hydrogen is water and gin.
4. Momentum: What you give a person when they are going away.
5. Vacuum: A large empty space where the Pope lives.
6. Germinate: To become a naturalized German.

Sure, go ahead and laugh. I might have given some of those answers in desperate sweaty moments when I took undergraduate final exams after skipping classes all semester. It's easy for smart people, especially scientists, to think of the rest of us as idiots. Their questions have only one correct answer. Look at these answers philosophically or artistically and you can appreciate the trend toward multiple intelligences, which is another way of saying that we're not all scientists. There is no single right answer in dealing with human beings.

Idiots: Real or Not Real?

Idiots in the workplace can either be real or imagined. If they are real, we need to deal with them. If they are imagined, we need psychiatric help. Former Secretary of State Dean Acheson wrote, "A memorandum is written not to inform the reader, but to protect the writer." Not if you're an idiot. Try some of these actual management comments on for size:

- "Teamwork is a lot of people doing what I say."
- "Doing it right is no excuse for not meeting the deadline."
- "My hope is that we can boil down these two documents and make three."
- "This project is so important, we can't let more important things interfere with it."
- "E-mail is not to be used to pass on information or data. It should be used only for company business."
- "We know communication is a problem, but the company is not going to discuss it with the employees."

There are two ways to ensure your words will be memorialized— say something exceptionally wise or exceptionally stupid. The managers who made the aforementioned comments thought their logic was as solid as Gibraltar. One even gave me a pamphlet a former employee had published, filled with his convoluted logic. He thought the publication was a tribute. I thanked him for the pamphlet and excused myself. I was late for a meeting back on Earth.

If you really want to know the answer to the question at the top of this chapter, "If Idiot Bosses didn't exist, would we create them?" you must first accept that it's a stupid question. Idiot Bosses do exist, by anyone's definition. The better question is, "How do you survive them?" A deeper and more ominous question is, "Am I really an idiot trying to live a life of denial and disguise?" Maybe I'm even projecting my own stupidity on an Idiot Boss, making him appear worse than he truly is.

It's in the blood

Genetics is yet another way we should be able to connect with our Idiot Bosses at some level. Some of us have Irish blood, others have German, or worse, Irish *and* German. What can you expect when you mix naturally conquering people with a weakness for alcohol? Most likely, Lutherans or Irish Catholics. Some people have Italian blood, some have French. You do the math. For most of us, if we trace the roots of our family trees deep enough, there are bound to be idiots in the woodpile.

Try looking at your I-Boss through a twisted lens for a change. The bloodlines are not in their favor. This explains their anemic comprehension skills. When you attempt to persuade an I-Boss to do something, your first task is to help him grasp the concept. Give him the benefit of the doubt. Idiot Bosses want to be liked despite the fact they are so dislikable. Keep saying to yourself, "He really means well." Not that saying it makes everything whole again. But at least it lifts the shroud of evil intentions. Compare your I-Boss to other boss types with truly evil intentions and you'll appreciate him more.

Good Bosses always mean well and generally have the intelligence to do well. Many Idiot Bosses would be Good Bosses if they could just hold a thought long enough without getting bored and trying to play management. The line that separates Good Bosses from I-Bosses is sometimes as thin as a few points on the intelligence compass. Good Bosses are concerned primarily with the growth and development of their team members because they know highly motivated people are highly productive.

The intelligence factor separating a Good Boss from an I-Boss includes recognition that meaningless tasks I-Bosses force on their team members are counterproductive to growth and development of the individual and, subsequently, to the organization. I-Bosses don't intentionally set out to thwart the performance of their team members, they just come by it naturally. I-Bosses give lip service to reaching company goals as they parrot the mantras of motivational authors. But, in the end, they muck up the works with irrelevant tasks, inappropriate evaluations of performance, and miscommunication. They don't grasp the notion that all of the minor chaos they create daily eventually adds up to major chaos. It's all in the blood analysis report.

Concept Avoidance

Intelligence, in the right hands, makes a Good Boss effective. Stupidity, in the wrong hands, will turn an otherwise effective organization into a circus. Good Bosses know the integrity of the 10th floor depends on the integrity of the nine below it. Imagine you're having a conversation with an Idiot Boss over lunch in the penthouse restaurant of a tall building he just helped complete.

"We saved money by mixing substandard building materials with the good stuff," the I-Boss explains as he tries to pick a sesame seed out of his first molar.

You stop your salad fork just short of your open mouth, blink twice, and set the loaded fork back on your plate. "Did you just say this tall building we're sitting on top of is constructed with substandard building materials?"

"A memo came down to cut costs," the I-Boss says, flicking the sesame seed over his shoulder. "I figured that meant cutting labor or material expenses, and with the union and all, cutting labor would have been tough, so I bought some brand X items." The I-Boss slathers butter all over the rest of his sesame roll and crams it in his mouth. "Got some great-looking stuff from a guy named Freddie the Palm," he mumbles through a mouthful of roll and butter. "Really cheap, too."

"Aren't you worried?" you ask, trying to avoid looking at what he's chewing.

"Heck no." The I-Boss swallows and takes a big gulp of water. "We came in on budget and they gave me a big raise."

"I mean, do you feel safe in a building made from inferior building materials?" you ask, scanning the walls and ceiling for cracks or other telltale signs of structural failure.

The I-Boss chuckles. "You must think I'm stupid."

"I didn't say that," you snap, hoping the thought, so present in your mind, didn't slip out.

"I'll have you know," he assures you, "that I used the highest quality steel and concrete here on the upper floors where the executive offices are located. The concrete and steel more prone to structural failure are on the lower floors where the peons work."

"That was a stroke of genius," you say pleasantly as you get up from the table and exit the building as quickly as possible.

Education is probably lost on a person too block-headed to realize the health and well-being of the big picture depends on the health and well-being of its component parts. A Good Boss gets it and cares enough to do something about it. A Good Boss consistently demonstrates intelligence, character, and common sense. Common sense alone can cover a multitude of sins.

Much of the frustration we experience when dealing with Idiot Bosses comes from expecting them to demonstrate common sense. Idiots' blood doesn't appear to be sufficiently oxygenated to mentally grasp the concept of common sense. They can do sensible things, but it won't be because something is sensible. It will be the result of your efforts to lead them in that direction.

Blood Sacrifice

I-Bosses can be distinguished from other boss types by more than the presence or absence of intelligence. Consider how intelligence is used. Persons in positions of power who truly believe they are gods combine delusional thinking with superior intelligence to produce the curious cognition cocktail that guides the behavior of God Bosses. The ability to focus and stay on task can be a God Boss' strongest suit, "as he understands himself." His primary task is not the achievement of organizational goals and objectives. A God Boss's cunning behavior seldom relates to what he is being paid to do.

I've noticed world leaders, as well as corporate leaders, who actually believe they are deity, tend to have underlying paranoid tendencies. That's the only way for a God Boss to stay in power. He must repress or eliminate anyone and anything who might point out he's a mere mortal. My mom always left out the part in the *Emperor's New*

Clothes where the child who exposed the ruse was arrested by secret police, imprisoned, and tortured. I know she was trying to protect me, but if she had left it in, I would have been better prepared for corporate life.

As I mentioned before, God Bosses can't allow reasonable people within their sphere of influence to have any voice or platform from which to expose them as frauds. But silencing people and disposing of their bodies without drawing attention requires cunning. A God Boss will demonstrate his intelligence in clever-yet-diabolical schemes necessary to silence seekers and speakers of truth. A God Boss's work is never done because there will always seem be someone with a natural desire to reveal the truth—except when filing income taxes, filling out job applications, or explaining to their spouses the real reason they arrived home late. It takes most of a God Boss's energy to build a ring of sub-God henchpersons who will round up anyone even suspected of not paying proper homage.

Although a God Boss will never overtly engage in paranoid behaviors the way a Paranoid Boss will, this hyper-vigilant self-protection suggests God Bosses know they're not really gods. Even with all of the God Boss' subjects genuflecting and singing psalms of praise, the God Boss is convinced most, if not all, of them pose a threat. If God Bosses were truly omnipotent and omniscient, they wouldn't feel the need to defend themselves against insurrections, real or imagined.

The God I believe in looks down on all the rebellion targeted against Him, shakes his almighty head, and takes a mighty aspirin. To Him, insurrection is a disappointment, not a tangible threat. God Bosses remind me of historical figures, some dating back beyond the Clinton administration, who ordered family members whacked just to make sure they wouldn't be assassinated at a holiday reunion. We all saw *Godfather II*, right? If God Bosses didn't exist, would we create them? Not likely. They are of no functional use to anyone.

Machiavellian Bosses also often apply their superior intelligence to evil purposes. There is nothing wrong with the desire to succeed, mind you. I hope every person has a desire to reach ever higher. Desire plays a tremendous role in creating the standard of living we enjoy in this great nation of ours. The difference between the typical standard of living in the United States and the standard of living elsewhere in the world is rooted in the definition of success. The former Soviet Union, for example, is essentially equal to the United States in terms of natural resources and labor pool. I believe their oil reserves are even larger.

Why, then, does the average American welfare recipient have a higher income, a more comfortable home, a larger color television, and a more reliable car than the average Russian shift supervisor? The last stats I saw indicated a single mother in the United States receiving Aid to Families with Dependent Children (AFDC), with all of her cash and non-cash public assistance combined, has a higher income than 90 percent of the world's population. That doesn't mean she's rich. It means the world is full of desperately poor people.

In the old Soviet Union, Boris was the victim of a dumbed-down definition of success. Dating back to the Tsar, success was defined by keeping your head down and doing what you were told to avoid arrest, imprisonment, and torture by the secret police. The Bolshevik Revolution put an end to all that. With the Communist Party in charge, the definition of success changed to keeping your head down and doing what you were told to avoid arrest, imprisonment, and torture by the secret police.

In the new Russia, success is the ability to traffic Calvin Kline jeans on the black market, Russian-made weapons and night-vision goggles on the international black market, or open a McDonald's franchise and use your profits to pay off the secret police to leave you alone. Only when you define success in the context of what you are capable of, not merely what you're allowed to do, can life become truly rich. Unfortunately, to Machiavellians, the desire to succeed is mutually exclusive with failure in others.

Whereas a God Boss will take out someone he thinks is threatening to expose him, a Machiavellian will take people out for merely standing between her and what she wants. God and Machiavellian Bosses, being intelligent and cunning, don't pitch high-volume, dramatic tantrums, drawing attention to their activities. As with my boss at Disneyland, God and Machiavellian Bosses strike with stealth and skill to surgically remove the offending parties quietly. God and Machiavellian Bosses go a step further to send a psychological message. A small drop of blood, left clearly visible on the victim's computer keyboard for the other team members to see, is a compelling reminder of the price of irreverence or interference.

Just as God Bosses have underlying paranoia, Machiavellian Bosses have underlying narcissism. Idiot Bosses have underlying cluelessness, which I'm amazed is not a diagnostic category according to the American Psychological Association. The fact remains, God, Machiavellian, and Idiot Bosses exist, so we don't need to ponder if we would or would not create them in their absence.

An Exception to Everything

If there is no one around the office to inflict pain and suffering, a masochist will do the honors himself—to himself. Even so, he need not look very far for someone to lend him a hand as long as there are Idiot, God, Machiavellian, and Sadistic Bosses around. Idiot Bosses usually cause pain and anguish unintentionally. God Bosses cause pain and anguish as a method of guaranteeing loyalty and support. Machiavellians cause pain and anguish in their ongoing struggle to transfer all that belongs to others into the Machiavellians' offshore accounts. Sadists love to cause pain and anguish.

I find Sadistic Bosses more tolerable than Masochistic Bosses. Perhaps, tolerable is not the right word. But they are more common and their behavior seems more natural in a demented sort of way. Masochistic Bosses are reluctant leaders until they realize the dramatic opportunities for self-abuse that leadership offers. A department full of team members can be turned into an angry mob with pitchforks if you annoy and antagonize them enough.

Sadists want to be bosses from the get-go because it's the perfect setup to punish and abuse unwilling victims. Masochists love working for sadists because the sadist provides a steady and reliable dosage of pain. Sadists, on the other hand, can't stand anyone who actually enjoys pain. As a result, masochists don't last long in sadists' departments.

Vertical Mobility and Trial Lawyers

With HR departments hedging against runaway labor litigation, the safest way to get rid of undesirable parties in your department is to help them get promoted. Nobody sues for being promoted. With incompetent knuckleheads being herded up the management ladder in an effort to get them out of working departments with a minimum of paperwork and reduced out-of-court settlements, the real working folks in the mushroom stem are supporting a cap increasingly populated with nutty, unproductive, self-defeating bosses.

Once the masochists are removed from a sadist's department, the remaining people have a natural reaction to pain—they scream. The Sadistic Boss now has the smorgasbord of victims she always dreamed of. The physical and psychological injuries sadists cause are difficult to prove in court. Sadistic Bosses keep team members working needlessly long hours, thus depriving them of precious time with their families. If a beleaguered team member tries to claim his or her divorce or loss of custody is directly related to prolonged absences from the home, a clever Sadistic Boss can testify in court how she heard rumors there was marital difficulty brewing and, despite her repeated efforts to send the team member home to rekindle his or her relationship, the team member instead took refuge from the marital friction in workaholism.

It's a brilliant tactical maneuver and as close to the perfect crime as one can get. The inhuman workloads Sadistic Bosses enjoy thrusting upon their team members can lead to sleep deprivation, malnutrition, or institutionalization. In each case, a shrewdly intelligent Sadistic Boss can claim under oath the team member was overly ambitious, which will only drive the team member deeper into despair and self-destructive behavior. If Sadistic Bosses didn't exist, would I create them? Definitely not. Give me an idiot any day.

Defying Explanation

I know of no body of physical or biological evidence to explain Paranoid Bosses. They exist in a theoretical or, more specifically, imaginative world of their own creation. Whether or not we ever develop the ability to explain them, Paranoid Bosses are insufferable. Nothing you can do will satisfy or please them and it's hard to stay motivated when everything you think, say, and do is under suspicion. As with most negative energy in the universe, the cycle of paranoia feeds on itself, becomes self-perpetuating, and takes on a life of its own. The perpetual motion machine might be a myth, but a Paranoid Boss's imagination will go on forever.

If a Paranoid Boss is difficult to explain, try a Buddy/Paranoid Boss combination. Not a Buddy Boss and a Paranoid Boss, buddy and paranoid personalities coexisting in one individual. Not a dominant and sub-dominant personality, but an even split. As we've discussed, there are numerous ways to approach and deal with every boss type on various issues. The buddy/paranoid personality stumps me entirely. If I say, "Hi, boss. It's good to see you," in order to appease the buddy personality, the paranoid personality will ask, "Why?"

"Oh," I stumble on. "I just am."

"Why?"

"Because..."

"Because why?"

If you can keep up your end of the Ping-Pong match long enough, he might give up and walk away. On the other hand, if you play to the paranoid personality and confirm that there is a conspiracy, the buddy personality is likely to freak at the possibility that a group of people actually don't like her. Talk about a multiple personality problem. If you're a business owner, you might consider selling out just to get away from the paranoid/buddy combo.

Extreme Measures

I don't recommend dissolving your company as a strategy to get rid of a problem employee. That would be like burning down the house to get rid of termites. Unfortunately, with certain problem people, blowing up the building with them inside might seem like a tempting way to resolve the issue.

When I was a teenager in a fledging rock band, we settled disputes with the "blow up/regroup" method. If someone became a problem, everyone else quit the band, moved across the street to someone else's garage, and re-formed without the accused. I did it on more than one occasion and had it done to me. As adults, we need to have better skill sets than that.

Buddy Bosses often resemble Idiot Bosses, but are not as clueless. Buddy Bosses can be quite intelligent. They're just lonely, which plays into the vulnerabilities of codependents like me. I-Bosses aren't sharp enough to realize that they're lonely. That's like being so poor you don't realize you're poor. If you have a Buddy Boss, take up a collection and buy her a dog.

A cat won't work. Cats will just ignore her and not give a rip if she's home or not. Dogs are much higher maintenance and might keep your Buddy Boss occupied long enough for you to sneak away for a weekend with your spouse and kids. Your Buddy Boss will eventually need to get home and feed the dog, greatly reducing the requests to spend long evenings with you. If Buddy Bosses didn't exist, I would leave well enough alone.

Pushed to the Brink

When an individual is disruptive to departmental efficiency and cohesiveness, and that person will not respond to conflict resolution efforts or extensive attempts to construct workable solutions, it's time for the manager to separate the wayward sheep from the flock. As unpleasant as termination is, it is sometimes the best solution. An untenable situation around a problem employee hurts team members more than it hurts bosses. Bosses have the power and the obligation to address personnel problems, team members must wait and hope. I didn't want to confront the chronically late technician at Disneyland, but the other team members deserved better.

One of the worst workplace scenarios imaginable is a disruptive and abrasive team member left to terrorize his peers and a boss who refuses to do anything about it. Chances are you've been in that situation. It's rough. Your boss is probably aware of the problem, although he might pretend he's not. To those who have never faced this situation as a boss, it's hard to explain.

Part of you doesn't want to admit you lack the skills to work it out. Part of you doesn't want to open a can of worms by addressing the problem and setting off a bomb only to find out that legally you can't dispose of it. You don't relish the thought of making an enemy out of this person. You hold out hope for some miraculous resolution to occur.

For a boss to go through the exhaustive and intricate process of terminating someone is about as pleasant as a root canal. But if you're one of the team members suffering while your boss wallows in indecision, you can do several things. Having studied what language your boss speaks and what drives his personality, you can approach him in the most diplomatic, well-thought-out manner possible and let him know how much the situation is thwarting the department's productivity and morale.

With different boss types, you'll need to determine to the best of your ability what constitutes disruption and an actionable problem in your boss's opinion. I hope you won't need to go over your boss's head to HR, but it is an option. Somebody in the organization is likely to care enough about productivity and morale to initiate some kind of action. Be reasonably assured you have identified that person before sticking your neck out.

Use caution when making an end run on your boss for any reason. If you're caught outside of your silo without a hall pass, that infraction might be more egregious to corporate muckety mucks than the real problem you're trying to bring to their attention. If you need to find someone in the organization with a spine, do your research. Find out if people have been terminated before. What was the offense? Which HR person handled it? Who is most likely to follow through?

I've taken problems to people on the organization chart who were ostensively supposed to handle them only to find out they lacked the fortitude to take action. Unfortunately, people who show more concern for the efficiency, productivity, and morale of the organizational population than for protecting their acre of corporate real estate are the exception, not the rule. The problem you're trying to bring to the attention of the appropriate parties might become the proverbial hot potato.

Assume you're on your own until you can find reasonable assurance you will be supported. Don't assume you will be supported, even if your organization's Standard Operating Procedures say you will. Any executive with sufficient power to assist you in the event you need to go over your boss's head will represent one of the major boss types. Know who you're working with before you expose yourself to retribution. Information is power. Nothing is stopping you from gathering as much as you can.

Be Thankful

If your I-Boss is not allowing an annoying and unresolved problem to abscess, rejoice. Regardless of any theoretical, theological, or biological explanations for Idiot Bosses, be grateful. Be glad they have no consciousness about the havoc they create and nothing to prick their consciences to keep them awake at night. Let them snooze. If we lose sleep hating them, it's nobody's fault but our own. I'm not saying if I-Bosses didn't exist I would create one. Let's not get carried away. But I would gladly substitute an I-Boss for a God, Machiavellian, Sadistic, Masochistic, Paranoid, or Buddy Boss any day.

With gratitude in your heart, practice generic compliments you can give your Idiot Boss. Word them in such a way so you won't be lying—exactly. Be prepared at any moment to say, "Gee, boss, you really make a difference around here." Or, "If you weren't around, things sure would be different." These comments have multiple meanings, allowing you to keep at least one foot in the truth.

Imagine the poor souls who haven't read this book. They're still blaming their Idiot Bosses for their career frustrations and plotting a coup. You, on the other hand, are an enlightened creature, realizing that, without your I-Boss, things could be much worse. Remember that next Thanksgiving when your I-Boss doesn't invite himself to eat at your house.

12

The Open Hand

Pretend for a moment you've just marched into your Idiot Boss's office in a righteous rage. You plant yourself directly in front of his desk with your feet shoulder-width apart. Clench your fist, shake it in his face, and say, "You miserable so-an-so. I'm smarter and more talented than you. I work harder and get more accomplished in one day than you do in a month. If you had half a brain you would treat me with the respect I deserve, double my vacation time, give me a raise, and beg me not to quit."

Feels good doesn't it? For a moment, it does. When you're driving on the freeway, do you shake your fist at other drivers and say, "You ignorant so-and-so, where did you learn how to drive? If I wasn't late for work I'd pull over and pound some sense into you"? When you arrive at the office, do you brag to your fellow team members how you cursed pathetic drivers on your way to work? Is that the high point of your day?

When we're stuck behind slow drivers, we hit the gas at our first opportunity and whip around them. If traffic is slow all over, we clench the wheel and simmer. When we're in a long line at the gourmet coffee shop or the bank, we fidget nervously or start a slow boil. If a clerk at the bank or the dry cleaners has the privilege of waiting on us after a slow traffic or cappuccino day, she just might get a piece of our mind that has nothing to do with her. Feels good, doesn't it?

Allowing steam to build up and blowing it off means living through long periods of mounting tension, interspersed with brief episodes of relief. Altering the way you value your time and effort means long

225

periods of fulfillment, interspersed with occasional moments of tension. Just because something feels familiar doesn't mean it feels good. Getting angry doesn't do you any good. What if you didn't get angry to begin with? How would that feel? To remain serene and calm in the face of otherwise pressured, tense, and aggravating situations—that feels good. That's how to work for an Idiot Boss.

Pretend again you've just marched into your Idiot Boss's office in a righteous rage. You plant yourself directly in front of his desk with your feet shoulder width apart. Open your hand up with fingers spread wide apart. Keeping it that way, shake it in his face, and say, "You miserable so-an-so. I'm smarter and more talented than you. I work harder and get more accomplished in one day than you do in a month. If you had half a brain you would treat me with the respect I deserve, double my vacation, give me a raise, and beg me not to quit."

Feels different, doesn't it? It's clenched fist vs. open hand, tight vs. loose, anger vs. appeal, rage vs. reason. When all is said and done, the 12-step program for recovering idiots will open your hand, your mind, and your options. Clenching something in your fist requires energy. Letting something go taps the energy of the natural universe. Clenching something in your emotional fist squeezes much of the life out of it. Holding it in an open hand allows life to flow into it.

Your reactive ego might prefer a two-fisted approach to life, especially with idiots. Your heart prefers the open hand. Your reactive ego wants to tighten up. Your heart wants to relax and let things flow. Your two-fisted self says, "I'm not going to give that so-and-so the pleasure and benefit of my best work or one drop of extra effort." Your heart says, "I can do what's in my job description with my eyes closed. I do my best work because it makes me feel good about myself. If it helps somebody else, so be it."

Do you want to thrive or just survive at work? If thriving sounds good, open your fist and let go. "But, Dr. John," you say, "I'm familiar and comfortable with anger, frustration, and resentment."

"Sure, you're familiar and comfortable with anger, frustration, and resentment," I agree. "But do they make you happy?"

Didn't think so. Open your fist and let them go. Every day, when you wake up with clenched fists, open them up and let go. By midmorning when the idiotic restraints, constraints, and pressures of the system make you want to clench both fists, let go. By lunch, when you feel like a week has passed and you want to shake your fist in somebody's face, let go. By mid-afternoon, when you've about decided living with open hands is for the birds, remember birds don't have hands.

Most creatures don't need opposable thumbs because they don't reflect on their circumstances and calculate how miserable and angry they are. Therefore, they don't need to clench fists full of anger, frustration, and resentment. They are truly in the moment, looking out for number one, living one day at a time, doing the best with what they have. Animals don't resent what they don't have.

Look at the good things in your life, the bad things, and give them all to your Higher Power. If you find you just can't live without anger, frustration, and resentment, there is plenty more available. Once you feel the difference between living with clenched fists and open hands, you'll relax your fingers as soon as you notice they're closing.

Give Away the Credit

In the workplace, as anywhere, the old saying applies: Compliments are like fertilizer. They don't do any good until they're spread around. Distribute them liberally. You can never go wrong by spreading encouraging words. They might be nothing more than fertilizer, but fertilizer can make things grow faster and bigger.

Don't act like a Machiavellian and feel as if you're robbing yourself just because you're allowing acclaim to flow to others. There is plenty of goodness for everyone. The more credit you give others, the more likely you'll receive some in return. If you extend credit for the sole purpose of receiving credit in return, you'll become resentful if nothing comes back. Give freely, expect nothing in return, and you won't be disappointed. Your emotional generosity, however, sets a tone that's likely to beget more generosity. If not, you have the satisfaction of knowing you did the right thing. There is no limit to how many times you can do the right thing and there's no limit to the satisfaction.

I've described how to give unwarranted praise to Idiot Bosses and others for the purpose of positioning yourself. Giving credit to others who deserve it is slightly different. It's always appropriate to congratulate superior effort and it's no more than you desire for yourself. Allowing credit for your ideas to go to someone else might make you feel like clenching your fists again, unless you put it in perspective. If you're living a big-picture life, you won't sweat the unimportant stuff and keep score when you do and don't get all the recognition you feel should be coming to you.

If you make it a personal policy to intentionally allow your boss and other team members the first drink from the cup of recognition, you will impress yourself. You will also impress anyone else who is paying attention. And even if no one else notices, you won't feel resentment because you are exercising your own free will. As some of my Baptist friends say, you're adding another jewel to your heavenly crown. My Jewish friends would say, you're being a mench. I say it's like putting on your own oxygen mask first.

Be Part of Something Big

No matter what work you do or what industry you're in, you can take pride in being part of the big picture. One of the times I premeditatedly and with forethought turned the credit for one of my ideas over to my boss was during a consulting assignment for a major defense contractor in California. I was hired to help integrate the technical trainers with the soft-skills trainers to create a unified training department. The task was similar to the cultural integration required to bring the audio and lighting techs out of the Disneyland Maintenance Division and into the Entertainment Division, and would have been simple if not for the web of hidden agendas, old grievances, and grudges built up over the years.

In my usual manner, I looked for commonality among the players. That's what sets the stage for cooperation among individuals and factions that, underneath the feigned civility of the white-collar workplace, really want to beat each other with tire irons. These people were so deep in their own tar pits they had long ago lost sight of the importance of the work they were doing. They built rocket engines for NASA. Their products propelled men and women into space. They were part of space exploration, past, present, and future. So, why did they walk around like post-lobotomy geeks with vinyl protectors in the breast pockets of their short-sleeved Oxford shirts?

My first thought was to restore these guys into pre-lobotomy geeks with vinyl protectors in the breast pockets of their short-sleeved Oxford shirts. As an outsider, I could see the forest and I tried to imagine what it must feel like to be part of something like the space program. When I worked for the Disneyland Entertainment Division, I felt proud to be part of something so extremely important and widely recognized.

In the Disney Way management programs Mike Vance initiated around 1970, management candidates spend time in the Park as Disney characters. It seemed like a cutsie idea when I heard about it. But it was more than that. I walked out of the various gates between the backstage areas and the onstage areas a dozen times a day. The signs at each gate reminded us we were going onstage. Underneath each sign was a full-length mirror. Even as a "suit" who drew no attention from Park guests, I had a sense that I was part of a proud culture.

Everyone did. Popcorn vendors, performers, and street sweepers, all felt the Disney pride when they went "onstage." Yet, I didn't fully understand it until I stepped onstage with my fellow Disney Way seminar participants dressed in character costumes. The costumes were assigned based on height. I wore Eeyore. We walked onstage in Frontierland near the Country Bear Jamboree. I had walked through that gate a thousand times before. This time, I saw everyone for 100 yards turn and light up at the sight of me and the other Disney Way participants. They charged us.

It took me almost a full minute to grasp what was happening. People of all ages and all nationalities ran up, hugged me, and started talking as if they'd known me their entire lives. Of course they were talking to Eeyore. One lady reached around and handed me my tail. "You need to hang on to this so you won't loose it again," she said in all seriousness. The same thing was happening to the other characters.

In those few minutes, I realized as never before how I was part of something woven into the fabric of people's lives the world over. In character costume, you don't talk. I just listened and experienced what it was like for my identity to dissolve into this much bigger thing. Harboring resentments and hostilities means it is all about you. When it ceases being about you and starts being about the bigger picture, resentment and hostility go away.

After I had helped move the theatrical audio and lighting functions from the Disneyland Maintenance Division to the Entertainment Division, but before my Machiavellian Boss had made his brilliant blitzkrieg move to seize power, an airline ticket holder was dropped on my desk. "What's this?" I quizzed the runner from the Walt Disney Travel Company, across the street at the Disneyland Hotel.

"You're on the 3:30 nonstop from LAX to Kennedy," he said as he headed out the door. I would have called after him, but my phone rang.

"Did you get your ticket yet?" It was the Show Development director, the one with the desk-diving secretary.

"Y-y-yeah," I stuttered. "What's this all about?"

"We just got the green light to do a target market tour starting in New York City, then Toronto, Winnipeg, Calgary, Edmonton, Vancouver, Seattle, and San Francisco. We need you to book theatrical venues in each of those cities. You leave for New York this afternoon. Good luck."

At 8 a.m. the following morning (5 a.m. California time) I was standing in front of Lincoln Center. I started trying doors. One building after another was locked. I walked around to the side street and tried the back doors unsuccessfully until I reached the stage door at Avery Fisher Hall. I tugged at the door handle and it opened. I walked inside and into the first open door in the long hallway. It was the office of the house manager—just the person I needed to see. "I need to book a theater," I said.

He stared at me as if to say, "Sure you do, kid. Pardon me while I call Bellevue and find out if there are any psych patients missing this morning." I wasn't sure why he doubted my sincerity. He looked more annoyed than amused as he reached for the telephone to call security. I pulled out my business card and laid it on his desk in front of him. He glanced at it curiously and stopped dialing. He picked up the card with one hand and hung up the receiver with the other. He looked at the card, then at me, and then the card again. The card featured a gold foil embossed Cinderella's Castle along with my name and the words "Disneyland Entertainment Division." I could almost hear him thinking, "This is a horse of a different color."

A radical attitude transformation registered on his face and within 20 minutes, I had my date and my venue. Less than 16 hours after the airline ticket folder had been plopped on the top of my desk in Anaheim, California I had booked a date at Avery Fisher Hall at Lincoln Center in New York City on the power of my business card and the company it represented. It was the world-renown reputation of Walt Disney and his organization that made people sit up and take notice.

Within the week, I returned to Anaheim with theaters booked from New York to San Francisco and all the way across Canada. In some cities, I landed, grabbed a cab into town, booked the hall, and immediately hopped a flight to the next city. No one questioned that business card. Nobody asked for additional identification or a down payment. They reacted to me as part of the Disney organization, not as John Hoover.

It wasn't until after I left Disney that I began to fully realize the incredible power I was able to wield as a member of that team. I had greater financial success after Disney than I would have had inside, but I never again achieved the pure status I had as a young person representing that firm. Like the space program, Disney was greater than the sum of its parts.

Lost Perspective Can Be Regained

Despite their place in history, some of the defense contractor people I later consulted had been on the job for 20 years or more and the thrill was gone. They had lost perspective on what they were part of. The bloom was off the rose. The rocket had lost its luster—literally. The cone-shaped rocket engine in front of the corporate headquarters building was nearly 20 feet tall and covered with bird droppings. Not one or two, here and there. The rocket had been a unisex toilet for our fine-feathered friends for a long time. They must have thought it was an enormous automobile.

I started dropping hints about how proud the space program people must be of the role they played in making history. The bird poop stayed. Finally I said, "If I was on the team that put a man on the moon and sends space shuttles around the earth on a regular basis, that rocket out front would be a symbol of my career accomplishments."

About a week later, the rocket had a gleaming new paint job and looked like it could be launched into orbit. It had a visible effect on the scientists. Everyone's spirits seemed to be lifted. The director of training was as pleased as punch that he had thought to initiate the rocket refurbishment. When he described how he had come up with the notion and gone "upstairs" to sell the idea of giving corporate pride a shot in the arm, I congratulated him.

It was important to make him feel good. I needed my paycheck more than I needed credit for the idea or the popular approval of the rocket scientists. That's who those people were, the Cal Tech crowd that hacks into the Rose Bowl scoreboard every New Year's Day. The Livermore Labs bunch. When people use the euphemism rocket scientist, they're talking about those guys.

I knew, as did my father, what it was like to be part of something bigger than any individual. He worked nearly 40 years in the public relations department at the Maytag Company. Everywhere he went and everyone he talked to mentioned their positive experiences with Maytag's legendary quality. After the character of Old Lonely was created in the mid-1960s, everyone Dad encountered talked about the loneliest repairman.

What Costume Do You Wear?

Do you wear the costume of Old Lonely, the Maytag Repairman? Real Maytag repair people across the United States are proud to wear the same uniform as Old Lonely. They're part of a legacy. For decades, the Maytag factories in Newton, Iowa, called Plant I and Plant II, shut down for two weeks every summer. That was vacation time for all of the plant workers who scattered to the four corners of the continent in their station wagons and camper-trailers. And nearly every station wagon and camper had a bumper sticker that read: "We're from Newton, Iowa—Home of Maytag—The Dependability People."

How many employees today would apply a bumper sticker to their vehicles as they head out of town on vacation proudly proclaiming where they're from and the company they work for? Maytag would have never achieved its remarkable reputation for quality if it wasn't for a dedicated and proud organizational population. Maytag pride and quality were part of them and they were part of every Maytag product.

If you're not from the northeastern part of the country and have never experienced shopping at a Stew Leonard's Dairy Store, do it the first chance you get. Stew Jr., Jill, Beth, and Tom are carrying on the inspired customer service culture their still active father started decades ago. More important than the world-class customer service and unique shopping environment at Stew Leonard's is the commitment to their employees; a commitment that earned them a spot as one of *Fortune* Magazine's top 30 companies to work for.

In Stew Sr.'s own words, "You can't have a great place to shop without first making it a great place to work." Visit *www.stewleonards.com* and you'll start feeling the energy. Request a copy of *Stew's News*, their bimonthly newsletter and you'll be amazed. It's an incredible effort for Jill Leonard Tavello and her staff; usually around 60 pages of news and stories about employees and their families, featuring hundreds of employee photographs are in each issue. But it's just one part of how the leadership at Stew Leonard's constantly recognizes and celebrates their employees. The net result is tremendous dedication and unsurpassed performance.

At Stew Leonard's, as with any culture of excellence, a uniform is more than thread and fabric. It's the way you feel about yourself and what you do. It's your cloak of connectedness. You might not wear an actual uniform the way UPS or Federal Express delivery people do. Police officers, firefighters, nurses, physicians, ball players, and soldiers wear clothing that is both functional and helps identify their trades. But that doesn't mean you can't feel similar pride. If you dress professionally, you're wearing the uniform of a professional.

You can not only find something to be proud of in what you do, you can also find pride in how you do it. You might not take as much pride in the firm that employs you as you take in the profession you represent. Are you proud of being an accountant, an ad writer, an engineer, an attorney, an electrician, or a mailroom clerk? A true thespian will take a small part and make the most of it. Proud professionals make something special out of everything they do.

Whether your costume is literally on your back or figuratively in your consciousness, it connects you to something bigger than you as an individual. You're never so unimportant that your job doesn't matter. Do your job poorly and you create a demand on others to compensate. Ask them if what you do matters. Do a fantastic job and it becomes more evident how much your contribution counts.

The heartbreak comes when your best efforts are not recognized by idiots up the ladder. That's when you have a decision to make. Is your job worth doing because you are the one doing it? Do you do your job with passion and fervor, despite the absence of appreciation, because that's the kind of person you want to go home with after work? It's up to you, not your Idiot Boss, to decide how you feel about yourself as a professional.

Be Part of the Best

For most of my adult life, I've felt a need to be best at something. I've never found anything I'm best at except being me. And I can always improve. I've found great peace in giving up my fantasy of being the best and brightest. That decision has lifted a tremendous burden from my shoulders. You can kill yourself trying to be the best.

If you no longer feel a Machiavellian-like drive to be the best at the exclusion of all others, then you won't feel a need to compete with your boss to see who's best. So many people these days are brighter, more talented, and more productive than their bosses. What does it matter? Your boss is still your boss, whether you're smarter and more talented or not. And bosses don't, as a rule, enjoy being shown up. Remind yourself your boss, like you, is only one component in the big picture. There is no need to compete.

Depressurize your situation by putting your efforts into making the organization, cause, or project you're involved in "the best." If it is about the organization, cause, or project—and not about you—the need you once felt to compete with your boss, idiot or otherwise, will dissipate. Allowing others to receive praise and affirmation will ultimately relieve enormous pressure and make your life more pleasant.

Be Realistic

If you're still trying to decide if you should give credit to your I-Boss for the good work you do, consider this: He's going to take the credit anyway. That leaves you with two options: You can fight your I-Boss for the spotlight or just let go. If you fight your I-Boss, or any boss for that matter, you'll have at least one hand tied behind your back. You might think you have the horsepower to outsmart or outmuscle your boss and you might be right, but only if your boss is all you have to deal with.

Focusing on the big picture and your role in it will put a new expression on your face. It's the kind of expression that makes high-level executives comfortable. There will be no death in your eyes. You will walk a little lighter and move more fluidly. You might earn the title, "company person." This will make you less popular with the cynics, but that's the miserable crowd the new you wants to distance from.

In reality, you have not given up who you are, unless being a resentful fist shaker is who you want to be. You've released the inner person to do your best work. What's changed most is why you're doing what you're doing. You're part of a grand scheme and can expand or contract your contributions (within reason) as your mood dictates. When you bring a proposal to your I-Boss, something he will attach his name or the department's name to, you give your ideas a better chance for adoption by getting your need for recognition out of the way. Recognition will come.

Organizationally speaking, to challenge your I-Boss is to put his higher-ups into an uncomfortable and potentially untenable situation. If they are so smart, why do they have idiots in their organizations? If they are idiots, whom do you think they're going to side with, you or your Idiot Boss? Even if they think you're right, the paperwork to move somebody in the organization is prohibitive. As I've already mentioned, firing people these days is next to impossible.

The more positive you feel about Idiot Bosses, the more comfortable they will feel around you. That's reality. Over time, you will no doubt have the opportunity to move up, not because of your talent and abilities, which your I-Boss wouldn't understand anyway, but because of how comfortable he feels around you. That, too, is reality. Once promoted, don't forget who promoted you. Be an effective servant-leader to your team members. Sympathize and empathize with their complaints about your boss and ask them to help you avoid the same pitfalls of anger and resentment. Stop the cycle of idiocy.

The Twelfth Step:
"These steps have me so jazzed, I want to share my joy with the world and apply them in all areas of my life."

In spite of the proverbial, "No good deed goes unpunished," giving credit to others ultimately brings blessings upon your head everywhere you go, not just at work. Once you've accepted the value of shining the spotlight on others, you'll do it at all times and in all things. Few things can revitalize a romantic relationship faster than letting go of the need to be right. The two words I've learned that restore vitality in any relationship, personal or professional, are: You're right.

That's the point of the 12th step. The investment in making such a tremendous shift in your personal paradigm must apply to all aspects of your life. If you think it's just about work-related issues, you haven't really changed. If you haven't really changed, the new behaviors at work won't hold up under pressure and you'll eventually lapse into the old attitudes and behaviors that caused you frustration to begin with.

You can be a nice person or a mean person, but not both. Don't buy into the myth that you can be mean at work and nice at home. One or the other is an act. You can be a truly nice person who tries to act like an SOB in professional affairs, the way I did by imitating Moe Green from *The Godfather*. If you can pull that off believably, you should go to Hollywood or Broadway because you have real talent. If you are an unscrupulous person and try to act like a nice person, dogs will growl at you when you walk by and mirrors won't reflect your image.

I prefer to deal with a surly, crusty, and cantankerous person over someone pretending to like me. When a telemarketer calls and asks me how I am doing, I start to simmer. I get mildly annoyed when people I know ask reflexively, "How are you?" They might really care if I tell them, although they'll be shocked. But a telemarketer doesn't know me, doesn't care anything about me except how to get my money, and yet tries to slide into an unsolicited conversation by befriending me. I'm not that desperate for friends.

If you're an unscrupulous person with the ability to convince people you really care about them, skip Hollywood and Broadway. Go straight into cold-calling sales and make some serious money. You have a histrionic personality disorder that's worth its weight in gold.

People are who they are and doing what most resonates with your essential nature will bring you the greatest sense of fulfillment. When you are doing things personally or professionally that fight your essential nature, you will be miserable and no fun to be around. If you want to survive and thrive despite your Idiot Boss, being a disnatured pain in the drain to others won't get it done.

I am guilty of staying in jobs I hated, working for people I despised, figuring I'd bide my time until I got promoted out of my misery. It never happened. I was an annoyance to everyone around me, especially my boss. Did I really believe someone higher on the food chain was going to say, "Hoover is a talented person with a pitiful attitude. Let's promote him so he can spread his ill will across more of our organization"? Talented and smart people, filled with anger and resentment, keep being passed over in favor of idiots because higher ups really hope they'll eventually take their attitudes and go away.

Terry

Your Idiot Boss might surprise you under the right circumstances. When Big Bill and I took over the audio/video production company in California, we hired a young woman named Terry as our receptionist. What a receptionist she was! On time every day, I could barely beat her to the office. If the phone rang at 8 a.m., she answered it. She was respectful and helpful with everyone and paid attention. She didn't know the words, "I don't know." If someone asked her about something beyond her immediate range of knowledge, she simply said, "Let me find out for you."

Terry kept information flowing. She knew who was in and out and could predict when people would return nearly to the minute. She was almost clairvoyant. To this day, I've never seen a sharper person with a more professional attitude. About five feet, four inches tall, she was slender and dressed well on a limited budget. She had a daughter in kindergarten and they both had a refreshing small-town, West Texas, *Last Picture Show* look.

Terry had the effect on Bill and me that any terrific team member can have on an Idiot Boss. We found ourselves trying to measure up to her. She set the standard for excellence in our offices more than we did. I was proud of her and through sheer association, I became more proud of our little company. There was no competition or resentment in her, only appreciation, gratitude, and focused good-natured professionalism.

I complimented Terry enough on her infectious attitude that she finally shared with me the joy she was finding in her 12-step program. You could have knocked me over with a paperclip. I didn't know anything about 12-step programs back then, except people joined them because they had some sort of problem. Terry left her problems in Texas, she said. She had been clean for several years and had a new lease on and passion for life.

Did she ever! I don't know how often she went to 12-step meetings, but her attitude was tuned up and running smooth and steady every day when she showed up for work. Terry had the brains and the organization skills to run our business as well, if not better, than I did. I admired how she could get her little girl up and off to school and still be so prompt and upbeat at the office every day. People with far less responsibility than she had far poorer punctuality.

We used to kid around about how we could set our watches by Terry. So, I wasn't totally surprised when she started looking a little tired. She's human after all, I thought to myself. I urged her to be a little more flexible with her time, perhaps even take time off if necessary to keep up with her daughter's needs. Acting almost embarrassed by my concern, Terry asked me not to worry and assured us all she was going to be fine.

She wasn't ever fine again. Terry finally had to call in sick. She came in less and less and, with each absence, we realized more and more how much her attitude and behavior had elevated our performance as a team. The doctors couldn't pinpoint any reason for her mysterious illnesses. In the mid 1980s, information and training in the medical community was limited when it came to the human immunodeficiency virus that had been incubating inside of her for years.

Eventually, Terry couldn't come to work at all. Our health plan took care of medical expenses and Bill had no problem keeping her on full salary. When Terry's situation started to worry us deeply, he really stepped up. Money concerns, Bill's perpetual issue, were off the table as far as Theresa was concerned. She had won us over that much.

I suspended my fretting over April's mothering as she spent most of every day at Terry's hospital bedside. We all took turns visiting her. Terry, her mind sharp as ever, reminded us of our various projects and approaching deadlines. The feelings of helplessness were beyond description. Her pretty West Texas face, with delicately chiseled features, swelled beyond recognition as her kidneys shut down and she was slowly poisoned by her own toxins. I was planning to make a hospital run one morning when April called to tell us there was no need to come anymore.

We all had to let Terry go. Clenched fists could never hold what she had given us. The only container appropriate for her spirit and passion for life is the heart.

You can use the maneuvers I've described in this book, the methods, techniques, and strategies. They're all effective, depending on the personalities and circumstances you're facing. You can do your research and gather knowledge. But I've never seen a better example of a self-actualized team member than Terry. None more dedicated, hard working, selfless, or content within herself.

In my mind, she remains the shining example of how to survive and thrive working for an idiot—with a heart and a spirit bigger than pettiness and personal pride. You and I don't need to worry about which one of us is going to interview God first and send back the answers to our list of questions. Theresa answered the most important ones before she left.

It's Your Move

How are you going to approach the rest of your day today? Will you start right now to take back the control over aspects of your professional life that you've abdicated to others? I'm not talking about trying to control the universe and everything that happens to you. Those things are generally beyond your control and trying to wrestle God's will to the ground is a losing proposition. However, He gave us all free will to do with our lives what we will.

Stop and consider how much of your free will you've given up. Free will is power—power no one can take away from you. Your personal and professional lives are intertwined and your power to make decisions is enough to change the course of both. You might consider all that I've shared with you about managing your boss and decide it's not worth it. If you decide to make a bold move, I hope it's an informed and not an impulsive decision.

If you decide to transition from resentful, angry subordinate to serene and appreciative team member, I hope you understand how difficult it might be. I, for one, still struggle against a return to the cynical days of endless criticism and complaining. Back then I thought I was making myself feel better. The fact was, I didn't know any better. Now I do, and so do you.

Being cynical and being realistic can appear similar in some aspects. However, being cynical engenders negativity. Being realistic is a foundation for making positive progress. Your cynical self might say, "I'm not happy about this and I don't see it getting any better." Your realistic self will observe the same thing and say, "I'm not happy about this and the circumstances might not change anytime soon. It's time to reposition myself physically, mentally, or both to make the best of it."

Growing New Rings

The longer a tree lives, the more rings it grows. As trees cycle through the seasons, growth slows, is stunted, even stops for all intents and purposes. New rings are formed as the growth begins anew. Although more sporadic and erratic, human life goes through similar start/stop and speed up/slow down cycles.

We can't undo bad decisions we've made in our lives any more than trees can go back and reform existing rings. Each of us grows new rings, whether we like it or not. But we have it all over trees in that we can influence the new rings we grow. We can change almost every characteristic of our new rings. What will the new rings look like? Will they be rings we can be proud of or rings we want to forget?

When you get out of bed tomorrow, do you want to remember today as a waste or a step in the right direction? The step in the right direction might mean turning back toward your Idiot Boss rather than running away and hiding from him. It might mean allowing, even encouraging, your better angels to talk to a person your demons would rather strangle. If you're like me, running away from people I don't like is easy. I take long, effortless strides. Approaching someone I have reservations about requires short, deliberate, and calculated steps.

Surviving and thriving an Idiot Boss is like climbing a mountain. You can't do it by proxy. Your success is contingent on the amount of effort you invest. Some days you will do well to hold position, like when the tree is dormant. Some days you'll climb 1,200 feet. Some days you'll only climb 12 feet. Regardless, every day will be a climb.

You can make a game out of managing your I-Boss, as many of my methods and techniques suggest. You can also turn it into a serious, strategic, challenging chess match. Either way, you need to play for keeps. Don't expect a lukewarm effort to produce satisfactory or long-term results. But expect that your passion will return to room temperature overnight. That's reality.

Each morning you must decide all over again if you're going to continue up the mountain. If you decide to continue your ascent, you'll need to poke at the embers of yesterday's passion and restoke the fire in your belly. Looking at your I-Boss as a human being, with all of the typical human shortcomings and then some, is something you might only be able to handle one day, one hour, or one minute at a time. Whatever your tolerance level, never forget that you can reboot as often as necessary.

Each time you reach out to climb another foot up the mountain, remember that you're doing it first for you; second, for those you care about and who care about you; and finally, for unnamed beneficiaries you might never meet. I believe God wants all of us to be happy and He gave us a powerful tool called empathy to transform gargoyle bosses into tolerable creatures. It's up to you to decide what the next right thing is—and do it.

Bibliography

Al-Anon's Twelve Steps & Twelve Traditions. Virginia Beach, VA: Al-Anon Family Group Headquarters, Inc., 1981.

Beebe, Steven A. and John T. Masterson. *Communicating in Small Groups,* Seventh Edition. Boston, MA: Allyn and Bacon, 2003.

Belasco, James, A. *Teaching the Elephant to Dance.* New York: Crown Publishing Group, 1990,

Belasco, James, A. and Ralph C. Stayer. *Flight of the Buffalo: Soaring to Excellence, Learning to Let Employees Lead.* New York: Warner Books, 1993.

Commons, Michael L. and Judith Stevens-Long. *Adult Life: Developmental Processes,* Fourth Edition. Mountain View, CA: Mayfield Publishing Company, 1992.

Cox, Danny. *There are No Limits: Breaking the Barriers in Personal High Performance.* Franklin Lakes, NJ: Career Press, 1998.

Cox, Danny and John Hoover. *Leadership When the Heat's On,* Second Edition. New York, McGraw-Hill, 2002.

———. *Seize the Day: Seven Steps to Achieve the Extraordinary in an Ordinary World.* Franklin Lakes, NJ: Career Press, 2002.

Crabb, Lawrence, J. *Understanding People: Deep Longings for Relationship.* Grand Rapids, MI: Zondervan Publishing House, 1972.

Frankl, Victor E. *Man's Search for Meaning,* Third Edition. New York: Touchstone/Simon & Schuster, 1984.

Gerber, Michael, E. *The E Myth: Why Most Small Businesses Don't Work and What to Do About it.* New York: HarperBusiness, 1995.

Hoover, John. *Can Television Shape Corporate Culture?* Ann Arbor, MI: UMI Dissertation Services, 1997.

Hoover, John and Robert J. Hoover. *An American Quality Legend: How Maytag Saved Our Moms, Vexed the Competition, and Presaged America's Quality Revolution.* New York: McGraw-Hill, 1993.

Hoover, John and Angelo Valenti. *Fearless Leadership: Lead the Way You Like to be Led.* Manuscript in submission, 2003.

Jarow, Rick. *Creating the Work You Love: Courage, Commitment, and Career.* Rochester, VT: Destiny Books, 1995.

Krames, Jeffrey A. *The Welch Way: Twenty-Four Lessons from the World's Greatest CEO.* New York: McGraw-Hill, 2002.

Miller, Keith J. *Compelled to Control.* Deerfield Beach, FL: Health Communications, Inc., 1992

Senge, Peter M. *The Fifth Discipline: The Art & Practice of the Learning Organization.* New York: Currency/Doubleday, 1990.

Vance, Mike and Diane Deacon. *Think Out of the Box!* Franklin Lakes, NJ: Career Press, 1997.

Index

About the Author

John Hoover, Ph.D., is a former executive with the Disneyland Entertainment Division and McGraw-Hill. He has consulted on a variety of projects for clients including Delta Air Lines, Hilton Hotels, IBM, Printronix, Sanyo Fisher, and Xerox. As managing partner of the second firm in the United States to publish commercial audio books-on-tape, he produced programs featuring such authors as Herbert Benson, Ken Blanchard, Harold Bloomfield, Jack Canfield, Terrance Deal, Peter F. Drucker, Dean Edell, Lillian Glass, Mark Victor Hansen, Tom Hopkins, Irene Kassorla, Norman Vincent Peale, Al Ries, Jack Trout, and Zig Ziglar.

Dr. John has previously coauthored six books and teaches university classes in business planning, communications, entrepreneurship, principles of management, and organizational behavior as an adjunct faculty member at several colleges in Tennessee. His background also includes several years on the California Board of Behavioral Sciences—registered marriage, family, and child counseling intern. He is cofounder of *Fearless Leadership,* a new organizational leadership development system (*fearlessleadership.com*), with Angelo Valenti, PhD. As a lightening rod for the treatment and prevention of stupidity in the workplace, Dr. John's columns and personal appearance schedule can be accessed at *idiotworld.org.*

Other Books by Dr. John Hoover

Leadership When the Heat's On (with Danny Cox)

Seize the Day: Seven Steps to Achieve the Extraordinary in an Ordinary World (with Danny Cox)

Can Television Save Corporate Culture?

An American Quality Legend: How Maytag Saved Our Moms, Vexed the Competition, and Presaged America's Quality Revolution. (with Robert J. Hoover)

Fearless Leadership: Lead the Way You Like to be Led (with Angelo Valenti)